"Miss Pedi~~~ ~~ ~murmured as he be~~~~ the words

T0208454

"I do believ~ ~~ ~ bit of a fraud. All show and little practical knowledge."

She shivered, feeling the way his lips touched the delicate skin of her ear.

"Don't you think it's time you sampled some of the real thing?"

"Real thing?"

"Baser emotions. Corporal pleasure."

Then he was shifting and his lips touched her own.

She was so startled by the contact—even though she'd been expecting it—that she didn't move. But as the fact sank into her brain that he was kissing *her,* his employee, she found that she couldn't shift away. The pressure of his lips was so soft, so sweet, so gentle—everything she had accused him of being incapable of displaying on the basis of his sex.

A faint moan came from her throat, and it must have pleased him, because she felt him smile.

"That's it, Miss Pedigrue," he coaxed. "Surrender to it."

When he took her hand, placing it at the side of his neck, she did not resist. Surprising even herself, she slid it to the nape of his neck, delighting in the way his hair fell over her fingers and tickled her skin. . . .

Reviewers Rave About Lisa Bingham and Her Incomparable Love Stories!

SWEET DALLIANCE

"A fast-paced, action-packed western romance that will leave readers breathless from its gait."

—The Paperback Forum

"An absolutely delightful story with unforgettable characters."

—Rendezvous

SWEET DEFIANCE

"Ms. Bingham writes a good yarn. Enjoyable, pleasurable reading."

—The Literary Times

"This sequel to *Sweet Dalliance* is every bit as delightful. Emotionally intriguing characters and a wonderfully arresting hero make this a must-read and will leave you breathless with anticipation for the final installment."

—Rendezvous

SWEET DECADENCE

"Sweet Decadence is a fast-paced, engrossing read destined to make readers wish there were more in this wonderful trilogy by the very talented Ms. Bingham."

—Romantic Times

THE BENGAL RUBIES

"A delightful read with just the right touch of humor."

—Romantic Times

"Lisa Bingham demonstrates her versatile and incredible talent with her usual deft touch. . . . *The Bengal Rubies* is filled with all the necessary ingredients that make for a memorable reading experience."

—Affaire de Coeur

Books by Lisa Bingham

Silken Dreams
Eden Creek
Distant Thunder
The Bengal Rubies
Temptation's Kiss
Silken Promises
Sweet Dalliance
Sweet Defiance
Sweet Decadence
Wild Escapade
Wild Serenade

Published by POCKET BOOKS

For orders other than by individual consumers, Pocket Books grants a discount on the purchase of **10 or more** copies of single titles for special markets or premium use. For further details, please write to the Vice-President of Special Markets, Pocket Books, 1633 Broadway, New York, NY 10019-6785, 8th Floor.

For information on how individual consumers can place orders, please write to Mail Order Department, Simon & Schuster Inc., 200 Old Tappan Road, Old Tappan, NJ 07675.

LISA BINGHAM

WILD SERENADE

POCKET BOOKS
New York   London   Toronto   Sydney   Tokyo   Singapore

An *Original* Publication of POCKET BOOKS

 POCKET BOOKS, a division of Simon & Schuster Inc.
1230 Avenue of the Americas, New York, NY 10020

Copyright © 1997 by Lisa Bingham

ISBN: 978-1-4767-1594-0

This Pocket Books paperback printing May 2004

10 9 8 7 6 5 4 3 2 1

POCKET and colophon are registered trademarks of Simon & Schuster Inc.

Cover art by Lina Levy

Printed in the U.S.A.

Prologue

Boston
March 10, 1859

My esteemed Captain Dalton,

I pray that this second letter finds you well and your health greatly improved. Once again please accept my condolences for the fire that ravaged your ship and killed so many of your crew members. I can only imagine the pain and grief experienced by those lucky enough to have survived.

As per your solicitor's instructions, I am reporting to you concerning your sister's progress at Miss Bodrill's School for Young Ladies. Regretfully, I find that I cannot offer you the reassurances that you are expecting.

I am well aware of the special circumstances which have brought Emaline to our institution. I empathize deeply with the child's plight and rue the horrors she has suffered. To be shipwrecked at five years of age is a tragedy. To be marooned with heathens for another four years before being found and brought to our school to await your return is the stuff of fiction. Unfortunately your dear sister is

1

proof enough that such terrors can also become the substance of reality.

Enclosed you will find a note Emaline wished to have forwarded to you. She has been told of your serious injuries and the reasons for her staying at our school, but I fear that understanding the reasons for your continued absence and accepting them are two different matters—which leads me to the point of this letter.

Captain Dalton, I fear that your sister's ordeals have prevented her from adjusting to Miss Bodrill's School for Young Ladies. I mourn with you over the calamity that has kept you in London and delayed your long-awaited reunion with your sister. Nevertheless, I feel compelled to be frank at this time.

As I stated in my earlier report, I am willing to make allowances for Emaline's lack of education thus far. Indeed, since learning to read, she is thriving in her study of art, literature, and French. She has a voracious appetite for knowledge and has made great strides in catching up with her peers. Her English has also returned to a near-perfect fluency despite her misadventures.

Having informed you of such happy tidings, it is with sincere sorrow that I must offer the rest of my report.

Captain Dalton, Emaline is not happy here. In the two months she has been in our care, she has shown no inclination to interact with the other children. She remains mulishly silent during mealtimes and exercise periods, and she responds orally only when called upon by her teachers.

In addition to her lack of social skills, your sister is quite unschooled in the daily rituals required by every young girl. The faculty and I have finally *convinced her of the necessity of dressing, but we have yet to keep her fully clothed throughout the day, shoes being a particular hindrance.*

Moreover, she stubbornly continues to eat with her hands, her grooming habits are nonexistent, and she bathes only when forced to do so.

Captain Dalton, I wish to emphasize that the teachers at Miss Bodrill's School for Young Ladies are doing their utmost to help your sister. However, I believe that our establishment is not conducive to her needs. From the depths of her heart, your sister longs for your return. You are the only living member of a family she hazily remembers.

I realize that your precarious health has been the reason for your absence, and I do not blame you in any way for Emaline's difficulties. However, I honestly feel that her disposition would be greatly improved if we could give her a date by which we might expect your return.

In addition, I trust you will forgive me for stating that I think Emaline is in need of a more constant companion than our teachers can be. If at all possible, I would recommend that the child's education be placed in the hands of a capable governess and that her personal care be overseen by a nanny. If a woman could be found who was willing to handle both sets of responsibilities, I would applaud such a relationship. I know that Emaline would form a faster relationship with one caretaker than with two. Indeed, she might learn to look upon such a mentor as a substitute mother.

I beg your forgiveness for interfering in family affairs, but your recent letters to the school and to your sister have convinced me of your deep love for Emaline. I know that you want the best for her.

I will await your instructions. Please rest assured that we will take care of Emaline to the best of our ability until this correspondence and your subsequent response can be forwarded.

Yours most respectfully,
Miss L. R. Bodrill

Chapter

I

May 1, 1859

Seven weeks. The letter from Miss Bodrill had taken seven weeks to reach him—and his answer would take at least that long.

Garrick Dalton pressed the heel of his hand to his uninjured eye. The pressure momentarily eased the aching of his head, and he exhaled in relief. After spending the morning poring over ledgers and receipts gathered from the London offices of the Dalton Shipping Company, he was weary and as weak as a kitten.

Dammit! He couldn't be ill any longer. He had to get home. Emaline needed him. Now.

Had it not been for the accident, he could have returned to New England months ago. As it was, he was forced to endure the restrictions imposed on him by his injuries. Just yesterday that quack of a doctor who visited once a day had proclaimed that Garrick shouldn't leave his bed for another fortnight.

And a sea voyage?

At that point the doctor had scowled and grunted. The arduous sea crossing would have to wait at least two more months.

Garrick's fingers curled around the arms of the leather chair that had been drawn close to the window of his bedchamber. Little did the doctor know that Garrick hadn't spent his afternoons resting for some time. Each day he pushed himself to the limits of his endurance both mentally and physically.

A small table had been brought upstairs to serve as a makeshift desk, allowing him to do some work—or rather, allowing him the opportunity to become irritated with the work he *couldn't* do. After several hours of bookkeeping, he would abandon the records and concentrate on strengthening the muscles grown weak from inactivity. Bit by bit he had progressed from prowling his room to pacing the halls and finally to negotiating the stairs. The whole process had taken nearly three months—and he had yet to step outside his London town house.

Garrick supposed he should be more content. After all, he was alive.

But as each day inched past, Garrick feared he would go stark raving mad if he didn't return to America soon. He longed to stride onto the docks of Addlemeyer Island, to breathe deeply of the honeysuckle-scented air, to step inside his boyhood home, knowing that this time he would not be alone there.

Emaline had been found.

Alive.

He tossed Miss Bodrill's letter on the table, massaging his thigh. Dear God in heaven, he yearned to see his little sister. He needed to reassure himself that she truly existed, that she was healthy, that she was glad to be away from the island where she'd been found. He longed to measure for himself how tall she'd grown and to gauge whether her features resembled their mother's as much as Garrick's resembled their father's.

Emaline. Sweet, adorable, chattering Emaline. Each time he thought of her, Garrick had to remind himself that she was nine years old. In his mind's eye, he envisioned her as she'd been that fateful day when she and their parents—Maureen and Thomas Dalton—and his three adolescent brothers had set sail for East Asia.

Little Emaline had been wearing a new frock—one made of blue wool and trimmed in black braid like her father's captain's coat. Sensing the impending confinement of the ship, she'd raced around the docks of Addlemeyer, climbing over crates and under nets, telling one and all that she was embarking on an adventure with her mummy and daddy. She was finally old enough to go to sea.

An ache gathered in his throat at the vivid recollection of waving good-bye to his family. Little had they known they would never be together again.

Garrick reached for Emaline's note, which Miss Bodrill had included with her own.

As soon as he saw the painstakingly printed letters, the tightness gripped his chest. At a glance he could see that writing was a challenge for her. But the sentiment of her words was clear: "Garik. Plees com tak me home."

Garrick's breath snagged in his throat. The sight of his name, slightly crooked and misspelled, was nothing less than a miracle to him. Emaline had not yet learned to read—let alone write—when she left. The ship had been slated to arrive in East Asia six months later, but mere weeks after its departure, *Dalton's Adventurer* had foundered in a storm and run aground.

All hands had died—or so everyone had thought. Last November Emaline Dalton had been discovered on a small uncharted island near Brazil, a mere twenty miles from the spot where it was believed the *Adventurer* had begun to take on water.

An acquaintance of Garrick's father had discovered Emaline. The man, who had once served as Thomas Dalton's first officer, had sailed to the island in search of fresh water. There he'd discovered a white-skinned girl who seemed somehow familiar.

When the child told the captain how she had washed ashore during a storm, he'd known immediately who she was: the youngest daughter of the late Captain Thomas Dalton. Speaking to him in halting English, she had described a giant who was once her brother. Someone named Garrick.

Not knowing what else to do, the captain had brought Emaline with him on his journey back to Boston, only to discover that Garrick Dalton was convalescing in London. The Dalton family solicitors had then enrolled Emaline in Miss Bodrill's School for Young Ladies while Garrick was notified of his sister's miraculous reappearance.

Garrick's thumb traced an irregular dot where the ink had smeared, his heart lurching as he realized the pattern could have been caused by a tear.

His jaw clenched, and he purposely ignored the weakness he had only just lamented. Garrick was going home, no matter what consequences he might suffer.

He was about to rise when he caught sight of another note addressed to him. Tearing the distinctive seal, he saw no heading, no signature, only these words: "Stay in London. Your health will improve greatly there."

Dammit, was he the victim of a conspiracy aimed toward making him follow doctor's orders?

Lurching to his feet, Garrick reached for the cane leaning against the wall. In a gait that was labored but determined, he strode forward.

Pain shot from the small of his back and down his legs as the new skin that had replaced his burns stretched with the unaccustomed haste of his movements. The muscles of his legs twitched from forced inactivity, and his thigh throbbed where it had been broken in two places, but he strained until he reached the door.

Planting a hand on the wall, he threw open the heavy door and bellowed, "Bickerstaff!"

To his surprise, Joshua Bickerstaff was already making his way down the hall.

"Calm down," the slighter, darker-haired figure retorted. He brandished a bottle of Irish whiskey in one hand and two small glasses in the other. "I was in the kitchen when the letters arrived. I figured you'd be hollering for me sooner or later."

Joshua Bickerstaff had been hired when Garrick was in his teens. At the time, Bickerstaff was expected to serve as Garrick's valet at boarding school, but the two men had never really adhered to the strict formality associated with a gentleman and his servant. Indeed, within months, the two had been fast friends, and that camaraderie had lasted long after Garrick finished his education and became a sea captain himself. Joshua had accompanied him on countless voyages, serving as a personal secretary, first officer, valet, drinking partner, and unofficial bodyguard.

Without a word, Bickerstaff ducked beneath Garrick's arm, shouldered some of his weight, and helped him return to his leather chair.

"I'm not an invalid," Garrick groused as Bickerstaff took a woolen blanket from the bed and draped it over Garrick's lap.

"So you say," Bickerstaff countered blandly, setting the glasses on the table and filling them with a healthy measure of whiskey before slouching in the opposite chair. "But you're still too feeble to throttle me, so I'll continue to help you until you are."

Garrick winced at the unnecessary reminder. The doctor kept exclaiming that Garrick's recovery had proceeded more swiftly than expected, but Garrick was far from convinced. He wasn't a patient man, and the long months of confinement he'd endured already had taxed his temper to the limit. The fact that his life had been spared when so many others had been lost still needled him with guilt and urged him to work that much harder.

Gradually Garrick became aware of the way Bickerstaff was staring at him. Blast that man and his evil eye. Garrick was as fed up with Bickerstaff's mothering as he was with the pain of his burns. It would be worth risking a return to sea if only to keep Bickerstaff occupied with something other than nursing.

"You haven't been sleeping, have you?" Bickerstaff chided.

Garrick's jaw clenched, but he didn't bother to answer. Bickerstaff would ignore anything he said to the contrary. Besides, the words had been uttered more as a statement than a question, and he knew Bickerstaff was well aware that the recurring nightmare of their last voyage still plagued him.

He took a quick gulp of whiskey, then closed his eyes as the fiery liquid burned a trail down his throat. The disturbing dream was always the same. He was at the helm of *Dalton's Pride.* Dawn streaked the sky with pink, and he could see the green shores of England glittering in the dim light.

Since he and his men would be docking in a matter of hours, and since a watery sun seemed determined to appear after nearly three weeks of rain and foul weather, he'd ordered the hatches opened to air out their cache of rum, distilled alcohol, and whale oil.

The moment the first cargo door was propped open, Garrick had smelled the thick, pungent vapor rising from belowdecks.

"Douse the lamps!" he'd shouted, his voice rising with urgency. "Douse the lamps!"

But his warning had come too late. A spark from a lantern had ignited the fumes. A fireball roared into the cavernous depths, setting off a series of explosions.

Garrick had managed a single shout, "Abandon ship!" Then the deck beneath him had exploded, and he'd been thrown into the sea. Surfacing, he'd desperately tried to help men cling to the broken timbers floating on the surface of the water, but another explosion caused the ship to disintegrate. He had been dragged under the waves and the world had dissolved into blackness.

When Garrick had finally regained consciousness, it was to find himself facedown on one of the beds in a clinic sponsored by the Dalton Shipping Company for its crews and family members. His body had been racked with unimaginable pain, and he remembered crying out, calling for his men. A singed and battered Bickerstaff lay nearby. Although he'd been reluctant to tell Garrick anything, Bickerstaff had finally confessed that twelve sailors had died that morning. In an attempt to help the crew, Garrick had suffered severe burns to his legs, back, and hands, three broken ribs, a shattered thighbone, and severe gashes above and below his eye.

"You can't blame yourself for what happened, Garrick," Bickerstaff said softly, interrupting Garrick's thoughts and wrenching him free of his memories.

"I should have checked the cargo hold earlier."

"We were all battling to survive the storm. It would have been dangerous to open the hatches during bad weather."

Garrick knew Bickerstaff was right. After all, Garrick had made a fortune of his own by taking such risks. Using the ship his father had given him on his twentieth birthday, he'd specialized in transporting barrels of distilled alcohol to England. Most seafarers demanded hazard pay for such goods since the barrels had to be loaded carefully and checked regularly. Otherwise, minute leaks formed by the rocking of the ship could allow fumes to collect in the air pockets, causing a dangerous situation for both ship and crew.

Not just dangerous.

Deadly.

"We all knew the risks before we signed on for the voyage, Garrick," Bickerstaff said. "There wasn't a sailor aboard who wasn't aware of the potential hazards of the cargo. Leave the past in the past." Bickerstaff lifted his index finger from his glass and pointed to the letters on the table. "It's time you concentrated on the future—and Emaline. How is the little imp, anyway?"

Garrick allowed himself to be distracted. Only time could cure him of his ills and his nightmares. Until then there were other problems to solve.

"Emaline wrote to me herself."

Bickerstaff's features brightened. "She's learned to print?" he asked incredulously. "Already?"

"Not just printing. She's mastered a bit of script as well." Garrick nudged the note in Bickerstaff's direction.

"Hell's bells," Bickerstaff exclaimed in delight. Then his grin faded as he absorbed the content of the note. "Damn," he whispered.

Garrick set his glass down and leaned forward. "I've got to get home."

Bickerstaff immediately shook his head. "A rough sea could set your recovery back months. The doctor has told me—"

"Dammit, Bickerstaff!" Garrick cried out, slamming his fist against the table with enough force to cause the whiskey bottle to shudder. "I can't stay here any longer. Emaline *needs* me."

Bickerstaff scowled, clearly torn between his concern for Garrick's health and his awareness of the needs of a frightened little girl. "What does that Bodrill woman say?"

"Look for yourself."

Impatient with the delay and with his own weakness, Garrick twisted to look out the window. But the pane of glass was mottled with the rivulets of rain pounding against the surface. The weather had been unbearable for weeks.

Just as it had been during the last crossing.

Seconds crawled by as Bickerstaff absorbed the report. When he spoke again, Garrick had managed to calm himself, but only slightly.

"The woman mentions your hiring a governess," Bickerstaff said. "Surely your solicitors could take care of the details until you return to America."

Garrick shook his head. "My solicitors are brilliant in regard to the law and financial matters, but I couldn't possibly trust them to hire a governess. Emaline needs a woman who will understand her difficulties and reassure her. Such a woman must be found by a person who knows my sister well enough to choose an appropriate companion."

"Or, as Miss Bodrill states, a kind of substitute mother."

Mother.

The word reverberated in Garrick's brain, and he slowly turned to stare at his friend.

Since learning of Emaline's return, Garrick had been tormented by his need to be with her. He'd sworn to himself that he would see to it that his baby sister was never alone again.

Unfortunately, the injuries that had kept him in England had also made him very much aware of his own mortality. What would become of Emaline if something happened to him? Eventually, he knew, she would grow to be an adult, marry, and have children of her own, but in the intervening years, she needed stability, a safe and secure home, and someone to watch over her should Garrick be unable to do so. She needed . . .

Her mother.

But Maureen Dalton was dead, and Garrick could not bring her back.

So that left him with hiring a governess to serve as a substitute parent, but even with careful screening, Garrick could not ensure that any woman he hired would stay with Emaline for a decade or more. No, he needed to find someone who would feel honor-bound to continue living with the girl.

He raked his fingers through his hair in disgust at his inability to concentrate.

Think, dammit.

It was a pity that Garrick and Emaline were the last in a long and distinguished line of Daltons. But no matter how much he might wish for the discovery of a distant relative, Garrick knew he couldn't pluck such a female from thin air. Nor could he create a sister or a . . .

Not a sister. A sister-in-law.

The words echoed in his mind as clearly as if they'd been spoken next to his ear.

Chills raced down his spine.

Of course. Why hadn't he thought of such a possibility before?

Suddenly restless, he pushed himself to his feet.

"What's the matter?" Bickerstaff immediately asked, but Garrick held up a finger for silence, trying to sort through the whirl of his thoughts.

A sister-in-law.

Since the two remaining Daltons had no family of their own, one would have to be created. The proud lineage must be ensured not only for Emaline's benefit but for the sake of the Dalton legacy—the shipping company, the acres and acres of family land. And the answer to both predicaments was so simple that Garrick wondered why he hadn't considered such an avenue before.

He was over thirty years old, and thoughts of an heir should have inspired him to marry years ago. But the lure of the sea and the fortune to be made had always persuaded Garrick to delay the inevitable.

Now he could no longer ignore the prospect. The time had come for him to find a bride.

But how? Garrick hadn't entertained a woman in more than six months, and he'd never taken any female's attentions seriously. He could list a dozen women he knew, but not a single soul to whom he could propose.

So what was he supposed to do? A man didn't simply put an advertisement in the paper explaining his need for a companion.

Or did he?

Turning, Garrick stared at the papers scattered on his desk. Miss Bodrill's advice about obtaining a governess for his sister suddenly had other, more lasting ramifications. After all, if Garrick's parents had lived, Garrick would have allowed them to make a good match for him from among the daughters of the company's business associates. His parents might have shared a love match themselves, but Garrick had long since given up such a notion in his own behalf. As far as he was concerned, love was a luxury, not a criterion for a lifelong relationship.

So why *couldn't* he hire himself a wife?

For the first time in months, Garrick felt alive. Time was of the essence. Plans had to be organized and arrangements made. He wasn't optimistic enough to think he could handle all of the tasks by himself, but he knew he could delegate enough of them so that he would be free to concentrate on his own recovery and his return to America. He wanted to be as hale and hearty as possible so that Emaline would not fear for his health.

"I have a job for you, Bickerstaff," Garrick said as he limped to the wardrobe.

Bickerstaff grunted. "I will not let you go home on some godforsaken conscription ship, so don't even bother to disobey the doctor's orders."

Ignoring him, Garrick tore a shirt from one of the hooks, then dropped his dressing gown and shrugged into the sleeves.

"I want you to go to the docks and find the first available ship returning to Boston."

"Garrick, you can't—"

"I want you to pack your bags and purchase passage for yourself."

For several seconds Bickerstaff stared at Garrick, his mouth agape. "I beg your pardon?"

"I want you to return to Boston immediately. As soon as you arrive, send word to Addlemeyer Island that Dalton Manor is to be readied for occupancy. Since Miss Fitch, my housekeeper, is the only servant currently in residence, I'll put you in charge of hiring the staff as well."

"Why Boston? I can find everything I need in Addlemeyer or, at the very least, Nantucket."

"I want the best, and Boston will give you more of a selection for your interviews."

"So I'm to hire your whole staff?" He shook his head in amazement. "Is that *all* you need me to do?" Bickerstaff groused good-naturedly, but it was clear that he was eager to return home himself even if it meant several weeks' worth of interviews to locate the servants required for Garrick's home.

"No. You're to finish the job within a fortnight of your arrival."

"A fortnight!" Bickerstaff complained in disbelief. "Why such a rush?"

"Because I intend to follow you to Boston. Then we will retrieve Emaline and bring her home, so I want the house ready."

Bickerstaff scowled. "The doctor told you to—"

"Damn the doctor to hell and back," Garrick growled, his jaw hardening as his strength of will returned. He reached for his trousers. "I'll heed the man's instructions to avoid a sea crossing for two more weeks. Despite what the two of you might think, I am completely aware of my own limitations. But by that time, the new schooner, *Emaline's Return,* should be finished. Aboard that ship I'll have the smoothest and fastest ride possible. I might even beat

17

you to Boston." He paused for effect. "But I *will* be leaving England."

Bickerstaff must have sensed that Garrick would not be dissuaded, because he didn't bother to argue any further. "Give me an idea of the servants you'll require."

"At least three stablemen, two grooms, five housemaids, a cook, a butler, a laundress, a coachman, and a full-time seamstress for my sister. If you wish, Nina Ellington, Jan's sister, can help you with the interviews."

Jan Ellington was Garrick's right-hand man as well as a close friend. He remained in Addlemeyer to oversee all aspects of the Dalton business whenever Garrick was at sea. Garrick would have been lost without him.

Bickerstaff grimaced. Nina Ellington had displayed an overzealous fondness for him in the past—a fondness that was not reciprocated. "Thank you, but no." Bickerstaff grabbed a stub of a pencil and began taking notes on a blank piece of ledger paper. "Anything else?"

"Yes. Emaline will need new clothes and shoes until the seamstress you hire can organize herself. I want you to contact Miss Bodrill for measurements as soon as you arrive, then buy Emaline anything she requires. My mother had accounts at all the major shops in Boston. They have never been canceled."

Reaching into one of the drawers, Garrick withdrew a pouch heavy with gold sovereigns. "Your passage to Boston will cost a pretty penny, but I'm sure the captain of the ship you choose will be happy to relieve you of this." He gave him another, smaller bag, "And this will serve you until you can arrange for more funds to be transferred. Have my solicitors in Boston handle the paperwork for you."

Bickerstaff weighed the money in his hands. "I can hire a staff without extra funds. I'll have no need of a transfer."

Garrick interrupted with "I'm afraid you will. Before Emaline is retrieved, there's another matter of business I would like you to handle. I want you to find Emaline a governess, then outfit the woman with all the books and equipment she desires to educate Emaline at home."

Bickerstaff weighed the bags in his hands as if considering the tasks. At long last, he nodded. "Finding a governess for Emaline shouldn't prove difficult, especially in Boston. I've always thought the town was flooded with spinsters lacking proper diversion," Bickerstaff said as he crossed to the door.

"Ahh," Dalton drawled, "but I need a particular spinster."

Bickerstaff twisted to look at Garrick over his shoulder, his brows lifting.

Garrick, carefully studying Bickerstaff's expression, delayed revealing his pièce de résistance.

"You see, I need a woman lonely enough, biddable enough, and desperate enough to succumb to my charms."

Bickerstaff's jaw dropped, and Garrick realized he hadn't mentioned women—or even one woman in particular—in regard to seduction in some time.

Garrick's lips spread in a slow grin, a devilish, maddening smile that he hadn't used since the death of his parents, but had adopted quite frequently in his youth.

When Bickerstaff appeared even more confused by the smile, Garrick couldn't resist the urge to startle him further.

"You see, I've always found meek women to be most vulnerable to my wooing," he said. "And Emaline's governess should be stuffed full of meekness. That way I won't have a difficult time persuading her to become my wife."

"Your *what?*" Bickerstaff breathed.

Garrick chuckled out loud, the sound rusty to his own ears.

"My wife."

Chapter
2

Patience Pedigrue clasped her hands tightly around her hymnal and tried her best not to fidget.

Long before the mourners arrived at the chapel, Patience's older sister, Constance, had sternly reassured her that the funeral services for their father would be as brief as decently possible. Patience had taken the words to heart, but at the time she'd forgotten that Constance's definition of "decency" was entirely different from her own.

After conferring with the clergyman, Constance had insisted on several musical selections, an extremely long passage from Scripture, an hour-long eulogy, and several testimonials.

Patience dug her fingernails into her palms to keep from screaming. As far as she was concerned, a person should not be required to sit still and review the glory days of a dear departed loved one for more than an hour.

Especially when the person required to endure the funeral ceremony was not particularly forlorn about the occasion.

Her eyes shifted as she searched the pews around

her for the proverbial lightning bolt. Surely, to think ill of the dead was evil, and to do so in the middle of a chapel bordered on blasphemy.

But when no otherworldly phenomenon occurred, Patience decided that even God was glad to be rid of Alexander Pedigrue. Heaven only knew that her father had reveled in praying morning, noon, and night. Perhaps the Lord was enjoying the sudden peace in the hereafter.

"Patience, please."

Patience started when Constance placed a hand on her knee. Reflexively, her leg had begun to bounce in an agitated manner.

Leaning toward her elder sister, Patience whispered, "How much longer?"

Constance pressed her lips together in disapproval, and Patience rolled her eyes. Constance could be such a prude when rules of propriety were at issue. Patience was just as diligent in maintaining her reputation as any true lady, but she drew the line at becoming obsessed with worry about whether people would talk.

At her other elbow, Felicity Pedigrue stifled a giggle and managed to lean close enough to murmur, "They won't finish until we're all stone cold from boredom."

A withering glare from Constance forced them into silence, and Patience willed her body to remain as stiff, proud, and unmoving as Constance's.

The attempt was a failure. Patience had never been a woman prone to quietude. She preferred to rush to whatever destination awaited her. She liked noise and bustle and crowds, a trait that had earned her father's disapproval—and occasionally his strap. In his opinion, genteel young ladies sat for hours on end with only their needlework to distract them. But then, Patience had never been overly fond of sewing, either.

Briefly she considered ending her torment by jumping to her feet and exclaiming, "My father was a miserly, awful old man who would have been happier with three slaves in his care rather than three daughters!"

But even *she* had her limits. She might struggle against a need to hurry, to experience everything, to complete tasks in the most efficient manner, but that didn't mean she had no understanding of etiquette.

Patience prided herself on her manners and polish. Indeed, she knew that the education she had received would rival that of nearly any man. In the "early years," as she'd grown used to calling her childhood, her father had doted on his children. He'd been strict, yes, but he had afforded them every luxury—tutors, nannies, governesses. He'd felt it a crime for a human mind—even that of a mere woman—to be wasted.

Unfortunately, as the Pedigrue sisters had entered adolescence, their father's mood had changed dramatically. The more they began to resemble young women rather than gangly girls, the more single-mindedly he'd striven to save them from "the disgrace of their heritage."

That disgrace didn't have to be explained. Patience had been five when her mother disappeared from the Pedigrue household. She remembered quite clearly how their father had explained that Louise Pedigrue had found younger, prettier, better-mannered children whom she loved far more than her own.

Patience had grown to hate her mother for such perfidy, and time had not dampened her rancor. With age had come experience, and now that she was an adult herself, Patience knew that her mother had probably been tempted to leave not for another set of children but for a lover. Even so, the woman's abandonment was unforgivable.

Her jaw clamped shut. Not once had Louise Pedigrue tried to contact her children, not even in the days since Alexander Pedigrue's death. Patience damned that tiny shred of hope which had insisted that finally—*finally*—Louise would show herself to the three daughters who had grown from children to young women to . . .

To spinsters well on the shelf.

Directing her eyes heavenward, Patience tried to ignore the sting of tears that pricked her eyes. The rush of sadness had nothing to do with her father or even with the mother who had deserted them all.

No, her grief was for the wasted years, the shattered dreams. For Constance who had wanted a life of glamour and had grown stiff and proud instead. For Felicity who longed for adventure but had been chained to her father's bedside as his own personal assistant.

And for herself. Patience's education had helped her to see that there were ways women could grow independent and free. She'd planned one day to take a position as a governess or a lady's companion so that she could travel the world. She'd fantasized being introduced to a host of gentlemen, one of whom would ask her to marry him, to become the mother of his children, and to oversee his philanthropic endeavors with the artists and scholars who would live in their home.

Perhaps her goals had been far too lofty for the daughter of a minister. Patience hadn't been daft enough to think her daydreaming had any basis in reality. But she'd also known that Alexander Pedigrue was not the pauper he pretended to be. He had more than a million dollars in land, business holdings, and gold—certainly more than enough money to supply proper dowries for his daughters.

But no. He hadn't wanted them to leave.

He hadn't trusted them to avoid following a path of sin like their mother.

"Patience!" Constance hissed.

Patience choked back a squeak of surprise, then stilled the leg that had once again begun to twitch under her skirts.

Focusing on the elegant carvings that framed the massive stained-glass window behind the pulpit, she offered a silent prayer for the hours to come: *Please, God, help me to endure the rest of this day—the funeral, the graveside service, the visitors, the mourners' supper.*

Blast, she wasn't going to be able to hold her tongue. She would have to bite it in half.

Conscious that her prayers had been interrupted by her own irritation, she quickly finished: *Lord, help me to appear grieved. Help me to feel some measure of sorrow.*

Patience waited, but the softer emotions didn't come. She was *glad* her father was dead, and so were most of the people gathered here, if they would only tell the truth.

Closing her eyes, she amended her pleas: *Thank You for liberating us from the hands of this tyrant. And please, if it wouldn't be too much bother, help me make something good come out of my father's death. Help me—help us all—to salvage at least a portion of our dreams. Give Felicity an adventure, Constance a taste of glamour, and me . . .*

Well, I realize the travel might be too much, as well the wealthy man and the children, the artists, the scholars . . .

But please, please, please *help me become independent enough to control my own destiny.*

*　*　*

25

Half a city block from the stone chapel, Louise Chevalier peered out the window of her carriage as she waited for the service to end.

Her vantage point and the blinds of her coach offered her a measure of privacy. Even the veil of her bonnet obscured her face from any curious passersby. Nevertheless, she clung to the shadows as much as possible.

Damn him. Damn Alexander Pedigrue to hell and back for what he'd done. As a naive and frightened youngster, Louise had offered the man her heart. Then he'd trampled on her love for him and for the three children she'd borne. In an effort to punish her for a supposed affair, he'd stolen their children away while she was attending a church quilting bee—a *quilting bee,* for Pete's sake. When she returned home, she'd discovered her house in shambles, her husband and daughters gone, and a note informing her that she would never see her children again.

Her hand crept to her throat as she realized how close Alexander's prophecy had come to being fulfilled. If one of the investigators she'd hired years ago had not seen her husband's obituary in the *Boston Times,* she still would have no idea where to find her girls. Her babies.

A tall, broad-shouldered man crossed the road in front of her, and she allowed her attention to be diverted. Unhooking the latch to the door, she waited until her bodyguard had climbed inside and resumed his seat before she spoke.

"Did you see him?"

He nodded, his dark eyes glittering in the shadows. "I was able to look inside the casket before the service began."

The muscles of her face grew rigid. "Is the man my husband?" she whispered, barely able to force the words from her throat. She had hated Alexander Pedigrue. She had vowed to find him and make him pay for his cruelty. To think that he was dead and completely beyond her retribution brought an odd combination of fury and relief.

"Yes."

"You're sure?"

"He wears the family seal."

Louise's own fingers clenched until the matching signet ring she wore on her left index finger dug into her skin.

She'd been fourteen years old when her parents—performers in a troupe of traveling actors—were killed in a railway accident. Devastated, alone, frightened, Louise had found her way to a local church where she had begged for help. While there, she'd met and attracted the attention of a visiting minister, Alexander Pedigrue, a man rumored to be the only living heir to a monstrous coal fortune.

Sensing that her only hope of survival might be to ally herself to such a man, Louise had not rebuffed Alexander's attentions. When he'd begun to court her quite seriously, she'd changed into the docile, subservient woman he'd thought her to be. Instinctively she kept her past as a performer a secret, witnessing time and time again Alexander's intolerance for any mode of entertainment not considered holy and meditational. When he asked her to marry him, she agreed, knowing that she could find a far worse mate than a man with money and influence.

But what she didn't know was that Alexander was a tyrant in preacher's clothing. He was possessive, malicious, cruel. He believed women were a manifestation of Eve's original sin and that all females should therefore be punished for their propensity toward evil.

In the first few years of her marriage, Louise had learned to make herself as invisible as possible. She'd buried her joy for life beneath layers of meekness and obedience, allowing her true self to surface only in the company of her three daughters. Her angels. Her saviors.

Then, one horrible day, the Pedigrues had been leaving church when an old acquaintance of Louise's had passed through town. Before she could warn the handsome juggler of the inherent danger of his words, he had informed Alexander that he'd worked with Louise and her parents as part of a traveling minstrel show.

Louise had expected an immediate outburst from her husband, but he'd grown deadly calm. Not a word was exchanged between them until the girls had gone to bed. Then Alexander backhanded Louise across the cheek and threw her to the floor.

"Harlot!"

"No, Alexander. Let me explain."

"You are the devil's seed. You come from the devil's seed. You have consorted with thieves and whores and idle men, and far worse, you've kept that life a secret from *me.* Your husband. Your master."

His hands curled into fists, and he towered over her. "Which of these women are you, Louise? A consort of the devil who flaunts her body in front of the lascivious eyes of rapists and miscreants? Or have you truly repented? Have you become the pious woman I have always thought you to be?"

She'd cowered away from him, anticipating another rain of blows. "I *have* repented, I swear."

"How can I believe you when our life together has been a lie? For all I know, you and the man who approached me today could have been lovers."

"No."

"How long has he been in town?"

Her body trembled with a fear like none she'd ever known. "I don't know. I—"

"You've lain with him, haven't you? He's been to this place before—only this time you were *caught* with your consort."

"No!"

He yanked her upright, his fingers bruising her arm and causing her to cry out. "Why should I believe you? You're a liar through and through. For all I know, the children you've borne aren't even my own!"

Her fear intensified. Alexander had a right to punish her, but not their daughters. *Please, dear God, don't let him hurt our daughters.*

"Alexander!" she cried. "You know you're the only man who has ever known me in that manner."

He glared at her, his eyes hard and cold. Then he snapped, "Prove your devotion to me and to God. Give me no more cause to doubt you."

"I promise." She eagerly nodded, willing to do anything to protect herself and thereby her children. When angry, Alexander punished those around him with a fanatical zeal.

The following day, upon the urging of her husband, she had gone to town to quilt blankets for the needy with the rest of the Ladies' Aid Society.

But when she returned home, her children were gone. . . .

The carriage rocked, drawing her mind back to the present.

Shifting to the seat beside her, Étienne touched her hands. "Forget the past," he murmured. "The man is dead."

29

Louise stared sadly out the window as the flourish of a pipe organ signaled the end of the service. "But his legacy of hate lives on."

Louise had hoped to rush to her daughters, to fold them in her arms and begin a reunion she'd dreamed of for nearly fifteen years. But in an effort to ensure that the obituary described the same Alexander Pedigrue she sought, Louise had managed to interview one of the former cooks in Alexander's home. The woman had heard stories of Alexander's wife—how the woman had abandoned God and found herself a lover and other children to satisfy her wanton desires.

Worse yet, the cook had described a joyless household and three young girls held hostage by their father's fanaticism.

"I have to help them, Étienne," Louise said to the man who had long ago become more than a bodyguard to her.

He shook his head. "I doubt they will even speak to you. They've been told for years that you deserted them."

She bit her lip to keep from crying out.

"Give them time, Louise."

"Time?" she blurted, near tears. "You don't understand. If I'm to make up for all the years I've missed, I have to do something *now*."

"Louise," he murmured placatingly, "a few weeks will allow their grief to ease so that—"

"No." She gripped his fingers in an effort to convey her panic. "I lived with Alexander for nearly a decade. I know how he thinks—thought." Even now it was hard for her to employ the past tense in regard to her estranged husband.

Taking a deep breath, she said, "I can guarantee that he'll use this opportunity to punish my daughters. Even in his last will and testament he won't offer them a portion of the family fortune—not until he feels they've earned it."

She gripped Étienne's fingers, her course of action suddenly clear. "We have to find that will and study it before it is read. There must be a clerk, a cleaning woman, someone, who can be bribed into helping us."

The double doors to the chapel opened, and she grew quiet, distracted by the figures who exited the building. The ache of misery increased as a simple pine box was carried out the front doors and taken to the waiting hearse.

I will win in the end, Alexander, Louise vowed silently as her husband's remains were lifted onto the beribboned conveyance. *You thought that your hatred would destroy me. But I will regain my girls and their love.*

As the mourners emerged from the chapel, Louise strained for a glimpse of her daughters at the head of the group. Without thinking, she searched for the darling imps she'd once known, then realized they would be grown women with women's bodies.

A trio of black-clad figures descended the church steps, and Louise held her breath. The deference offered to the women by the rest of the group told her clearly enough that she was looking at her children, but her daughters had also worn mourning veils, and she was offered little more than a glimpse of their willowy forms.

They turned to climb into the carriage positioned behind the hearse, thereby presenting their backs to the woman who watched.

Disappointment flooded through Louise's body, making her weak. *Please. Let me see just* one *girl's face. Please!*

As if some angel had heard her prayer, a gust of

wind dislodged a pallbearer's hat, whipped at the minister's robes, then rushed past the veils of the Pedigrue sisters' bonnets. Improbably, miraculously, one of the organza pieces lifted high in the air, affording Louise a glimpse of a woman's delicate features and a head of brilliant red hair.

Patience.

Louise bit her lip, a choked cry of joy escaping her lips.

My darling, misnamed, impatient little Patience. How you've grown. . . .

Chapter

3

Garrick Dalton planted his feet securely on the pitching deck of his newest schooner, a ship he'd christened *Emaline's Return,* in honor of his little sister. Deftly, he called out orders to the sailors who were lashing the vessel to the thick timbers of the pier. But once the lines were fast, he quickly surrendered his authority.

"You're in charge, Mr. Rosemund."

"Aye, sir."

"Have the cargo unloaded and wait for my further instructions."

The man nodded, then turned to shout orders to the crew.

As he strode along the pier, Garrick lifted his cheeks to the warmth of the sun, knowing that the man he had become at sea bore little resemblance to the invalid Bickerstaff had left in London. The new schooner, an easy crossing, hard work, fresh air, and the thought of soon seeing his sister again had worked wonders with his constitution. His legs and arms had regained most of the strength he'd lost after his accident. The burns had all but completely healed, the new skin still tender, but much more supple. Then—probably his proudest accomplishment—he'd long-since thrown his cane into the sea.

Admittedly, there were times when his thigh throbbed. On days like this one, he was forced to wear a patch over his injured eye when the sun was at its height. His back bore the scars of his injuries and some of the worst-hit areas were angry and pink. He still grew impatient at the thought of the obstacles that remained before he could be reunited with his sister, but a stiff wind in his sails and the refined design of *Emaline's Return* had reduced the length of his voyage substantially.

Cutting easily through the cluster of stevedores, hawkers, and merchants crowding the landing, Garrick hailed a hansom cab and ordered the driver to take him to Dickerson, Dickerson, and Smee. Although he ached to rush to Miss Bodrill's and retrieve his sister, he knew it would be foolhardy to go to the school first. The weeks at sea might have improved his health, but they had done nothing for his appearance. His chin was covered with a soft beard, his hair was too long and hopelessly wind-blown. Much of his body was tanned and wind-burned, but bathing in salt water had done little to truly wash away the grime.

As soon as Garrick had conferred with Bickerstaff on the progress of the governess hunt, he would book a suite at the Bristol Hotel, take a thorough bath, trim his hair, and shave. By dinnertime, he would be on his way to Miss Bodrill's.

Lighting a pipe with shaking fingers, the man backed into the alley opposite the offices of Dickerson, Dickerson, and Smee.

He would have to notify his colleagues in Addlemeyer that the captain had arrived in Boston and would soon return.

And then what?

When he and his companions had decided to rid themselves of Garrick Dalton, they hadn't dreamed that his sister would be returned as well. The girl would not be allowed to stand in the way of the fortune that awaited them all as soon as the Dalton children were gone. The man knew his colleagues wanted to kill the girl. He shuddered. He drew the line at murdering children. He had suggested that they take Emaline back to that island near Brazil and leave her there to rot.

He dragged deeply on the fragrant tobacco, hoping it would settle his nerves. The smoke offered little comfort, however, and he choked on a cry of impatience and something akin to fear.

The master was about to return home, and there was no doubt in his mind that Captain Dalton would bring his sister with him. As soon as they stepped onto Addlemeyer's shores, disaster would follow. The man knew that as well as he knew the sun would rise and set.

But what could he do to prevent the tragedy? He certainly couldn't go to the captain, and there was nowhere else to turn.

Squeezing his eyes shut, he took quick, jerky breaths and willed himself to grow calmer.

After all, there was nothing he could do to delay the inevitable. He would have to follow through with the original plan and pray that the reward he received for his treachery would be worth a few more days of fear.

* * *

I've always found meek women to be most vulnerable to my wooing. And Emaline's mistress should be stuffed full of meekness. That way I won't have a difficult time persuading her to be my wife.

Bickerstaff groaned and massaged his temples.

"Garrick married." He said the words aloud in the empty conference room loaned to him by the solicitor Septimus Dickerson.

Bickerstaff had half expected the sound of his own voice to make the statement more real to him, but he experienced no such effect. As many times as he had pondered Garrick's outrageous announcement, he still hadn't been able to picture the words becoming reality.

The situation didn't fit the man Bickerstaff had come to regard as the nearest thing he would ever have to a brother.

Garrick had never been the marrying kind. He was the variety of male more suited to quick, tempestuous affairs than a lifelong romance. He was much too devoted to the sea and his ships to ever settle down enough to make a woman happy.

But then, happiness wasn't necessarily part of the bargain, was it? Bickerstaff realized.

If any other man had approached Bickerstaff with such a cold-blooded method of matchmaking, Bickerstaff would have challenged the man. But to hear such a proposal from Garrick didn't surprise him in the least. Since the death of his parents, Garrick had abandoned any softer emotions he might have possessed. He'd taught himself not to love—and thereby not to be hurt.

Had it not been for Emaline's return, Bickerstaff feared Garrick would have become a hardened, ill-tempered, lifelong bachelor. Fortunately, however, the news of his sister's survival had tempered his flinty reserve. Garrick adored his sister now more than ever, and for her he would do anything. Even marry a stranger.

Bickerstaff supposed he had no right to complain about Garrick's methods. Even in these enlightened times when romantic novels were the rage, arranged marriages were quite common. The fact that Garrick had asked Bickerstaff to screen the candidates was nothing more than asking him to . . . cut off his right arm and hold it temptingly in front of a lion.

Bickerstaff took a deep breath to settle the sudden roiling of his stomach. The pressure to find the perfect woman—for Garrick and for Emaline—was more than he could bear.

He'd begged Garrick to change his mind and wait until he was settled at Dalton Manor before contemplating wedlock, but Garrick had been adamant.

A woman must be found.

Immediately.

Bickerstaff frowned. Even at that point in Garrick's plan, he could have come to terms with his conscience. He would have been more than willing to delicately intimate to the women he interviewed that their prospective employer was seeking a kind, resourceful female for a bride.

Unfortunately, Garrick had insisted that Bickerstaff keep that information secret. Under no circumstances was Bickerstaff to let on that Garrick would be watching the woman with a great deal of personal interest. Her family, her prospects, her education, and her looks wouldn't matter. Emaline's needs would always be paramount.

Garrick's needs could always be met elsewhere.

So Bickerstaff had been left with the task of finding a woman who was kind, sensitive, firm, knowledgeable, serene, and infinitely loving. She must also be presentable enough for Garrick to woo her.

Bickerstaff had salved the prickings of his conscience about Garrick's cold-blooded approach to matrimony by insisting to himself that the woman could refuse Garrick's advances at any time.

A snort that was half humor, half disgust, escaped his throat. As if any female on earth would refuse Garrick anything. The man had a notorious reputation for seducing ladies—and the ladies rarely complained.

Bickerstaff wasn't sure why Garrick was so successful in persuading even the most pious female to abandon her values for an evening of lovemaking. Garrick's tall, broad frame, sharply chiseled features, and cold blue eyes should have sent them scurrying. Instead, members of the gentler sex were drawn to him like lemmings to the sea. They wanted to ease the hardness of his lips or tame the thread of savagery buried in his nature.

Women adored Garrick.

They'd always adored him.

So why was Bickerstaff hesitating? Why hadn't he chosen one of the dozens of women he'd interviewed thus far? Surely the parade of sallow-faced, pinch-lipped, holier-than-thou governesses had supplied him with a plethora of candidates. Why did he feel as if the woman he chose might be Garrick's last chance at true happiness? Why did he feel driven to find a woman who would meet Emaline's needs *and* her brother's?

As if such a lady existed. In order to catch Garrick's heart, such a female would have to be witty, smart, and confident. She would need a streak of stubbornness and a will of iron to match Garrick's. Otherwise he would dominate any conversation, any argument.

Garrick had also requested someone meek, but Bickerstaff knew full well such a quality would bore the man.

But did such a woman exist? And if she did, could she possibly be waiting in the anteroom of Dickerson, Dickerson, and Smee?

A discreet tap at the door brought his head up. Bickerstaff smoothed his vest, then his hair, realizing that the lunch break was over and the parade of women was about to continue.

"Yes?" he called, his voice filled with the same authority Garrick's solicitors might employ, since Bickerstaff was using their offices for the interviews he'd scheduled throughout the day.

The highly polished door opened without a squeak, offering a distorted reflection in its depths before Bickerstaff's attention was caught by the man standing on the other side of the threshold.

Automatically Bickerstaff stood. The stranger's dress and posture proclaimed him to be a gentleman or, at the very least, a person of importance and wealth.

"Please come in," Bickerstaff said with a sweeping gesture.

The gentleman advanced, shutting the door as he went. When he shook Bickerstaff's hand, his grip was firm, powerful. His body rivaled Garrick's in size, but the diplomatic pouch tucked under his arm gave him a very official air.

"Monsieur Bickerstaff?"

The accent was thick and very French, causing Bickerstaff's curiosity to increase.

"Yes, I'm Joshua Bickerstaff."

"I've been told you are interviewing for the position of governess for a Mademoiselle Emaline Dalton."

"That is correct."

"Très bien."

Without being asked, the stranger settled his large frame in one of the leather chairs opposite the desk, forcing Bickerstaff to sink into his own seat as if he were the one about to be interviewed. Bickerstaff and Garrick might share a casual, friendly relationship, but such attitudes were rarely manifested by those who knew him to be a paid servant.

"You will pardon me if I do not give my name for the time being," the stranger continued, tugging a pair of leather gloves from his fingers. Clasping them in one hand, he used the other to lay the diplomatic pouch in his lap. He opened the flap, giving Bickerstaff a clear view of a sheaf of legal documents and a very large, very nasty-looking pistol.

"How can I help you, Mister, er . . ." Too late, Bickerstaff remembered that the man wished to remain anonymous for the time being. "How can I help you, *monsieur?"* he said lamely.

"I have a copy of your advertisement with me." The gentleman removed a clipping from his valise. "Here you've stated that Monsieur Dalton is looking for a woman of quality to serve as a governess, the time limit of the position being indeterminate."

Bickerstaff nodded slowly, schooling his face into a bland mask. Had someone unearthed Garrick's plan? Was Bickerstaff about to be challenged for the hidden agenda buried beneath Emaline's need for a companion?

"I was asked to approach you on behalf of my own employer, a person of some renown—thus the need for anonymity."

Bickerstaff didn't bother to respond. In truth, he was somewhat startled by this man's appearance and definitely confused as to the Frenchman's intent, but he listened intently.

"My employer has become aware of the daughter of a friend who is looking for a position similar to the one you have advertised. Her name is Patience Pedigrue."

In an effort to fill the silence, he offered, "They are well acquainted, I take it, your employer and Miss Pedigrue?"

The Frenchman chose his words carefully. "Actually, my employer prefers to approach this entire situation from a distance."

"Do you mean to say your employer is serving as some sort of . . . benefactor to Miss Pedigrue?"

"In a way," the Frenchman conceded as if Bickerstaff had missed the answer to a very simple riddle. "Perhaps I should be plainer," he offered.

"Please."

"Let me start at the beginning. My employer was once very close to Miss Pedigrue and her two sisters. Indeed, she was considered very much a member of the family. Sadly, when Miss Pedigrue and her sisters were quite young, my employer lost touch with the girls. For years she had no knowledge of the children. Then, two weeks ago, she happened to stumble upon the obituary of their father, Alexander Pedigrue."

Bickerstaff still had no idea how such a tale involved him.

"It is at this point that I must ask for your discretion, Mr. Bickerstaff," the Frenchman said. "If the details I am about to tell you ever became known in society . . ."

"You have my word that nothing you say will leave this room."

"Good." The Frenchman's eyes became dark and

piercing. "Arriving in Boston during Alexander Pedigrue's funeral, my employer happened to speak with one of the solicitors appointed as executor of the estate. After a good deal of . . . convincing, he was persuaded to talk about the contents of Mr. Pedigrue's will."

Bickerstaff couldn't help but smile. So the Frenchman and his employer weren't above using chicanery to meet their own ends.

"Am I to understand that money changed hands?" he murmured.

"An enormous sum of money," the Frenchman concurred.

"To what end?"

"It was imperative that my employer discover the contents of the will before it was read."

"And were the results worth the expenditure?"

"Very much so." The Frenchman's blunt jaw hardened even more. "We soon discovered that Alexander Pedigrue had kept his children in servitude for most of their lives. Except for infrequent errands in town, they were imprisoned in their father's home. At first, as children, they were given the finest education that money could buy. But as the Pedigrue sisters grew to adulthood, their father became more and more tyrannical in his demands."

When the Frenchman paused, Bickerstaff shrugged. "I have yet to see how any of this is connected with my business here today."

"I am nearing that very point." The Frenchman withdrew a set of legal documents from his valise. "This is the original will. The plight of the other sisters is irrelevant to my visit, but you will note the passage marked for your inspection. In order to receive a measly inheritance of five hundred dollars,

Miss Patience Pedigrue was told that she must complete a year of servitude in a nearby asylum."

The words were bluntly spoken, shocking Bickerstaff just as they had been meant to do.

"You must be joking."

"No, *monsieur.* I am afraid I speak the truth. Moreover, Alexander Pedigrue—a man worth over a million dollars—expected his daughters to prove their worthiness to him even after he'd gone to his grave. For their diligence, they would receive little more than a yearly stipend and his permission to live in the family home."

Bickerstaff skimmed the document, noting immediately that what the stranger said was true.

"But if the woman has been sent to work in an asylum—"

"Miss Pedigrue never received those instructions, Mr. Bickerstaff. My employer managed to intercept the will and replace it with an altered copy."

Bickerstaff's brows rose. "A fact which must have caused even more money to change hands."

"I am glad you have understood the . . . nuances of my story, Mr. Bickerstaff." He collected the will and tucked it in the pouch on his lap. "When the altered testament was read, the Pedigrue sisters were surprised to discover that each of them had been granted a . . . wish of sorts. Rather than being burdened with their father's prescribed tasks, they were offered a chance to spend a year indulging themselves in an occupation more suited to their needs and interests."

"So Miss Patience Pedigrue . . ."

"Has often expressed a wish to be free of Boston, to find the means to support herself, and to live a life completely different from that which she led so far."

A life completely different from that which she has led so far.

Bickerstaff felt the quickening of his pulse. Did that mean she longed for the adventure that could be found in the company of a sea captain? Had she longed to meet a man who was gallant and fierce? Would she wish to live in a house filled with luxuries and to possess a fortune beside which her father's would pale in comparision?

Bickerstaff tamped down his enthusiasm. He knew nothing of this woman save her dire circumstances. Besides, she had a protector. A person of renown as this Frenchman had stated.

"So your employer would like for me to interview this woman for the position open in the Dalton household?"

The Frenchman dipped his head in agreement. "My employer believes that Miss Pedigrue would benefit from a long-term situation such as the one you are offering."

A long-term situation? Meaning a *permanent* situation?

The stranger continued, "Even so, my employer intends to ensure that Miss Pedigrue's future employment will be of the highest quality."

"What makes you think the position I offer is one of quality and endurance?" Bickerstaff replied, his pulse still thudding in his ears with excitement at the possibilities being presented to him.

"My employer knows the Dalton family is above reproach."

Bickerstaff took a moment to digest everything he'd heard so far. "If I understand the purpose of your visit correctly, you would like for me to hire this . . . Miss Pedigrue without even conducting an interview?"

"Not at all. We are well acquainted with the circumstances surrounding Emaline Dalton's return to the United States. We wouldn't dream of interfering with her education. But we would appreciate your efforts if you would *strongly* consider Miss Pedigrue for the position. She has impeccable manners, a firm foundation in the classics, musical training, a—"

"And no real family to speak of?" Bickerstaff asked with seeming nonchalance, wondering if the Fates were about to smile. So far, the governesses he'd interviewed had been competent, but each of them had mentioned ties—children, elderly parents, nieces, nephews. If Garrick's plan was to succeed, Bickerstaff would need to locate a woman with as few entanglements as possible.

The Frenchman's eyes narrowed as he considered his answer. "Not really. As I mentioned earlier, she has two sisters, each of whom has also been given a chance to follow her heart's desire. Whatever other relatives Miss Pedigrue might have are quite . . . er, distantly removed."

The response was exactly what Bickerstaff had hoped to hear. At the very least Miss Pedigrue wouldn't have an irate father appearing at Dalton Manor when he discovered the precipitate nature of his daughter's courtship.

A slow smile spread over Bickerstaff's lips. Only moments earlier he'd been bemoaning his task. But he might—*might*—have found a solution to all the problems presented. If Miss Pedigrue proved presentable, Emaline would have a mother, Garrick a wife, and Miss Pedigrue a home and family.

"I would be very happy to interview the woman, Monsieur . . ." Bickerstaff allowed his words to trail away, making the Frenchman aware that the time for anonymity had now passed.

"Renoir. Étienne Renoir."

Étienne Renoir? Upon Bickerstaff's arrival in Boston, he'd collected all of the local newspapers and periodicals to satisfy his hunger for fresh news. He'd been inundated with articles describing the famed actress Louise Chevalier. The woman had arrived unexpectedly in Boston for a short holiday. Nearly an entire wing of the Palace Hotel had been devoted to her entourage of servants, one of them being her personal bodyguard, Étienne Renoir.

Choosing his words carefully, Bickerstaff said, "Miss Chevalier must be very fond of Miss Pedigrue to have you come to me in this fashion."

"As I stated before, Miss Pedigrue probably does not remember my employer at all. Miss Chevalier's interest in her is sentimental."

"Would Miss Chevalier be visiting Miss Pedigrue should she be employed by Captain Dalton?"

The Frenchman grew thoughtful. "Very doubtful. She has a busy rehearsal schedule, and as I said before, my employer wishes to remain anonymous for the time being. Once again, I hope I have your word that no mention will be made of my visit."

"I will keep all of the information given to me in strictest confidence."

"Thank you."

Bickerstaff wanted to throw his hands into the air and dance a jig, but such a reaction would have tipped his hand.

"I thank you for bringing the woman to my attention, Monsieur Renoir."

The Frenchman gathered his things and closed his valise. Standing, he extended his hand, but this time he held Bickerstaff's grip a moment longer than necessary. "If Miss Pedigrue happens to be chosen as

Emaline Dalton's governess, do I have your word that she will be treated well?"

Bickerstaff fought an inexplicable urge to grin. "I believe that I can safely say she will be welcomed like a close member of the family."

This time it was the Frenchman who allowed himself the smallest hint of a smile. "My employer will be extremely pleased."

"Will you offer her my warmest regards?"

The Frenchman tugged his gloves over his hands. "I will be happy to pass on your sentiments. Thank you for your attention." He touched a finger to his brow. "Good day."

The man left as abruptly as he'd come.

As soon as the door closed, Bickerstaff rushed to sift through his papers for the mention of Miss Patience Pedigrue.

Smiling smugly to himself, he noted that she was scheduled for the first appointment after lunch.

Chapter

4

Patience Pedigrue covertly studied the women who sat like iron statues on the uncomfortable chairs lining the office walls.

Blast it all, they looked so much more qualified than she. They were grim and stern and no doubt highly experienced, while she had not even considered seeking employment until her father died.

She pressed her lips together and fought to keep her expression implacably blank. In the weeks since Alexander Pedigrue's funeral, she had been unable to summon any tears for her father's passing, and she supposed she would be damned to the fires of hell for such disrespect. But how could she feel bad when her father had done his best to strip all vestiges of joy from his daughters' lives?

Patience remembered that the Pedigrue sisters hadn't always been entrusted to their father's sole care. She had vague memories of her mother, a beautiful woman who had brought laughter and joy to every person she touched.

Then she had left her children for a lover and a new family.

At first Patience had refused to believe Louise Pedigrue capable of such betrayal. As a child, she'd insisted over and over to herself: *Mama would never abandon us. Never.*

But the years had proved her childlike faith to be false. Alexander Pedigrue had taken his daughters to his birthplace in Boston, then had secluded them in the old Pedigrue home to "protect them from the evils of the world." No word had ever been heard from Louise since.

In the early years the loss of their mother had been the only hardship. Nannies and governesses had been hired, and special tutors had been brought into the home. But as the girls grew to resemble the pictures of their mother hidden in the attic, Alexander Pedigrue had become more embittered and intractable. One by one, servants were dismissed and Felicity, Patience, and Constance Pedigrue were expected to assume the household duties.

That was how Patience knew of her father's wealth. It was she who had shown a talent for bookkeeping, so on rare occasions she was allowed to spend the day in Boston proper running errands for her father. Once outside his scrutiny, she rushed down the cobbled streets to the market by the wharf, where she sated her curiosity about unusual ships, foreign people, and strange cargoes. She'd known all along that someday she would board one of those ships and sail into the sunset.

Unfortunately her limited freedom had always come to an end far too soon, and she'd had to rush home to avoid a scolding or, worse yet, a beating.

Patience slammed the door on her musings, not wanting to remember how Alexander Pedigrue had made his home unbearable for his girls. Even now, after his death, he was doing his best to rule them from beyond the grave, refusing to part with even a shred of his vast fortune until his girls proved themselves worthy of the yearly pittance he was willing to spend on their behalf.

She gritted her teeth. Five hundred dollars a year. Of the fortune he possessed, her father had offered his daughters only five hundred dollars a year and the use of the home once owned by his own parents. As an added insult, he'd stipulated that even this small allowance would be awarded only to those girls who proved themselves worthy of it. Felicity had been sent out west to teach school, Constance had journeyed south to New York to serve as a seamstress, and Patience was to devote herself to some unknown family as a governess.

Since Alexander Pedigrue's solicitors were named as executors of the estate, they had been responsible for finding Patience a suitable position. So far, Patience had been sent on a dozen interviews, each of the proffered positions being worse than the last. The first had involved a household of six boys, hooligans all. The second situation had offered three sets of twins under seven, the third an uneducated herd of children with hair redder than Patience's and tempers to match, and the fourth . . .

No. She didn't want to think about her prospects anymore. She was tired of jumping to obey her father's commands, even posthumously. If she'd had one penny of her own, she would have struck out into the world to obtain the only thing she had ever wanted: a chance to see the world outside Boston.

Patience had refused to commit herself to one particular family—although, to be honest, no one had offered her more than an interview and a firm goodbye. Over and over again she'd been told she was too young, too inexperienced, too ambitious, too willful, too tall, too thin, too naive.

A sigh rose in her throat, but Patience tamped it down. She kept hoping that somehow, some way, she would stumble upon a position that might fulfill her desire for independence. Then she would perform the twelve months of service her father had demanded, collect her five hundred dollars, and strike out into the world beyond Boston.

But her father's solicitors had sent her on one more interview—this time to a family who hadn't even seen fit to question her themselves. Instead, they'd sent a friend of the family—the master's valet, if the whispers in the waiting room were to be believed.

Shocking. Absolutely shocking.

Despite the unorthodox arrangement, the solicitor's office was crowded with hopeful prospects, especially since the position advertised involved only one child, a nine-year-old.

Please, please, let me make a good impression this time, Patience prayed silently. *To have only one tidy, polite little girl to watch over would be heaven.*

Especially in contrast to the three sets of twins.

"Miss Pedigrue!"

A stout clerk stepped into the doorway, then motioned for her to accompany him.

Steeling herself in an effort to look calm, cool, and collected, Patience followed him down a dim hallway to a richly paneled door.

"Wait here, Miss Pedigrue," the clerk said as he ushered her inside. "Mr. Bickerstaff is due back from his lunch break any moment."

Patience stifled an irritated sigh. Thus far, she'd spent two hours in the offices of Dickerson, Dickerson, and Smee without encountering anyone directly connected to the Dalton family. She was tired of waiting, tired of remaining quiet, still, and proper. If she had her wish, she'd tear the pins from her hair, strip away the itchy wool basque she wore, and run uninhibited through the park across the street.

Drawn to the window, she gazed out at the expanse of green lawn and flowering shrubbery. A pond glittered enticingly, reminding Patience that her father had not allowed such frivolity as swimming or cavorting in public.

"Who are you?"

The barking demand came from the doorway behind her, and Patience whirled, a hand automatically touching her throat as if in an attempt to block her automatic outcry.

Instantly she focused on one of the largest men she had ever encountered. He towered well over six feet, the width of his shoulders dwarfing the doorway. His clothing was rough and worn, his sleeves rolled up to his elbow, his hair long and windblown. Overall, he looked more like a dockside ruffian than a man intent on grilling prospective governesses. Indeed, the black patch he wore over one eye gave him a piratical appearance.

Horrified to be caught so blatantly woolgathering, she hastened to explain, "I—I was merely enjoying the view."

"Undoubtedly."

He didn't seem at all pleased by such an admission, so she hastened to explain, "I was sent here to wait."

"Oh, really."

She fought the urge to huff indignantly. The man was being rude. He spoke to her as if he'd caught her reading private papers, not looking out the window. Moreover, as he took a step into the room and slammed the door behind him, there was no escaping the aura of authority he brought with him. His bearing, his manner, his expression of hauteur, declared eloquently enough that he was a man accustomed to giving orders and having them obeyed.

So this was Joshua Bickerstaff? The man reputed to be Captain Dalton's valet?

Impossible. This man could never have been a servant of any sort, let alone a gentleman's gentleman.

Then who was he? And what right did he have to scrutinize her so discourteously?

As the man's eye swept over her frame for the second time, Patience stiffened. She'd long since grown weary of the way interviewers studied her as if she were a specimen in a bottle. She'd grown all too aware that some found her youth a disadvantage, her red hair a distraction, and her inexperience a complication. But that did not mean she had to endure an inspection that bordered on . . .

On what? Intimacy? Indecency? Why, the man looked at her as if he hadn't seen a woman in months.

"Mr. Bickerstaff," she began boldly, "I wish you would—"

She had no opportunity to finish her request. Instead, the man grinned at her—a naughty, mischievous, mocking grin that sent a rash of gooseflesh down her spine.

"I'm not Joshua Bickerstaff," he said bluntly, then chuckled to himself as if the whole situation were a rich joke. "As a matter of fact, I'm looking for the man myself."

Garrick Dalton watched the color seep from the woman's cheeks, causing her skin to appear even paler, her hair even redder. It was obvious that she was startled by his appearance, just as he was astounded by hers.

He'd arrived at his solicitors' offices less than a half

hour after docking in Boston, only to discover that Bickerstaff had left minutes before in search of lunch.

Since Garrick had been impatient to groom himself in preparation for retrieving Emaline, he'd asked his solicitors for a current report on the governess hunt. He'd never dreamed that the post was still unfilled. He couldn't imagine why it was taking Bickerstaff so long to choose a teacher for Emaline and a bridal candidate for him.

But once he'd stepped into his solicitors' waiting room and seen the gaggle of women who had appointments, he'd understood at least a portion of Joshua's delay. Never in his life had he seen such a collection of prune-faced, brittle-boned, sour old maids and widows. When the clerk informed Garrick that one of the prospects was waiting for her interview in the room reserved for Mr. Bickerstaff's use, Garrick had resignedly agreed to question the candidate himself. He'd been sure he would find yet another woman well past her prime and relegated to a life of servitude.

Instead, he'd discovered a woman with hair the color of fire.

Garrick moved to lean on the desk. Amused, he watched as she countered his advance by crossing toward one of the leather chairs and gripping its back.

"If you aren't Mr. Bickerstaff, then who are you, sir?"

Garrick was sure that she'd meant to sound like a queen deigning to speak to a beggar, but when he began to study her even more closely, a breathiness had feathered her tone.

Her expression became immediately wary.

"I'm a friend of Mr. Bickerstaff's," he replied noncommittally, but the fact that he'd avoided giving his name did not escape her notice.

"He hasn't returned from lunch yet," she offered archly, as if she knew all about Mr. Bickerstaff and his habits.

"Then I suppose we'll have to wait, won't we?"

Clearly she found that remark less than comforting.

"I suppose you have business with the man?" she said, but he sensed she spoke more from want of something to fill the silence than from a need for an answer.

"Yes, I do," he replied, but gave her no more information than that.

To his amusement, she pursed her lips in irritation. This woman had a short fuse to her temper, he would wager. She would be the sort of woman who was icy on the outside, but blazingly hot when she dropped her guard.

Offering a soft huff, she turned away from him to stare out the window again. He wondered if he should inform her that her attempt to discourage his interest had failed. Instead, he found himself freely studying the fragility of her shoulders, the tiny circumference of her waist. She wasn't a busty woman by any means. Unlike the voluptuous women considered most fashionable by current society, she was thin and willowy and had made no attempt to hide that fact.

"You haven't answered my question," he said after a few minutes of silence.

She tried her best to ignore him, but finally relented and haughtily demanded, "What question might that be?"

"Who are you?"

She glanced over her shoulder, openly peeved and ready to point out that she'd asked his name and hadn't received a reply. But since the alternative to answering him appeared to be a tension-fraught silence, she said, "My name is Patience Pedigrue. I have come to be interviewed for the position of governess to the sister of Captain Garrick Dalton. I wouldn't suppose you'd know him."

"We've met."

Her brows rose in patent disbelief.

"I suppose you've had scads of experience," he inquired.

Her response was breezy. "I've taught dozens of children."

Looking at her, Garrick was sure that she hadn't been out of short skirts all that long herself. She couldn't be much more than eighteen or nineteen years old.

"Really?" His doubt was blatant.

"My, yes." She faced him completely, waving dismissingly. "I've developed quite a reputation for my work."

"How extraordinary."

This time his low drawl brought a frown.

"You sound surprised," she said challengingly.

"It's merely that you appear so young."

"Looks can be deceiving."

He nodded, conceding the point. "So where did you acquire all this experience?"

She took a deep breath, seemed to grope for words, then said, "I've spent most of my time in Europe, actually."

"Which parts?"

She shrugged as if such a petty detail didn't matter. "France, Italy, Belgium. I even served as governess to a Russian count at one time."

"My, my. You have been busy." He knew she was lying, and he was quite sure she was aware of his opinion, but she didn't back down.

"Idle hands are the devil's workshop," she said.

"Are they?"

This time she glared at him. "Yes," she stated firmly, in a way that reminded him of his own governess. "They are."

Garrick couldn't remember the last time he'd sparred with a woman in this manner. He was so accustomed to having females fall all over themselves in an effort to please him that this woman's honest reaction was incredibly refreshing.

Nevertheless, he wouldn't want a steady diet of such spiritedness. Would he?

Wishing to stifle the woman's challenging nature, he stated bluntly, "You don't look like a governess."

Her frown deepened to a scowl. "Since we have not yet been introduced, Mister . . ."

Ignoring her ploy to obtain his name, Garrick continued. "All of the other women applying for the job seem much more . . . advanced in years."

She didn't immediately speak, but her lips were so tightly pressed together that he knew she longed to utter a pithy retort.

"Aren't you a trifle young to have had so many employers?"

"I've lived more than two decades," she said with a proud tipping of her chin.

Twenty years? Or more?

"So old?"

"I'm not in my dotage."

"No, I suppose not. Pity."

He wouldn't have thought such a reaction possible, but her posture grew even more rigid.

"Some would look upon my youth as an advantage."

"How so?"

"I can identify with children more readily."

"And have you?"

"Have I what?"

"Identified with many children? What about your Russian count? We both know you've never even *seen* a Russian count, let alone his offspring."

The color, which had been absent earlier, now flooded her cheeks at having her fabrication pointed out to her.

"Have your charges come to look upon you as a friend as well as a governess?" After a pause, he added, "Have you even *had* any pupils?"

"Mmm," she offered noncommittally.

"I don't think I heard you properly."

Her knuckles grew white against the leather of the chair. "I don't believe I am required to give you an answer. Such details are best left to Mr. Bickerstaff's formal interview and not to idle conversation. If you aren't affiliated with Mr. Bickerstaff or the Dalton family, I fail to see—"

"At first glance, I would have assumed you'd never worked a day in your life. I'd picture you more as a woman bent on philanthropic exercises. You know the sort—those who gather charity baskets or linens for the local orphanage."

She was breathing more quickly now, her hands dropping to her sides, her fingers curling into fists. "I—"

He didn't give her time to continue. "In fact, you have the fragile, porcelainlike air of a woman who has never wanted for anything." He prowled toward her, unsure why he felt driven to push this woman to the limit, but if the women in the antechamber were representative of his bridal candidates, this woman was by far the prettiest of the lot. Nevertheless, he had to know if her facade of steely resolve was too deeply ingrained to accommodate the meekness he required in a wife.

He did need an heir, after all. She would have to

submit to him in order to supply him with a son to carry on the Dalton name or a daughter to dote upon.

Miss Pedigrue must have sensed a change in his manner, because she began to back away from him, making her way slowly but steadily toward the door.

"I believe that I would prefer to wait for Mr. Bickerstaff in the—"

"Am I right, Miss Pedigrue? Are you a pampered thoroughbred filly intent on amusing herself by playing teacher-for-a-month? Or are you honestly interested in the well-being of the children who may come to regard you as something of a mother?"

To his surprise, Patience Pedigrue halted in her tracks. Her chest was heaving in anger, her green eyes snapping in indignation.

"How dare you?" she hissed. "How dare *you*—a man who can't even tend to the most basic grooming needs—judge me?"

One tiny foot stamped the floor as she whipped a long, pointed hat pin from her bonnet and brandished it in his direction like a sword. "Get away from me this instant, or I'll make you rue the day you ever crossed me, sir."

He automatically took a step backward, causing her to relax a bit. When she spoke again, her voice was more controlled, but only slightly.

"I don't care if you're connected with the Dalton family or not, Mr. Whatever-Your-Name-Is. As far as I'm concerned, you have no right to speak to me, question me, or insult me, no matter who you are. Frankly, I think that *you* are in far more need of an education in manners than any nine-year-old girl. As for me, I am a woman of simple means and high values, and I will *not* stand here and allow you to insult me any further. Good day, sir!"

With that, she readjusted her bonnet, jabbed the

hat pin into the crown, and stormed from the room—
just as Joshua Bickerstaff attempted to enter.

In an attempt to appease the woman, Joshua Bickerstaff flattened himself against the wall. Open-
mouthed, he watched the stranger march down the
hall, her skirts twitching in patent indignation. Then
he moved through the doorway and regarded Garrick
inquisitively, obviously less than surprised at Garrick's unannounced arrival.

"What in hell's name happened here?" he asked,
regarding his longtime friend.

"Hire her," Garrick ordered as he began to search
the desk for some sort of liquor.

"Who?"

"Patience Pedigrue."

A long silence punctuated Garrick's statement.
Then Bickerstaff said, *"That* was Patience Pedigrue?"

"So she said." Garrick had finally located a bottle
of brandy, and he offered Bickerstaff a firm stare. "Go
get her and hire her."

"After you rattled her so completely? Even *I*
wouldn't take a job from you if that's the way you
conclude an interview."

"I didn't interview her in the strictest sense of the
word. Nor did I give her my name. For all she knew, I
was a stranger off the street. Therefore, the last few
minutes should not dissuade her from accepting a
position as Emaline's governess."

Bickerstaff couldn't speak. His jaw dropped again,
and he wondered why on earth Garrick even wanted
the woman, judging by the temper she'd just displayed.

"Dammit, Bickerstaff," Garrick said. "Go find the
woman, offer her the job, then send her to meet with
me at the Bristol Hotel in an hour. I'd like to collect

Emaline from Miss Bodrill's as soon as possible, and I think Miss Pedigrue should join us all, but I've got to bathe and shave first."

"An hour! But—"

"Please, Joshua," Garrick interrupted, his voice filled with concern. "I have to get to Emaline. We've been separated far too long as it is. As soon as you've notified the governess of her responsibilities, head to the docks and get a report from Mr. Rosemund. He hopes to ready the ship by morning, but if the customs officials delay him . . ."

"I know, I know," Bickerstaff grumbled. "There will be hell to pay. You want to take Emaline to Addlemeyer as soon as possible."

At the mention of Emaline, Bickerstaff stared at Garrick consideringly. "Did you bring some appropriate clothes with you from London?"

Garrick peered down at himself, then scowled. What he'd brought with him was merely more of the same rough attire.

Before Garrick could reply, Bickerstaff held up a hand. "Shall I find you something to wear on my way to fetch the governess? If you appear in that getup, Emaline will think *you're* the one who's been marooned on an island."

Bickerstaff was right, but Garrick's frown grew blacker. "Buy whatever I need. Just hurry."

With that, Garrick swallowed the last of his brandy and exited the room as abruptly as Miss Pedigrue had done, leaving Bickerstaff to wonder when and how he would tell his employer about the circumstances that had brought Patience Pedigrue to this office in the first place.

Chapter

5

Addlemeyer Island

"A letter! A letter from the master!"

Willie Burton hurried from the dock into the mercantile and made a beeline for the postal counter located in the rear corner. With trembling fingers, he handed the vellum missive to Mrs. Gray, the postmistress.

Edda Gray's lips twitched excitedly as the shop grew silent around her. Everyone present—from Alvin Harris, the owner of the establishment, to seven-year-old Miranda Polski, who swept behind the counters—knew that a letter addressed to the postal office could mean only one thing: Captain Garrick Dalton was about to announce his return.

Mrs. Gray took great enjoyment in pausing and extracting a handkerchief from the top drawer of her desk. As if she hadn't a care in the world or the slightest reason to hurry, she dabbed at her nose.

She knew her leisurely manner was maddening to those present, and in truth, she was burning with curiosity as to the intent of the letter awaiting her inspection. But by thunder, she wouldn't give these . . . commoners a reason to chatter about her manners.

"I suppose we should read it straightaway," she murmured.

Willie stared at her as if she'd lost her senses.

Nonchalantly searching the drawer, she chose a minute pair of scissors. With utmost precision, she slit the sealed flap and withdrew the single sheet of paper.

Naturally, she—as well as the rest of those present—assumed that Captain Dalton had written to them himself, so it was with a good deal of disappointment that she noted that the signature was that of the captain's upstart valet. Nevertheless, she allowed no hint of distress to mar her brow. Slowly, silently, she read the curt note, which announced that the captain would soon return. The house and the shipping company books were to be ready for his inspection.

Without a word or a hint of emotion, she folded the sheet, reinserted it in the envelope, then slid the entire packet toward Willie again. "Take this to the shipping office, then on up to Miss Fitch at Dalton Manor."

Since Willie couldn't read, he took the note, then waited expectantly for Mrs. Gray to continue.

Adopting the dignity of a queen, she braced her meaty hands on the counter. Her chins trembled as she surveyed her expectant audience.

Sighing as if supremely pressed, she announced, "The master and his sister are coming home."

A furor of excitement billowed through the room, finally reaching the woman who had entered the establishment mere moments earlier and stood unnoticed near the pickle barrels.

The master and his sister are coming home.

The words reverberated in the room amid exclamations of excitement and joy.

Moving carefully to avoid attention, the woman slipped out the back door, then took deep drags of air to calm an inexplicable frantic urge to run.

It wasn't as if the announcement had come as any sort of a surprise. News of the explosion at sea had reached them months ago. Close on the heels of such tidings had come the announcement that Emaline Dalton had been found alive.

She'd known that it was only a matter of time before the Dalton children were reunited and returned to the family estate. Even so, she'd dreaded that day. Dreaded it, planned for it, prepared for it.

Discovering that Emaline had been boarded at a school for young girls, the woman had begun her preparations in Boston, hiring a clerk at the customs house to watch for Garrick Dalton, his ships, or his men. A fortnight earlier, she had received the first report: Joshua Bickerstaff had arrived in America and had begun interviewing servants for Dalton Manor.

That tiny piece of information was all that was needed for her to send her colleague to Boston. The months of scheming were about to be put to the test, and she was ready for the challenge.

Looking up, the woman squinted against the bright glare of the sun, noting the way the light winked over the house on the hill. The sight, so familiar and disturbing, caused a pang of regret.

So beautiful. Dalton Manor stood like a rare diamond in its setting of green, beckoning with a siren's song of might-have-beens.

The brief wave of sadness faded beneath a burst of anger, then the icy calm of resolve.

The master of the house would take up residence at

Dalton Manor, the woman reminded herself silently. But the master she referred to was not Garrick Dalton. No, it was time for the real heir to the Dalton legacy to step forward and be heard.

Pivoting in the direction of the shipping company, the woman began to hum.

Garrick and Emaline Dalton were both in America, she repeated over and over to herself. The news must be spread quickly so a proper welcoming could be organized.

Patience stepped into the gilt-and-marble foyer of the Bristol Hotel in Boston, then stopped in her tracks, her jaw gaping ever so slightly.

Never in her wildest dreams would she have imagined that a place such as this existed in all the world, let alone the city in which she lived.

Heedless of the guests who flowed past her, she gazed in wonder at the black marble floors streaked with gray and white. Mahogany gleamed from the front desk as well as the paneled walls and elegant furniture. Then, lest the room prove too dark, bright patches of red peeked out at her from the brocade on the overstuffed chairs, the fringe on the draperies and pillows, and the vibrant peacock blue of the runners and area rugs.

The grand surroundings immediately dampened the triumph she'd felt since Joshua Bickerstaff had arrived on her doorstep a mere fifty minutes ago. After explaining that he regretted missing their interview, he'd flabbergasted her completely by explaining that she had been recommended to him by a friend and that if she wished to take the position, it was hers for the asking.

Take it?

A position that involved only one child, an exotic

seacoast location, and a mysterious sea captain? She would have been daft to refuse.

Against her elder sister's objections to the haste involved, she had packed the few personal items that had not already been readied for storage. Then she'd hastily dressed in her finest wool suit and bonnet and all but raced to the Bristol Hotel to meet her new employer.

Captain Garrick Dalton.

Such a noble sounding name. In her mind's eye, she envisioned him as she was sure he would be. Wise in the ways of the world, steeped in tradition and responsibility. A touch of silver would grace his dark hair, and lines of experience would crease a thoughtful brow. No doubt he smoked a pipe, took long walks in the evening, and never, ever allowed a coarse word to escape his lips.

"Move out of the way, lady!"

Too late, Patience realized that she'd blocked the entrance to the hotel and become the object of a newsy's glare.

"Pardon me," she murmured, feeling a heat singe her cheeks.

Dash it all, Patience, she silently scolded herself. *This is no time to be woolgathering.*

She had a job to do. A paying job. One that did not involve catering to Alexander Pedigrue's every whim.

Moving decisively to the front desk, she surrounded herself with an air of stern civility, knowing from experience with her own childhood governesses that such an expression was favored by such women.

"May I help you?" a sallow-faced gentleman asked from behind the marble-topped counter.

"I have been told to meet with Captain Dalton. May I have his room number, please?"

The man blinked, then lifted the pince-nez held to

his vest with a gold chain. "You want the *captain's* room number?"

"Yes, please."

"You're not his usual type."

"Type?"

The man shrugged as if the fact were no concern of his.

"Room one-seven. Up those stairs and to the right."

"Thank you."

Aware that the clerk still regarded her through his spectacles, she walked stiffly to the wide spiral staircase. Halfway to the top, she heard a soft giggle and, looking up, saw a gentleman descending the steps, a woman of rather liberal values clinging to his arm.

The clerk's words rushed into her brain: *You're not his usual type.*

The heat of embarrassment that had only just receded thundered through her veins again. Surely that man didn't think that she . . . that the captain . . . that . . .

Filled with righteous anger, she glanced over her shoulder, then glared at the sallow-faced clerk.

Immediately contrite, he ducked his head and began to leaf through the registration book, but even his obvious contrition didn't mollify her. Perhaps she should have insisted that the captain meet her in the lobby—someplace public and respectable.

But she hadn't considered such a thing, and even if she had, she couldn't require her new employer to dance attendance to her whims. Such outlandish behavior would have her on the streets in no time—and her five-hundred-dollar stipend sent to some charity in her father's name.

No. From this moment on, she would have to guard her every word and her every action. She must be calm, biddable, obedient, and respectful. But she must also guard her reputation like a treasured jewel. At no time should she give rise to gossip. If she really intended to use her wits to garner a position as a lady's traveling companion, she would need references, and Captain Dalton's might prove to be the most important recommendation of all.

Stiffening her spine, she pressed her lips together as Miss Grundle, her music teacher, had been wont to do. Then, straightening her bonnet, she jabbed her hat pin more securely through the rope of braids at the nape of her neck, tugged her bodice into place, fluffed her lace-edged collar up, and knocked on the door of room one-seven.

"Come in!"

The muffled bark could not be construed as anything other than a summons, so Patience took a deep, steadying breath and twisted the glass doorknob.

You are a proper, dignified governess.
Act like one.

Prepared to find a gruff seaman dressed in a blue woolen suit piped in black, she was disappointed to find that the door opened into an unoccupied sitting room furnished in the same lush palette as the foyer downstairs.

"Is that you, Bickerstaff?" A deep voice bellowed from beyond a doorway at the far end.

Patience briefly debated how she should respond.

Had she come too early? Too late? Should she have sent someone from the desk to inform the captain she was here?

Before a proper greeting could pop into her head, a shadow fell across the doorway. Then a huge shape filled the opening, blocking the light that had once streamed through the aperture.

Then, just as quickly, came the rest of the details and impressions gleaned by her stunned senses.

The man wasn't wearing any clothes. Except for the bath towel wrapped around his hips and the dark patch over his eye, he was as bare as the day he'd been born. Even so, there was no mistaking his resemblance to the oaf she'd met at Dickerson, Dickerson, and Smee.

"You!" Patience gulped in surprise.

"Miss Pedigrue, I assume?"

The voice was low, dark, and deep, sending a rash of shivers through Patience's body.

Sweet heaven above, *this* man was her employer?

The man was huge, the effect made even stronger by the muscular shape of his naked arms and chest. His skin was tanned, his fingers long and tapered. Pinkish scars dotted the skin on his upper torso, forcing her to look up, up, up, into a face that was craggy and hard and implacably grim.

"Mist . . . Captain Dalton?"

She'd meant for her reply to be firm and without hesitation, but it emerged as a question.

Vaguely she noted that despite his ablutions, his hair was still longer than was fashionable, the wet strands waving to a point beyond his shoulders—a legacy, no doubt, of his months at sea. The whole effect was slightly pagan.

Now, where had that thought come from? Patience wondered in horror. But even as she condemned the purely feminine response as incredibly foolish, she was reaching up to check her bonnet and the sweep of hair drawn back to the nape of her neck.

The tall, wheat-haired giant stared at her long and hard—as if he hadn't seen her that very afternoon, wearing this very suit, waiting to be interviewed for the position as Emaline Dalton's governess.

Then, just as quickly, came the thought that this man had been wearing something else.

Clothes.

Horrified that she had burst in on her employer—no, on that oaf from the solicitor's office—she whirled, presenting her back to him and covering her cheeks with her fingers.

She would be fired for certain now. The man would never wish to have an employee in his household who had seen him in such a state of dishabille.

Thankfully, before the man could speak, the outer door burst open and a wiry gentleman appeared, carrying an armload of bundles.

"I managed to buy something for tonight, but as for tomor . . . row . . ."

His statement trailed into silence as he looked at Patience, then Garrick.

"It's about time you got here, Bickerstaff," the captain's deeper voice responded. "Come show me what sort of trappings you've chosen this time."

To her immense relief, Patience heard the two men disappear into what must have been the bedchamber.

The slam of the door made her jump. Closing her eyes, she flattened a hand over her heart and willed her pulse to stop its tumbling gait. But the deep breaths she took had no effect. Nor did the silent count from one to ten.

Constance had been right. Patience should not have run willy-nilly into this situation. As usual, she had followed her instincts, acted hastily, and now would be forced to endure the consequences. If only she had summoned the captain to the front desk. Or waited for *him* to open the door. Or called out his name to warn him a woman was nearby.

If, if, if. *If*s never did a body any good. The deed had been done. She'd caught the man in the moments after he'd stepped out of his bath.

Not much more than seconds, she would suppose, judging by the water dappling his shoulders.

Her mistake could not be erased.

Just as the picture of his sculpted chest and taut, washboard stomach would be impossible to banish.

She would merely have to live with the results.

And with that man. In his house. Days. Nights.

A squeak of distress burst from her throat.

"Is anything wrong, Miss Pedigrue?"

Her eyes flew open, and she found herself looking into the reflection of the captain's face in the mirror hanging next to the fireplace.

An iciness swept through her body, then a blazing heat. Gone was the rough-clad tormentor who had taunted her in his solicitor's offices. Gone was the pagan body of the man who wore nothing but a towel. The wheat-gold hair had been savagely combed into place. A snowy white cravat hung untied beneath a clean-shaven jawline. And the giant's body had been disguised with a shirt, a half-buttoned brocade vest, faun breeches, and shiny black boots.

His brows lifted ever so slightly.

"You look quite stunned, Miss Pedigrue. Should I pirouette to reassure you that I am properly—and completely—clothed?"

Blast the blush that scalded her cheeks, and blast this man for drawing attention to the very fact she wanted to forget.

Bickerstaff entered and began to finish dressing the captain.

Stiffening her shoulders, she said, "I suppose the offer of the governess's position was in jest—an exchange of embarrassments."

"Embarrassments?" he echoed in honest confusion.

71

"I'm sure the dressing-down I offered in the hallway of your solicitor's office didn't sit well with you and you devised this little . . . charade for my benefit."

His eye narrowed, but there was no mockery in the icy blue depths, only a certain thoughtfulness. "I hate to disprove such an intellectual theory, Miss Pedigrue. But I can assure you that I found your remarks this afternoon to be less than memorable and hardly a . . . 'dressing-down' as you refer to them."

"Then . . ." She bit her lip when she realized that she'd impetuously jumped from one anthill to another.

His grin was impudent. "The position is yours, Miss Pedigrue—providing, of course, that a more thorough interview reassures me of your suitability for the job. Then you need only hope that my sister approves."

"Approves?" she echoed weakly.

"If you're to be her daily companion, don't you think she should have some say in the matter?"

"Yes, of course."

"Haven't your previous employers demanded much the same thing? And this time, let's avoid the realm of fiction, hmm?"

"My . . . previous experience did not occur under quite these circumstances." The answer was so vague that she was sure he would require her to explain, but for the moment she couldn't seem to force herself to confess that she'd never served as a governess before.

"Ahh."

Patience wasn't sure why, but she didn't like the way that single drawled word left his lips. It was as if he knew full well that she was stalling.

Bickerstaff had finished tying the captain's cravat and buttoning his vest and now helped his employer slide his arms into a wool jacket trimmed with velvet. When he was finished, he quietly slipped out of the room.

Gesturing for her to move closer to the intimate arrangement of settees and chairs, the captain said, "Please, sit down."

"I would prefer to stand." The words burst from her lips before she could stop them, and she cursed herself for her foolishness. She was the employee here. It was up to her to impress this man with her somewhat limited qualifications. She shouldn't be thwarting him at every turn.

But to sit down and have him towering over her would be completely rattling.

To her immense relief, the captain shrugged as if he didn't care what she did. "Suit yourself."

Crossing to the sideboard, he poured a measure of brandy into a glass. "Would you care for anything?"

She shook her head. "No. Thank you." Even she wasn't harebrained enough to accept liquor during an interview.

"I thought it best that we speak privately, Miss Pedigrue."

Patience thought that any necessary discussions they might have would be better suited to his solicitor's office, but when she met her employer's drilling scrutiny, she didn't object. "Very well, sir."

He rested his free hand on his hip. Very slim hips. Narrow. Clad in an expensive wool that appeared butter soft to the touch, not rough and scratchy like her own. Even so, the cut of the trousers was not entirely correct. No honorable gentleman would wear apparel that clung so close to his body, so completely. To muscled thighs. Long legs.

Patience jerked her attention away from the man

73

who stood before her and focused instead on the ornate pattern of fern fronds embroidered into a pillow on the settee.

The captain was the first to move. His footsteps silent on the carpet. Patience's face flamed as he made a slow circle around her body, appraising her from all angles.

"You look strong."

The comment was low and probably meant for his ears alone, but after such an insulting inspection, she couldn't prevent herself from saying, "Are you sure? You might want to check my teeth first."

Immediately she snapped her jaw shut. When would she learn to hold her tongue?

The captain's eye narrowed, glittering with an emotion she couldn't decipher—amusement, anger?

"You've got a sharp tongue in your head, haven't you, Miss Pedigrue?"

Since she'd dug a hole for herself already, Patience decided she might as well jump in. "I was led to believe that you were looking for a woman of education, not a weak-willed mouse."

He didn't immediately respond. Unfortunately, he didn't look away, either.

"Just what education *do* you have, Miss Pedigrue?"

"My father hired the finest of private tutors."

He nodded, and she knew from his expression that he approved.

"You are familiar with such classics as *The Iliad* and *The Odyssey*?"

"Yes, sir."

"You can speak French?"

"As well as Italian and a passing amount of German."

"Do you dance?"

The odd question took her by surprise and when she didn't answer, he repeated the question.

"Do you dance, Miss Pedigrue?"

"When it's necessary to do so." As a matter of fact, the only dancing she'd ever done had been when she and her sisters had bumped around the attic mimicking the steps they'd seen through their neighbors' window during a Christmas ball. But she didn't bother to inform him of that. As far as she was concerned, there were limits to what an employer needed to know.

"Have you had any experience caring for children?"

Again she hesitated. She'd been asked to tend to her neighbors' offspring on occasion when their mothers had committee meetings. "Yes, sir. But not as a means of employment. I have only been thrust into service during the past month."

"Why exactly have you decided to work, Miss Pedigrue?"

"I'm sure your solicitor gave you the form I filled out before my interview."

"That isn't the point. I wish to ask the questions and see your reactions to the answers. Besides which, it would be remiss of me not to interview you myself, wouldn't you agree? I might sense a character flaw that such a piece of paper would miss."

Patience bit the insides of her cheeks to keep from erupting in anger. The man had all but accused her of having a warped personality.

"Why were you in need of a job?" he repeated.

"My father recently died. In his will he stipulated that I should work as a governess for a year."

"He did, did he? Why?"

Patience tamped down an irritated sigh. "He didn't bother to explain his motives."

"But you're such an obedient daughter that you've blindly followed his wishes?"

"Not at all, Captain Dalton." She couldn't control the stiffness that entered her tone. "I am merely trying to fulfill the requirements I have been given in order to claim my inheritance."

"How much?"

He folded his arms over his chest, looking down at her from his immense height. Patience supposed she should have been intimidated by him, but the all-out gall of his question was enough to get her dander ruffled.

"I don't see how that is any of your concern."

"It is of immediate concern, Miss Pedigrue. I need to know from the start if you plan to win my sister's affections then flit away again as soon as you have your money. Such an abandonment would scar her delicate sensibilities for life."

She balled her hands into fists. Did she honestly look like the kind of woman who would do anything that . . . that . . . *heartless?*

"Captain Dalton, I would be the first to admit that I have plans for my future. But the five-hundred-dollar yearly stipend offered in my father's will would barely allow me to survive. Therefore I am resigned to working for my keep for the rest of my life. Indeed, I relish the idea *and* the independence it offers me. Nevertheless, there isn't money enough on this earth to tempt me to toy with the tender emotions of an . . . an innocent child."

"Well, then. I suppose we should fetch Emaline and inquire as to her opinion of your qualifications."

"Fetch her?"

"My sister is currently a resident at Miss Bodrill's School for Young Ladies. Our reunion has been sadly delayed, but not for much longer."

"Reunion?" Patience had been told nothing about Emaline and her brother except that the girl needed a governess and the brother doted on her.

"Come along, Miss Pedigrue. I've waited years for this moment, and I don't care to wait a second longer."

Chapter

6

Emaline Dalton stood on tiptoe, peering out of the window into the darkness below. The air—considered balmy by the other girls in the dormitory—felt chilly against her bare legs. She was used to hot tropical nights that sapped the strength from her body and filled her with laziness.

Sighing, she pressed her forehead against the glass, searching the street—first one way, then the other.

A note had been sent to Miss Bodrill's indicating that her brother would arrive within the next few weeks. Emaline had already waited so long. Surely Garrick would hurry to her as fast as he could.

Emaline was tired of this place. The girls were mean, the teachers distant. Since her arrival, she had been told what to do and what to say. She'd been forced to don uncomfortable clothing and restrict her activities to the dormitory and school. She'd nearly frozen to death during the winter months, and now she wanted to be out in the sunshine and fresh air.

Miss Bodrill frowned on what she called "too much nature," but Emaline was sure her brother would disagree. Unfortunately, upon Emaline's arrival at the school, she'd been informed that Garrick was sick, that he'd nearly died in an explosion at sea. The news had brought back the nightmares of her own horrible experience with shipwreck.

She didn't want to stay here any longer. She wanted to go home.

Her lashes fluttered, and her gaze fastened on the cobblestones below. Squinting, she saw that the man was standing there once again.

For the past week, as soon as the other girls were asleep, Emaline had slipped from her bed and crept to this window to watch for her brother. During her second such vigil, she'd noted a man walking toward the school, and her heart had leaped in anticipation, then had thudded to her toes. The gentleman was too small to be her brother. She remembered Garrick as a giant of a man—tall, broad, and strong. This man was stoop-shouldered and old.

She didn't like the way he waited among the trees across the street. Emaline wasn't sure what he hoped to find, but she knew he would stay there until dawn, smoking on an odd-shaped pipe. She had never seen the stranger's face. Once, however, when his match flared, she'd been able to see that his pipe was made of ivory carved into the shape of a woman's face—much like the figureheads on Papa's ships.

Tears stung the backs of her eyes, but she pushed them away. Mama and Papa were gone, as were Paddy, Joseph, and Peter. She'd been aboard the ship when it ran aground on a reef in bad weather. She'd watched the boat break up, the impact throwing her father onto the rocks. Mama, panicked, had tried to reach him, but one of the beams had fallen, crushing her legs.

A fire had begun below deck, and Emaline could hear her brothers' screams for help, but she hadn't known what to do. Running to her mother, she'd been flabbergasted when Mama pointed to a barrel Emaline had used as a throne in her games of make-believe.

After Emaline dragged the barrel closer, Mama had helped her tie a length of rope around one of its staves and fasten the other end to Emaline's waist. With her face contorted in pain, Mama had ordered Emaline to drag the barrel to the opposite side of the ship where the deck dipped into the swirling waves.

"Keep your head above water," Mama had ordered her as she hugged Emaline close. "Hold on to the barrel. As soon as he can, Garrick will find you and bring you home."

A wave had washed over them both, grasping Emaline and the barrel and tugging them irretrievably away from the burning ship. She'd tried to get back to her family. She'd paddled with her hands and her feet, but the waves had pulled at the barrel and she'd grown so tired . . .

From that point on, she had only a few hazy memories. She remembered waking off and on and becoming aware of the stickiness of salt on her face, the ache of her arms from being wrapped around the barrel. Sometimes she was completely submerged by the water; then she popped free like a cork. She didn't know how many hours—or even days—passed. Her head hurt. Her eyes stung. Then, when she least expected it, she'd been jostled into awareness when her knees hit something solid. Land. Then the world had grown black again, the sensation accompanied by a chattering in some unknown language.

Swiping at the moisture that insisted on plunging down her cheeks, Emaline peered even harder into the darkness. For years she had clung to her mother's promise, holding the images and memories of her family clear and bright in her head so that she would never forget the love she'd had in the past. Deep in her soul, she knew Mama would not have lied to her. Garrick would come one day to take her home.

So she'd waited. First on a strange exotic island, then here at Miss Bodrill's.

But how much longer would she have to endure the delays?

"He's never coming, don't you understand?" whispered Grace Harrington from her bunk a few feet away.

Emaline's face screwed into a mask of fury, but she refused to acknowledge she'd heard the girl. Of all her schoolmates, Grace had been the beastliest.

"You're such a fool, Emaline," the girl continued when she received no response. "Haven't you the brains to see what has happened? Your brother is dead. He died in that fire. He won't ever come to get you."

Whirling, Emaline growled and dived onto Grace's bed, pushing her onto the floor. Yanking at the girl's hair, Emaline shouted, "Take it back! Take it back!"

Around her, the dormitory dissolved into chaos.

"We'll take a carriage, Miss Pedigrue."

Still dazed by the sudden turn of events and the way the pace of her life seemed to gallop inexplicably out of her control, Patience nodded.

She doubted Garrick Dalton had even seen her agreement. He had already turned to Bickerstaff to issue instructions.

"I want Captain Rosemund—"

"I know, I know," Bickerstaff interrupted. "You've told me what to do already. Go get your sister so that you can relax from this state of near-hysteria. If you don't, I swear I'll send for a doctor."

Patience's eyes narrowed. Never in her life had she seen anyone less in need of a doctor than Captain Garrick Dalton. His figure was taut and muscular and . . .

She grew still, looking past the facade of strength the man presented to the world. For the first time she noted a pinched quality around his lips, the odd pallor that lingered beneath his tan.

Had the captain been ill?

Immediately, the scars she'd seen sprang to mind, and she found herself looking for other evidence of injury. Above and below the eye patch he wore, a paler ring of flesh made her wonder if his use of the patch was fairly recent.

A hired carriage rolled to a stop next to the curb.

"Come along, Miss Pedigrue," Captain Dalton said with a sweep of his hand.

She hesitated. "Wouldn't you rather greet your sister in private, Captain? I could wait for you here if you'd like."

"No, Miss Pedigrue. I think it's important that a bond be formed between you and Emaline from the very beginning."

Patience still felt like an interloper, but she reluctantly acquiesced. "Very well."

She was stepping toward the carriage when a figure bolted from the alleyway bordering the hotel. Running past Patience, he shoved her roughly to one side, and she cried out, falling to the ground.

A shout split the night air. A woman's scream.

Twisting, Patience turned toward her employer in time to see that the assailant had tackled him, throwing him beneath the traces that tethered the jittery horses to the carriage.

The wheels rocked with the driver's efforts to control his mounts. Heedless of the danger, the assailant drew back his hand. In the gleam of the hotel's lanterns, Patience caught a glimpse of a bloodied knife. Then Bickerstaff was diving into the fray, pulling the attacker off the captain and flinging him toward the curb.

The shrill whistle of the doorman combined with the horses' squeals and the shouts of the gathering crowd, caused the figure to leap to his feet. Within seconds he'd disappeared into the night.

"Garrick! Dammit, man, are you hurt?"

Patience clumsily fought the layers of her skirts and pushed herself to her feet. Stumbling toward the carriage, she grabbed the captain's free arm and helped Bickerstaff pull him out of the way of the wheels and the horses' hooves.

Somehow in the fracas, the captain's patch had been dislodged, exposing a nasty scar that split his brow and the top of his cheek. But when he opened his eyes, they both appeared miraculously unscathed and clear.

"Who was he?"

Bickerstaff placed a hand on Garrick's chest to keep him from speaking. "I don't know. He ran off before anyone could give chase. I could . . ."

When the valet's voice faded into silence, Patience looked at him questioningly, but Bickerstaff was already addressing himself to the crowd.

"He's fine. Nothing but a bump or two. No need to worry."

"It's a shame the way the beggars have taken control of the streets," one man muttered.

Another agreed.

The onlookers began to disperse, and Bickerstaff leaned close to Patience. "Tell the driver to stay. There's a gold coin in my watch pocket. Offer it to him as payment if he'll draw his carriage into that alley there and wait until we have need of him. I'll take the Captain upstairs."

Patience stared at him blankly.

"Go on, now. Get the coin and do as I say."

But it was only the captain's impatient command, "Do it, Miss Pedigrue," that forced her to move.

Slipping a finger into Bickerstaff's watch pocket, she retrieved the coin, all the while lamenting a world that caused strangers to carry knives for the sake of robbing innocent people on the street.

Summoning what shreds of composure she could manage, Patience offered the driver the coin. After the man agreed to wait, she stood on the curb to see that he positioned his horses in the alleyway as directed instead of galloping away with the money. Then, under the watchful eye of the doorman, who had stayed nearby to prevent yet another mishap to one of the Bristol Hotel's guests, she returned to the lobby.

Aware of the many eyes that followed her progress, she made her way upstairs and knocked at the captain's door.

In seconds, it whipped open to reveal Bickerstaff's pale face.

Without a word, he took her wrist, pulled her inside, then slammed the door again and locked it.

"Grab the whiskey from the sideboard," he said abruptly, gesturing to the sideboard. "Then follow me."

He disappeared through the doorway opposite, and Patience heard mumbled snatches of talk.

Patience stood rooted to the floor. Whiskey? What about Emaline?

Just as quickly, the scene outside the hotel flashed through her mind, and she remembered the glint of the blade in the glow of the lanterns. A bloody blade.

Spurred into action, she hurried to fetch the bottle, then grabbed a stack of tea towels from a corner table.

She rushed into the captain's bedroom just as Bickerstaff helped him to remove the jacket he'd worn over his vest. A dark crimson stain was already spreading down his ribs from a gash located beneath Garrick's left arm.

"Help me," Bickerstaff ordered.

Setting the liquor and the towels on the bedside table, she held Garrick's arm up while Bickerstaff unbuttoned his vest, then used a knife to cut away his shirt.

"You have a hard time keeping the clothes I buy you in good repair," Bickerstaff commented as he slid the garments from Garrick's good arm, then gestured for Patience to finish the task on the other side.

"Too . . . bad . . ." Garrick said between clenched teeth. "I rather liked that vest."

"And it was the only one in Boston ready-made to fit someone of your size, I can guarantee you."

Bickerstaff helped Garrick turn and lift his legs onto the bed.

"Brace your back against the headboard."

"I'm not an—"

"Invalid. I know, I know. But you are wounded." Bickerstaff turned to Patience. "Help him slide toward the wall; then brace some pillows behind him."

Patience automatically did as she was told, but she could not stifle the gasp that escaped her lips when she saw the angry pink welts puckering Garrick's back.

"Old wounds, Miss Pedigrue," Garrick stated before she could comment.

Knowing that now wasn't the time to ask how such wounds had been inflicted, she stacked the pillows as she'd been told, then stepped out of the way.

Hissing in pain, Garrick draped his arm over his head, allowing Bickerstaff a clearer view of the gash.

Patience felt her stomach churn. The blade had gone nearly to the bone.

"I'm going to have to stitch this," Bickerstaff announced.

A blackness began to gather at the edges of her vision. There was so much blood.

"Catch her!"

Bickerstaff whirled in time to wrap an arm around Patience's waist. As her senses returned, she groaned in mortification. Now was not the time for swooning. This man needed help.

Carefully leading her into the parlor, Bickerstaff said, "Take the key from the sideboard and go downstairs. See if the clerk can round up a sewing kit."

The thought of what Bickerstaff intended to sew caused her stomach to roil, but she firmly set her mind on the task rather than the intended outcome.

"Very well," she whispered. Then more strongly, "I'll hurry as fast as I can."

Wriggling free of Bickerstaff's support, she snatched the key from the marble counter and slid it into her pocket. She was already marching toward the door when she saw a scrap of paper lying on the carpet.

Curious, she bent and retrieved it, automatically reading the scrawled message: "Next time I'll kill you, Captain."

Gasping, she turned and held the paper out to Bickerstaff. "What is the meaning of this?"

Chapter

7

Nothing. Absolutely nothing. The captain has merely been targeted by some fool intent on stealing a large sum of money.

That was the explanation Bickerstaff had given Patience for the attack and the subsequent note. At the time, that explanation of the bizarre turn of events had struck her as inadequate. But now, in the cold light of day, Patience supposed that Bickerstaff was right. What better way to extort money than to threaten a wealthy man's life unless he paid a handsome fee? Even so, she could think of far more efficient methods of blackmail.

But then, efficiency had always been one of her strong points. A talent that Miss Bodrill would do well to develop.

Glancing at the clock over Miss Bodrill's desk, Patience realized that she had been inside the School for Young Ladies for thirty minutes and still had received no word as to when she could expect to see Emaline Dalton. She was severely tempted to march through the school herself until she found her charge.

Patience had tried to impress upon Miss Bodrill

that time was of the essence. Although she hadn't mentioned Captain Dalton's being attacked, or the fever that now raged through his body from his wound, she had pointed out that the captain was anxiously waiting for his sister to be delivered to him.

"Anxious" wasn't precisely the correct word, Patience realized as she winced at the memory. He was furious. After the knifing he'd received, then the threatening note beneath his door, he'd been ready to tear Boston apart with his bare hands in order to find the man responsible.

Luckily, Bickerstaff had plied him with ample amounts of whiskey. The captain had passed out midway through the stitching of the wound, and Bickerstaff hadn't bothered to wake him once the task was complete.

Instead, he'd met with Patience who was waiting anxiously in the sitting room. He'd instructed her to take the carriage to her home, pack what things she would need for her new life on Addlemeyer Island, then have the luggage delivered to the wharf. As soon as decently possible the next morning, she was to go to Miss Bodrill's School for Young Ladies, retrieve her charge, and make her way back to the docks where the captain would wait for her upon his ship, *Emaline's Return.*

Patience had spent a worrisome, sleepless night pacing the bare confines of her father's house. Felicity had long since left for Saint Joseph, Missouri. Constance had left at dawn for New York.

To Patience's surprise, when she left her father's house, closed the door, and firmly locked it behind her, she had discovered the same carriage driver waiting to take her to Miss Bodrill's. As an added precaution, Bickerstaff had provided two sailors from Captain Dalton's ship to serve as escorts.

She drummed her fingers on her chair. The captain had already endured so much in his efforts to be reunited with his sister. Thank heavens Joshua Bickerstaff had seen fit to apprise her of the accident that had scarred her employer and forced him to recuperate for months in England. Even now Patience found it hard to believe that so many tragedies could strike a single family—the loss of *Dalton's Adventurer*, Emaline's being washed ashore and marooned on an uncharted island for years until her discovery, the explosion on Garrick's ship, and now the attack on a quiet Boston street.

What was the world coming to? Sheer chaos and bedlam?

Her toe hesitated in its irritated tattoo against the floorboards as she remembered the awful wound Captain Dalton had sustained. And then that note . . .

She shivered as the words echoed in her brain: "Next time I'll kill you, Captain."

No. She wouldn't think of such things. The whole ordeal was a case of mistaken identity, she was sure. The attacker had not meant to wound the captain. He'd been after some ingrate with a build similar to that of Garrick Dalton.

Another giant? Not likely.

A robbery, then. The plight of the poor had caused many instances of crime if the newspapers were to be believed. In any event, such matters were not Patience's immediate concern. She had a job to do, and by thunder, she would see it executed as quickly as possible.

Squelching her own misgivings, Patience studied the office of the headmistress of Miss Bodrill's School for Young Ladies with growing disapproval.

The cause of the interminable delay she'd experienced so far was quite obvious. Judging by this room, the woman in charge of the establishment displayed a distinct lack of tidiness. Papers had been scattered willy-nilly on her desk. Books were stacked haphazardly on their shelves or, worse yet, piled on the floor. There was a layer of dust on nearly every surface and an even thicker layer of soot on the windowsill.

How could anyone with such habits claim to be the proprietress of a girls' finishing school? Granted, the woman had seemed truly concerned about Emaline, but young ladies of Emaline's background needed so much more.

Tearing her gaze away from the unsightly scene, Patience focused on the picture hanging over the headmistress's desk—that of a Botticelli-like woman offering succor to a dying child. Patience's lips thinned. In her opinion, it was not the sort of artwork young ladies should be exposed to—and certainly not Emaline Dalton. She'd already seen more than her share of death.

The steel of Patience's spine strengthened even more. Thank heaven Captain Dalton had decided to liberate his sister from this place.

"Miss Pedigrue!"

The headmistress burst into the room, obviously breathless, her lace cap slightly askew. Behind her, there was a horrible commotion, a screaming and pounding as if one of her charges was having an apoplectic fit.

"I'm so sorry to keep you waiting," the woman said. "We had some trouble finding Emaline . . . Emaline's . . . things."

The explanation sounded weak to Patience's ears, as if something important were being kept secret. Patience considered investigating the situation, then abandoned the idea. Right now the only detail on her mind was retrieving a nine-year-old child and putting this place behind them both.

Patience opened her mouth to inquire how much longer she would have to wait for Emaline's care to be transferred into her own hands. But Miss Bodrill—who had begun to sink wearily into her chair—rose again, smiling widely and gesturing to a spot somewhere behind Patience. "There she is!"

Twisting, Patience saw a demure young adolescent framed in the doorway. She was dressed in the uniform of the school: black gown, black hose, black snood, and white pinafore. Except for a pair of scratches on her cheek, the girl was incredibly pretty. Porcelain fine, delicate, demure, yet curiously unlike her brother in coloring.

Standing, Patience held out her hand. "Good morning, Miss Dalton. I am your new governess, Miss Pedigrue."

The child regarded her in confusion, then looked beyond Patience to the headmistress.

"No, no," Miss Bodrill said hastily. *"That* isn't Emaline Dalton. This is Grace Harrington, of the Boston Harringtons."

Grace's lips pinched together. Tipping her nose into the air, she announced, "Miss Bodrill, I was told to inform you that Emaline's trunks have been loaded on the carriage. Miss Whippleton said Emaline is free to go at any time."

"Thank you, Grace."

The girl cast one more burning glance in Patience's direction, then huffed and stalked away.

At the same moment Miss Bodrill nodded her head to a spot farther on, and Patience allowed her gaze to slide regretfully from Grace Harrington to the staircase.

As soon as Patience realized what she was seeing,

her eyes widened in horror. Three grown women—teachers, probably—were literally dragging a girl her way. The child was kicking and screaming and biting the hands that gripped her. Her long hair was matted, her dress torn, her stockings falling down around her ankles. As she drew closer, it was obvious she hadn't had a bath for a good long time.

Patience's eyes squeezed closed in silent prayer. *That untamed creature was Emaline Dalton.*

Sighing, she swept a despairing gaze up and down the child. At this angle, Patience didn't think Emaline needed a governess so much as a stiff cleaning, and from what Patience understood, those sorts of tasks were supposed to be relegated to a nanny. *Or a mother.* But since Emaline had neither, Patience supposed that she would have to see to the task herself. Her only regret was that she wouldn't have time to tend to the child before taking her back to captain Dalton. Somehow she doubted he'd envisioned his sister in a state such as this.

Knowing there was no time to dally, Patience stepped into the hall.

"Miss Dalton," she proclaimed in her most regal tone. "My name is Patience Pedigrue. I am the governess your brother Garrick hired. It is my task to make a lady of you." She didn't add that since she had never before served as a governess, her reputation—as well as any opportunity for future advancement—would depend on her success in this matter.

At the mention of her brother, Emaline ceased her struggles.

"Garrick?" the child whispered, her eyes—the same ice-blue as her brother's—growing wide. Instantly some of the wariness eased from her expression.

Pleased that Emaline apparently remembered Garrick and was eager to join him, Patience said, "Come with me." She held out her hand, indicating that the girl should take it.

Emaline frowned in suspicion. "Where's my brother? I was told he would come for me himself."

Not about to give the girl time to begin another tantrum the likes of which Patience had already seen, she said sternly, "You'd best hold my hand, Miss Dalton. Otherwise you may have some difficulty keeping up with me. It is my duty to see you are taken to the captain within the hour. Then you will be going home."

Home. The girl didn't say the word aloud, but her lips moved. After wrenching free of her captors, Emaline became inexplicably docile, slipping her hand into Patience's and turning to glare at Miss Bodrill.

Although she was startled by the girl's obedience, Patience did not allow her surprise to show. She nodded politely to the open-mouthed teachers and the equally stunned Miss Bodrill.

"Good day, ladies."

As she walked out the door, she overheard one of the women whispering, "Do you really think she'll make anything out of that savage?"

Patience firmly closed the door behind her, sure that Emaline had also heard the comment. Squeezing the girl's hand, Patience did her best to control the anger that rose in her breast at the insensitivity of Emaline's former instructors.

Silently she uttered the only possible reply: *Yes. I will.*

Leading Emaline to the waiting carriage, Patience resisted the temptation to glance behind her. The prickling of her scalp told her that Miss Bodrill and the other teachers were spying on her from the windows, but Patience refused to pay them any heed.

Good riddance. The school certainly hadn't over-extended itself to help Emaline adjust to society. The dirt under the child's fingernails was proof enough of that.

Accepting the hand offered by one of Captain Dalton's sailors, she took the seat opposite Emaline. Knowing that the next few minutes would set the tone for their relationship, she smiled brightly.

As soon as the carriage rolled into the street, she said, "Well, now. Did you have time to say good-bye to your friends?"

Emaline pressed her lips together and folded her arms in open rebellion.

Ignoring the reaction, Patience continued as if she hadn't been openly snubbed. "When I was your age, I would have jumped at the opportunity to have so many other girls nearby for playmates. My sisters were my only companions."

Emaline's eyes had narrowed suspiciously.

"Is something wrong?" Patience inquired as sweetly as she could. This mulishness was a trait that would have to be quashed straightaway.

"Who are you?" the little girl whispered.

"I've already introduced myself. I'm Patience Pedigrue. I'm to be your governess."

The child suddenly scrambled to her knees and pressed herself into the corner. "Who *are* you?" she demanded more loudly.

"Emaline, I'm—"

"You were sent by the man with the pipe, weren't you?" Her voice rose with each word. "That's why he was watching the dormitory! You've come to take me away so that Garrick can never find me."

Patience leaned forward to touch Emaline's hand,

but the girl cringed away, then began to scream—a high-pitched wail that caused the hairs on Patience's arms to stand on end.

"Emaline, please!"

Instead of stopping, the driver of the carriage urged his team to a faster pace, throwing Emaline to the floor and causing Patience to bounce against her seat. Righting herself, she reached for the youngster, but when Emaline tried to bite her, she huffed in impatience.

"Honestly," she muttered to herself. After the wrestling match she'd seen at the school, she had no desire to resort to fisticuffs, besides which, physical confrontation with a child was beneath anyone with civilized manners.

Unfortunately, Emaline hadn't been around civilization in four years.

Doing her best to ignore Emaline's unseemly behavior, Patience began to talk, speaking in the same manner she might have used if she and Emaline had been sharing a quiet tea. "I was introduced to your brother yesterday. He arrived on his ship in time to interview me for this position."

Quickly skipping the fact that the meeting had taken place in a hotel room after she'd caught Captain Dalton wearing nothing but a towel, she hurriedly continued. "Did you know that he's named his newest ship *Emaline's Return,* after you? I overheard the sailors talking when they came to fetch me this morning. Isn't that sweet? I can't think of another little girl in all of Boston who's had a ship named after her. Certainly none of those girls at your school."

Emaline was still screaming bloody murder, but Patience sensed a slight decrease in volume.

"I never had a brother," Patience said. "If I had, I think I would have wanted one like yours. My red hair caused a good deal of teasing from the neighborhood children, and I would have enjoyed living with a giant of a man who could come to my . . . aid."

At the word "giant" the screams diminished in volume, then faded completely away.

Emaline still sat huddled on the floor, her arms wrapped around her knees. When she looked up, her cheeks were tearstained, her expression heart-wrenching. Obviously, she was afraid to hope that her years alone would come to an end.

"Yes, he's very handsome, with hair the color of wheat and eyes the same snapping blue as your own."

Emaline began to inch toward her.

"Of course, you mustn't be alarmed that he hasn't come to get you himself. He woke this morning with a slight fever."

Emaline's brow puckered in concern, and she climbed onto the seat beside Patience.

"In my opinion, his malady is due to overwork. Did you know that he moved heaven and earth to get back to you as soon as he did?"

Again she thanked Providence for the gossip exchanged by the sailors.

Moving slowly so that she wouldn't startle Emaline, Patience wrapped her arm around the girl's shoulders and drew her close. "He's very fierce to look at—but then I suppose you remember that much about him."

Emaline nodded her head.

"I sense that he has a good heart. After all, how can anyone who loves a sister as he does be bad?"

Emaline tucked her feet up beside her, then rested her head in Patience's lap. Concerned, Patience noted the weary pallor of the girl's skin beneath the grime.

"Emaline?" She kept her voice soft and soothing. "You said a man was watching the dormitory." Unbidden came the memory of the stranger who had attacked Captain Dalton with a knife. "Do you know who he was?"

Emaline shook her head.

"You called him the 'man with the pipe.' What sort of pipe did he have?"

Emaline shrugged.

"How long did he watch the dormitory? All night?"

But there was no answer. Emaline's lashes fluttered against her cheeks, and she fell into a deep, exhausted sleep.

The sight of her, so small, so defenseless, caused Patience's heart to twist. The fact that this girl had survived her many ordeals at all was a miracle. To have done so with her wits intact was an even further blessing.

Glancing out the window, she watched the horizon thin of its houses and buildings until she caught a glimpse of the sea and the busy wharf.

The sailors directed the driver to the proper berth, and the carriage shuddered to a halt.

This is your last chance, Patience's inner voice warned her. As soon as she stepped aboard the captain's ship she would be obligated to stay with the family for at least a year in order to receive her inheritance.

Was that really what she wanted to do? To ally herself with a huge man bent on getting his own way and a child who was untamed and willful?

But what other choice did she have? To interview for more positions, which would be filled by women who had years of experience? Moreover, now that she'd seen Emaline's vulnerability, how could she turn her back on the girl?

The door to the carriage was wrenched open, and

Captain Dalton's shape crowded out the sun. In an instant, after one brief glimpse of Captain Dalton's expression, Patience made her decision.

These people needed her.

"What's wrong with her?" Captain Dalton demanded, his eyes clinging to the tousled child curled on the bench.

Patience held a finger to her lips in a tacit bid for quiet. "She's worn to a frazzle, poor lamb. I don't think she's slept for some time."

Garrick regarded Patience with something akin to panic, and she was stunned that he would even allow her to see such an emotion.

"She spoke of a . . . man with a pipe who has been watching the dormitory for the past few nights. I'm sure there was nothing truly ominous about the experience, but she was frightened nonetheless. When I arrived without you, she was afraid I was taking her away so that you could not be reunited."

The captain cursed under his breath, then reached out and gently scooped Emaline into his arms. Skillfully, he brought her against his body, resting her head on his shoulder.

Tears stung Patience's eyes, and her throat grew tight as she watched Garrick hug his sister tightly, rocking her slightly as if she were still the four-year-old he'd last held in his arms.

Then, lifting his head, he surreptitiously wiped one eye and offered gruffly, "Rosemund, let's get out of here."

"Aye-aye, sir," a florid-faced man with a white beard responded. Then, turning to the men, he shouted, "Let's hear it for the captain and his sister. Together at last."

As one, the crew yelled, "Hip, hip, hooray!"

Patience winced, sure that the noise would rouse

Emaline and cause her to start screaming again. But the girl's lashes flickered, and she stared briefly into her brother's still-damp eyes.

"Garrick," she whispered, a soft smile curling her lips. "You've finally come to take me home."

Then, lifting one small hand, she patted his cheek and promptly fell back asleep.

Chapter
8

Garrick urged his horse into a gallop after leaving the shipping offices where he'd paused only a moment to announce his arrival and say hello to his workers.

The men had been overjoyed to see him, questioning him about his ship, his sister, and his recovery. Under normal circumstances, Garrick would have stayed much longer. But he had sent Miss Pedigrue, Bickerstaff, and his sister toward the house, and he wanted to catch up to them as soon as possible.

As the horse's hooves thundered on the packed-earth track, Garrick marveled at how much his sister had grown since he'd seen her last. She'd changed so much—for better and for worse. He was relieved to find her healthy and strong, but the shadows in her eyes and the fear she'd displayed on the journey home had nearly brought Garrick to his knees.

Midway through the sea journey, Emaline had awakened from her exhausted sleep. Garrick had been at her bedside in an instant, eager to talk to his sister and reassure her that she had not dreamed his presence. But the moment she became aware of being on a ship, she'd become hysterical, screaming and thrashing as if she were being attacked by the hounds of hell.

The noise had brought Miss Pedigrue from her own quarters where she'd been sleeping, then Bickerstaff from his walk on the deck. None of them had been able to calm the little girl. Finally, in desperation, Garrick had ordered Bickerstaff to fetch a glass of the elderberry wine he'd brought with him from England. Telling Emaline that it was a special punch, he'd managed to coax her to drink enough for the alcohol to enter her system and put her back to sleep. Then, shaking and upset beyond measure, he'd gathered his sister in his arms and rocked her until her breathing became deep and regular.

Throughout the night, he'd cursed himself for being so insensitive. Why hadn't he realized that putting her aboard a ship again might bring back horrible memories? But then, the old friend of his father's who had taken Emaline to Boston had never mentioned her terror.

Taking a deep breath, Garrick marveled at Miss Pedigrue's poise through the entire episode. After she realized that Garrick meant to hold his sister until their arrival in Addlemeyer, she'd changed back into her woolen suit and had brought pencil and paper so that she could question Garrick about Emaline's future schedule.

The no-nonsense talk had helped him to relax and allowed him to see that Emaline's fragile emotions would not be strengthened in a day. Holding his sister's hand, studying her grimy fingers, he'd realized that Emaline's rebellion against Miss Bodrill's social and hygienic regimens might stem from one simple fact: a fear of water.

Turning a corner, Garrick finally caught sight of the

carriage. Instantly, his thoughts went to Emaline, then bounced to Miss Pedigrue.

The woman might not have experience as a governess, but so far she had shown an empathetic kindness and a common sense that Garrick valued much more than years of practice. His instincts had been dead right when they'd prompted him to hire her—despite her lack of meekness.

But now that he was faced with a flesh-and-blood woman rather than his own notion of what Emaline's governess would be, he was confronted with yet another question. Should he go through with his plan to woo the teacher, wed her, bed her, and legally declare her his sister's guardian?

She wasn't at all hard on the eyes. Her coloring was dramatic, but he was drawn to the exotic contrasts provided by her red hair, pale skin, and green eyes. More than that, she was practical, passionate about her views, and sensitive to her pupil's needs. Her mercurial temperament and lust for life should entertain him for years to come. Perhaps even a lifetime.

At that moment Patience tipped her head back and laughed, the sound floating through the air and wrapping around Garrick's heart. So many years had passed since he'd heard a woman's laugh that he found himself craving more. Swift on the heels of that thought came a yearning for everything else a woman brought to a man's home—a sense of peace, comfort, vitality, and warmth.

Yes, Garrick decided, she would make a very acceptable companion. For his sister and for Garrick himself.

Barely a quarter of an hour had elapsed since Captain Dalton's schooner docked at Addlemeyer. The moment the vessel was secured in its berth,

Garrick had carried a crying, exhausted Emaline from the ship's cabin to his office near the quay. There he'd arranged for a carriage to take Emaline and Patience to the house, a horse for Bickerstaff, and another for himself. Then the captain had left them briefly, stating that he needed to have a word with his staff, and he'd sent the carriage—with Bickerstaff riding guard—on ahead of him.

From a point behind her, Patience heard the approach of a horse, and dared a quick glance to confirm that it was the captain rejoining their group. Her gaze met his—briefly, disturbingly—before she looked away. At the same instant the carriage turned into a narrow lane and the imposing brick house belonging to the Dalton family came into view.

Patience's fingers trembled in sudden nervousness as she noted the feverish activity at the front of the house. Servants carrying valises, trunks, and crates made antlike queues into the house, then came out again, unencumbered, for another load.

Astride his horse to the left of the carriage, Bickerstaff gestured to the chaos and explained that most of the servants had been hired in the last week and had arrived earlier that morning on the supply boat from Nantucket, thirty miles to the south.

Pointing to the view of the entire island seen from the open carriage, he explained, "The Daltons have owned this island for two generations. Addlemeyer is only a little over twenty miles long, but its location is ideal for maritime commerce."

"Then why isn't it used as much as Nantucket?"

"Because Addlemeyer Island is privately owned and used exclusively by Dalton Shipping. We're rather isolated from the rest of the New England shoreline due to the treacherous currents surrounding the mainland. That's why the supply ferry comes only once a week."

The thunder of approaching hooves signaled the arrival of Captain Dalton. Even so, Patience couldn't prevent herself from starting when he reined his horse to a walk.

"Enough, Bickerstaff," Garrick interrupted. "Miss Pedigrue has plenty to remember without your adding a history lesson."

Patience stiffened when the captain's horse skidded into line beside them. Automatically she glanced at Emaline to gauge her reaction to this newest phase of her journey. The girl had recovered from her latest bout of panic and now sat gape-mouthed as she studied her surroundings. Her obvious joy told Patience that she recalled this place quite vividly despite her early age when she'd last seen Addlemeyer Island. It wouldn't be long before she would be itching to explore old play areas.

Nevertheless, Patience had already decided that the first order of business was a bath for the girl. Since no one had dared interrupt her sleep, Emaline still looked as dirty and untidy as a beggar.

Digging into her reticule, Patience withdrew a clean handkerchief, dampened it with the tiny vial of toilet water she kept in her purse for such tasks, and leaned forward. "We really must see to it that you have a bath straightaway."

At the mention of a bath, Emaline slapped Patience's hand away. "No!"

"Emaline," Garrick scolded, the height of the horse giving him an air of added power.

Emaline's lip began to tremble and her eyes filled with tears.

"I think you should apologize to your governess for your rudeness."

Emaline eyed Patience, then stuck out her tongue.

"Emaline!" Garrick barked.

Thankfully, the carriage stopped at the same moment, and Garrick's attention was drawn to the groom who rushed to take the reins from the driver.

Before dismounting Garrick leaned forward to release the latch on the carriage's door. As he did so, a huge shaggy dog ambled through the front door and paused at the head of the marble steps.

"Oscar!" Emaline shouted in joy.

The dog lifted its head and sniffed the air.

Squealing in delight, Emaline jumped from the carriage and rushed toward the animal. Startled, Oscar lunged in the opposite direction, his toenails scrabbling on the slippery marble before he managed to gain enough of a foothold to dart through the gate to the garden at the side of the house. Emaline followed, swift on the animal's heels.

Patience was so stunned at the girl's sudden disappearance that she couldn't move.

A rumbling laugh came from the captain as he swung to the ground.

"Don't fret, Miss Pedigrue. She's a heathen, to be sure, but she's healthy and full of spirit. As for the dog, Oscar and Emaline are old friends. In fact, they share the same birthday."

As the captain spoke briefly with Bickerstaff, a group of servants rushed from the house and quickly lined up in single file. Standing at attention, they waited to be introduced to the owner of the house, stiffening even more when a woman dressed completely in gray regally made her way to the head of the queue. Bickerstaff joined the groom as the boy walked the horses to the stable.

"Captain Dalton," the woman in gray murmured, offering a smile that barely moved her thin lips. "How good it is to see you."

"You're looking well, Miss Fitch."

"Tolerable. Thank you, sir."

She turned to the group assembled on the stairs. "All of the servants who were hired in Boston are present and accounted for, although many have not yet had time to don the uniforms you provided."

Garrick nodded. "Will you introduce them, please?"

"Of course."

While Miss Fitch led Captain Dalton down the line, Patience hesitated, then made her way to the side gate in search of Emaline.

"Miss Pedigrue!"

At the captain's shout, she turned, her cheeks burning when all eyes fell on her to the exclusion of everyone else. There was something disturbingly intimate about his gaze.

"Yes, sir?"

"I will expect to see you again this evening after you've rounded up my sister and given her a bath."

"As you wish."

She walked away from him as smoothly and calmly as she could—even though her knees had a curious quiver to them and she knew he was staring at her every step of the way.

"Dinner at seven o'clock, Miss Pedigrue."

"Yes, Captain," she replied without breaking stride.

"Don't be late. I despise tardiness."

"I shall do my best to meet your high expectations, Captain Dalton," she said as she stepped through the squeaky iron gate into the garden.

* * *

Garrick Dalton's eyes narrowed as he watched Patience Pedigrue's skirts swish through the narrow opening.

He'd been at sea too long. Much too long. How else could a person account for the fact that a prim and proper governess had the power to prick his interest so quickly? Somehow his original plan had not taken into account that he might find someone like Patience Pedigrue.

"Captain?"

Aware that Miss Fitch was waiting to continue with the introductions, he pulled his attention away from his sister's governess. There would be plenty of time for her later. At dinner.

Seven sharp.

Patience didn't know why the captain had been so insistent about announcing the time he expected Patience and Emaline to join him for dinner. The man barely left them alone all day. It was he who encouraged a game of tag with Emaline and Oscar, he who took his sister exploring in the nearby woods, dismissing Patience so that she could settle into the governess's room next to the nursery.

Then, just when she was beginning to wonder if she should go in search of Emaline to meet her seven-o'clock appointment, the captain carried his sister to her room and laid her on her bed. Sighing once, she rolled on her side and fell asleep.

"I doubt she's slept well in a month," Garrick said indulgently.

"I'll watch her tonight," Patience murmured.

The captain shook his head. "You've got to eat, Miss Pedigrue. I don't expect you to hover over Emaline twenty-four hours a day. I'll speak to Miss

Fitch about having one of the maids check on her now and again. Then I'll expect to see you in the dining hall as planned."

"But it isn't customary for a governess to dine with her—"

"Be there, Miss Pedigrue. We have things to discuss."

Patience opened her mouth to decline, then realized that the pretty phrase had disguised a blatant order.

"Yes, sir."

As soon as the captain left the room, Patience's starched posture melted away, leaving her weak.

While in Boston, there hadn't been time for her to think of what her life would be like at Dalton Manor. She'd been completely occupied with the attack and then with her pupil. But now she realized that she would be living in the same house as Garrick Dalton. They wouldn't merely share the space offered by the manor's enormous rooms. Their lives would actually intertwine, especially since Emaline's care would involve complete cooperation and communication between them.

Pacing to the mirror, Patience began to tidy her hair. Steadfastly, she ignored the flush that tinged her cheeks and the sparkle in her eye, which proclaimed she wasn't as unaffected by the captain as she pretended to be.

After all, he was just what she'd always dreamed of in a man—wealthy, dashing, experienced. He had seen exotic ports and could tell her everything she ever wanted to know about life outside Boston.

But she couldn't allow herself to think such things.

Captain Garrick Dalton was her employer.

And that was all he could ever be.

* * *

The clock in the hall had just chimed the seventh hour when Garrick glanced up from his own tiny timepiece to find a figure in the dining room doorway.

"You're on time," he commented to the woman garbed in black. Black gown, black slippers, black mitts. It should have been a somber costume. *Should* have been. But on Patience Pedigrue it had the opposite effect, suggesting an almost exotic quality. He noted with interest the way the inky shade made her hair gleam as bright as a candle flame and gave her skin a velvety sheen.

For some odd reason Garrick found himself imagining what she would look like in the same gown if it wasn't buttoned up to her throat. She might even be considered pretty if she wore a more fashionable décolletage—one that hugged her bosom and left her shoulders bare. He could imagine her that way, wearing jet or pearls—or perhaps even rubies.

Yes, she would make a beautiful addition to his household.

"Good evening, Captain Dalton."

He knew immediately from her high-and-mighty tone that Miss Pedigrue was determined to keep her distance. The fact didn't dissuade him. There was something invigorating about clashing wills with his sister's governess. Most females tended to concede to his every whim.

"Please come in," he said, gesturing for her to approach.

As she moved toward him, he continued to study her carefully, wondering why she hadn't worn something softer and more feminine, since she was essentially off duty.

"You're wearing a different gown than you did this morning."

Before he could continue, she interrupted with "It

109

is now evening, sir. This afternoon I was wearing an *afternoon* dress."

The tone she used was one he remembered his own governess employing when she wanted to maintain her role as a hired professional. Garrick couldn't resist baiting Patience even more.

"Oh, really? What, pray tell, is the difference?"

"An afternoon gown is worn during the . . . afternoon." It was obvious she thought his question absurd.

"If that's the only difference, then how is one supposed to tell them apart?" he continued with his baiting. They both knew full well that he already was aware of current fashion customs, but Patience didn't challenge him.

He saw the way she pursed her lips as her green eyes flashed in the candlelight. A red-haired, green-eyed vixen. How many women could lay claim to such an interesting combination?

"Dresses worn in the day are of a sturdier, more practical fabric."

He pretended to consider the point. "And that one is made of . . ."

"Taffeta," she supplied shortly. He could see the way she'd buried her hands in the folds of her skirt.

"May I see?" he inquired.

"See what?"

"The fabric."

The spark of annoyance he'd witnessed was replaced by suspicion.

"Why?"

"I'm interested in its quality," he said matter-of-factly, as if she should find that point perfectly logical. "I am in the shipping trade, after all."

It was quite apparent that she didn't want him to scrutinize her gown or anything else, but she finally moved toward him, the rustling of her dress accompanying her like the whisper of autumn leaves through the grass.

"Lovely," he murmured when she stopped a foot away. "I have always enjoyed the sound made by a woman's skirts brushing the floor."

"I'm sure you have," she said tightly, intimating with her tone that she believed him to have entertained scores of swooning ladies.

Before she could take another step, he grabbed her wrist, pulling her forward so that her skirts filled the space between his knees. Then, with his free hand, he rubbed the ebony fabric between his thumb and forefinger.

"Very nice, Miss Pedigrue."

"I'm so glad you approve." There was no disguising her sarcasm.

She pulled away, and he let her go. Instinctively, he knew Miss Pedigrue was on the verge of losing her temper. Nevertheless, it was a pity that she hadn't lingered for a few seconds longer. The scent of her perfume had wafted his way, and he'd been drawn to it in an inexplicable way.

"Should I sit, sir?"

When she drew his thoughts back to the present, he settled a little more comfortably in his seat, his fingers caressing the stem of his wineglass. "Please do."

He waited until she'd taken her place before saying, "I've noted that you always wear black." He could see the way she stiffened. "Am I to understand the somber color is due to your father's recent passing?"

"I *am* in mourning, sir."

"Ah." He appeared to think about the strictures of her observance, then sighed with something akin to regret.

"Be that as it may, I would prefer it if you would not wear black."

Her lips thinned. "Propriety demands—"

"Propriety be damned."

He saw her cheeks pinken at the curse, and her blush intrigued him. Of late he hadn't spent much time in the company of women who could still blush. Taking a breath, he said more calmly, "Miss Pedigrue, I apologize if my request seems unreasonable. But there are already too many reminders of death and dying in this house. Emaline is excited about being home, but the fact remains that she will soon remember that there were others who will never step through these doors."

He paused to clear his throat when a telling gruffness entered his tone.

"As I was saying," he continued after sipping from his wineglass, "Emaline is a delicate child."

He noted the way she snorted ever so slightly at the term "delicate."

"She may be a trifle unruly—"

"Unruly!" she echoed, then snapped her lips closed.

"Is there something you wish to say, Miss Pedigrue?"

"No, Captain." But her tone was only slightly conciliatory.

"Then I will continue with my original point. Since my sister was discovered, she has been faced with many disappointments. The fact that she and I were only recently reunited has shaken her trust in the future and her feelings of security. I know my request is completely unreasonable. As a grieving daughter, you have every right to wear what you wish. I am merely . . . suggesting that black not be your choice for the next few weeks."

Garrick rang the silver bell beside his plate, signaling that dinner should be served, and lifted the bottle of wine. "May I pour you some?"

She was regarding him so suspiciously he could have been offering her a bit of arsenic. "I don't drink wine or spirits."

"Why not?"

His question took her by surprise.

"They are ungodly."

"In what way?"

"They cause one to . . . lose control."

"Is that a sin?"

"It can lead to sin."

He smiled. "It can also lead to a good deal of pleasure."

He filled her glass nonetheless, and the green of her eyes hardened in displeasure. Garrick was astounded by how such a reaction pleased him. She was a strong woman. Strong enough to think for herself and to stand up to her own convictions.

Bickerstaff entered the room, his thin, wiry frame clad in formal livery.

"What the hell?" Garrick inquired.

"I've promoted myself from valet to butler."

"Whatever for?"

"A higher salary."

Garrick stared at the man, wondering what his true motive might be. But since Bickerstaff would be joining him later, he said instead, "Bickerstaff, since Miss Pedigrue has strong convictions about wine and spirits, be so kind to bring her a glass of fresh milk, would you?"

"Of course, sir." After setting bowls of thick steaming soup in front of them both, he withdrew.

Slipping his napkin over his lap, Garrick motioned for Patience to begin eating, but she seemed reluctant to do so. It was clear that she was somewhat piqued by his insistence that she be brought a glass of milk as if she were the child instead of the governess.

He took his own soup, stirring the thick, creamy concoction with relish.

"Despite what you may have been told already, Miss Pedigrue, there are one or two points about my sister that you should know."

He had her immediate attention.

"I'm sure that you are aware that my family has been in the shipping business for generations."

She tentatively lifted her spoon, tasted the soup, then wrinkled her nose. Without comment, he handed her the saltshaker.

"Early on, my father made it a habit to take his family with him during his sea voyages. He couldn't bear to be parted from my mother or his children for long periods of time unless it could not be avoided. Therefore, on his last journey to East Asia, even though I was unable to join them, he took my mother, my brothers, and my little sister aboard. The ship ran aground, was destroyed, and only Emaline survived."

He knew by the darkening of her eyes that Patience had been told as much already.

"How long ago did this occur?" she asked softly.

"Four years this fall."

"And she was alone on the island where she was discovered?"

"Except for a tribe of natives who cared for her."

Miss Pedigrue's spoon dropped against her bowl.

"As we have both seen, her experiences have made her a bit . . . willful. Some might even say untamed. It is a quality I would like to have softened, but not at the expense of her spirit. Obviously that high-priced finishing school wasn't up to the task."

"I'll do my best, Captain."

Even though the reply was meekly uttered, there was no meekness in her expression.

"This brings us back to the my earlier comment about your black garments."

Her expression became unreadable, and he wondered what thoughts were racing through her head.

"For the next few weeks my sister will be particularly vulnerable. Since I have recently suffered through a similar accident at sea, I have reason to believe that Emaline may begin to feel guilty at having survived where others did not. The black clothing may remind her of things better forgotten."

"Then why did you send her to a school where the teachers as well as the students wore black uniforms?"

His eyes narrowed. He was impressed. There weren't many men who would question his judgment, and even fewer women.

"I was not aware there *was* a uniform," he said slowly. "I appreciate your apprising me of the fact."

At his gentle rebuke, Patience flushed. "I'm sorry, Captain. That was rude of me. I would be happy to soften my attire, but this is all I have."

"You have only one dress?"

"No, Captain. I have three. But they have all been dyed black."

It wasn't hard to imagine this woman, bent over a vat of bubbling ebony dye, pushing her dresses into the inky mixture.

Although he'd wanted just such a paragon of virtue to instruct his sister, he couldn't help thinking that such strictures were a crime against nature. Especially for this woman. She should wear jewel tones with that hair and skin.

"If you are agreeable to the arrangement, I'll see to it that you're given something else to wear. If you insist on maintaining a semblance of mourning, I can order clothing in the blues and browns acceptable for such observances."

Her frown was immediate. "I couldn't possibly accept so personal a gift, Captain."

"Why not? I'm your employer."

"That doesn't matter."

"My maids and kitchen staff don't seem to mind their livery."

"That is an entirely different matter."

"How so?"

"Uniforms are exempt from such restrictions."

"Fine. Then I'll develop some sort of . . . uniform for you to wear if you wish. A special governess's livery."

She eyed him suspiciously, but now that he'd persuaded her to come this far, he wasn't about to let her back down.

"It's settled. Come morning, I'll see that you're outfitted. In the meantime, eat up before your soup grows cold."

Patience eased into her room, collapsing against the door. Would Captain Dalton never cease to surprise her? What other governess would be told on her first night when to eat, what to drink, and how to dress? Never in her life had she experienced such an emotional encounter. Such a meal.

Such a man.

Taking a deep, calming breath, she stood and began to remove the pins from her hair, relaxing ever so slightly as the weight on her scalp was eased and the thick plait fell down her back. Digging her fingers into the strands, she quickly combed her tresses free so that they were loose and far less aggravating.

A glance at the clock proved to her that she had been gone for less than an hour, but she felt as if she'd been imprisoned in the dining hall with that man for days, weeks.

He was very strange and compelling, she decided. In his evening attire, he'd cut a figure that was quite sophisticated and dashing.

Impatient at her own inner ramblings, she lit the lamp and began to strip off her black gown—a gown that was soon to be relegated to the depths of the wardrobe, if Captain Dalton had anything to say about it. She still wasn't sure whether she should allow him to buy her clothing of any sort—uniform or not. But even if her pride had demanded she refuse, she would have no funds of her own with which to purchase new garments until she received some of her wages. And she would not do anything to hurt Emaline further.

She pulled a face as she tossed the garments onto the bed. She wouldn't be all that sorry to see them replaced, although she would be loath to admit such a thing to Captain Garrick Dalton. She hated the black clothes, hated the hypocrisy they represented, because she didn't really mourn Alexander Pedigrue's passing. Not in the way she should. He'd wanted his children to be boys. All three of them. Girls were useless to him except as servants to cater to his whims.

That was why this position at Dalton Manor was so important to her. It was a means for Patience to prove to herself that she was capable of taking care of herself.

Dropping her nightgown over her head, Patience was about to move to the washstand when she was startled to see a shape huddled in the corner of the room next to her bed.

The lamp cast such deep shadows that she was unable to see more than a tangle of hair. Thinking it was Oscar, the sheepdog that Emaline had chased into the garden, she sighed, wondering who had let the creature upstairs. But as she drew nearer, she realized it wasn't an animal but Emaline. She was curled up on the rug, little more than a tattered blanket wrapped over her frail body. Beneath that, she was naked, which to Patience was shocking in the extreme—not that the child wore no clothes but that the maid who had been assigned to check on her hadn't seen to it that Emaline was properly clad.

Patience knelt beside the girl. "Emaline?"

When there was no response, she nudged her shoulder. "Miss Emaline, you need to get off the floor. You'll catch a chill."

But the young girl was impossible to wake. Indeed, she could have been unconscious if not for the very unladylike snorting noises she made.

At a loss as to what to do, Patience sighed and hefted Emaline into her arms. She gazed longingly at the fluffy pillows and soft featherbed, but Emaline's deadweight was already taxing Patience's strength and she doubted she could carry the girl all the way to her own nursery cot. Patience would merely have to exchange sleeping arrangements with the girl.

Emaline mumbled in her sleep, "Matumba."

Frowning, Patience settled her amid the blankets, wrapping her securely in extra quilts to keep her small body warm, then padded into the nursery. When she saw the short, babyish cot that had been laid out for Emaline's use, she could only sigh in disbelief.

What sort of sins had she committed to deserve *this?* And what did "Matumba" mean?

Garrick entered his study, his body throbbing with a weariness that had been building inside him for far too long.

He was pushing himself too hard. The journey to

Addlemeyer, the tension, and his recent wound had left him as weak as an infant. All he wanted was a few minutes of peace to gather his thoughts. Then he would summon enough energy to climb the staircase to his room. In the meantime he would have given anything to surrender himself to the quiet, but he wasn't foolish enough to think it would continue.

Just as he'd feared, there was a tap on the door.

"Come," Garrick commanded wearily.

The knob twisted and Bickerstaff entered, holding a tray with a single cup and a pot of coffee. "Sir."

Bickerstaff shut the door noiselessly behind him, then took a deep breath, unbuttoned his coat, and sank into the settee, propping his feet up on the hassock.

"I hate this uniform."

"Then don't wear it," Garrick suggested.

Bickerstaff grimaced. "It gives me an air of authority, don't you think?"

"I think it makes you look like an ass." Garrick's lips tilted in a rare grin. "Which is probably the point. I assume you have a reason for becoming the household butler."

"Mmm." Bickerstaff took the cup from the tray and filled it with coffee, drinking deeply. "Nectar of the gods."

"You should try the brandy."

He shook his head. "I intend to stay alert."

The question waiting to be asked hovered in the air between them. Sighing, Garrick surrendered to the inevitable.

"I suppose you're doing this in order to get the run of the house and therefore hover over me as some sort of unofficial bodyguard?"

Bickerstaff grinned. "I always suspected you were more clever than you looked."

Garrick shook his head. "I don't need anyone watching over me."

"Tell that to the man who approached you in front of the Bristol Hotel."

"An isolated incident."

"Come now, Garrick. There's no need to lie to me."

Garrick rubbed his lips with his fingers, then finally conceded to Bickerstaff's concern. "Who do you suppose is responsible?"

Bickerstaff sipped again, all humor dropping from his mien. "You're a wealthy man, so extortion is always a possibility. But I doubt that's the issue here."

On that Garrick agreed with his longtime friend.

"Unfortunately, that leaves us with only two possible motives for the attack."

Garrick nodded to encourage the man to continue.

"Either someone related to one of the sailors on your last ill-fated journey has decided to dabble in revenge . . ."

"Or?"

"Or we have a fanatic on our hands with a reason to hurt you. Something beyond our own logical deductions."

"There is a third possibility," Garrick suggested.

"Oh?"

"The man who attacked me may simply have wished to scare me. This whole affair could blow over within the next few days."

Bickerstaff peered at Garrick over the brim of his cup. "I hope you're right." He allowed a moment of silence to pass, then said, "But I don't think either one of us puts much faith in that theory."

"So what should I do? Go running back to England? Force Emaline to take an extended journey on a ship when the mere thought of water terrifies her?"

His friend shook his head. "No. You know as well as I do that such a move would aggravate your sister's problems and prolong the danger. I don't want you to underestimate the damage your foe is capable of doing, Garrick. He's already had one swing at you, hasn't he?"

Garrick shifted uncomfortably, reminded of the knife that was rammed into his side as he was thrown to the ground. The moment his back had come into contact with the rough gravel of the street, his newly healed body had protested with a fierce spasm of pain, immobilizing him.

"I want to look at your side," Bickerstaff said when Garrick didn't respond.

"Leave it alone, Bickerstaff."

"I will not. Not after all the trouble I went through to stitch up the wound." When Garrick said nothing, he added, "You might as well get my fussing over with, Captain. I can be just as stubborn as you."

Unfortunately, Garrick knew that fact all too well. Sighing, he stood up and stripped off his jacket with only the barest of winces. Then he dragged off his shirt, not bothering to untuck it, but allowing it to hang from the waistband of his trousers.

Bickerstaff set his cup on the tray and stood. Crossing behind Garrick, he made a clucking sound with his tongue. "The bandage is bloody. You've ripped open the wound again."

"Just take a look at the damned thing and be done with it," Garrick growled.

"I don't think so," Bickerstaff said as he removed the strips of cotton he'd put there only that morning. "It will need to be resewn."

Garrick nodded toward a cabinet. "Second drawer."

As Bickerstaff passed, he handed Garrick the bottle of brandy, which had been left on the corner of the desk. "Here. You'd better start drinking."

"Why?"

"You'll want to be drunk for this. The wound looks like hell. Last night was a waltz in the park compared to what you'll feel tonight."

Garrick didn't need to be told that. His side already hurt like hell.

Bickerstaff took a wicker sewing kit from the drawer, pausing. "Your mother's?"

"Yes."

Garrick took a swallow of the brandy, as much to wash away the tightness of his throat as the sting of his wound.

"I don't think she would approve of the way you've been pushing yourself so hard lately, Garrick."

"I'm home now. I'll get the rest I need."

"Are you sure?"

The needle pierced Garrick's flesh and he hissed, taking another healthy swallow of brandy.

Ignoring Bickerstaff's question, he tried to focus his mind on anything other than the pain.

Patience. He would think of his sister's governess. Of her red hair and flashing green eyes. Tomorrow he would begin to woo her.

Time was of the essence. By this time next month he intended to have her as his wife.

Chapter

9

"Tell me, Miss Pedigrue. Do you often sleep in your charge's bed?"

Patience's eyes sprang open, and she focused on a wall papered with delicate hobbyhorses and cabbage roses. For a moment she was completely confused by her surroundings until the memory of the previous day flooded into her head. With it came the identity of that voice. A voice like liquid midnight. Captain Garrick Dalton.

Twisting her head against the pillow, she ignored the twinge of pain that accompanied the movement. Somehow she'd fallen asleep with her head cocked at an awkward angle.

Almost afraid of what she would find, she pushed the waves of hair out of her eyes, wishing she'd taken the time to braid it the night before. But after such a hectic day, she'd been exhausted. Even sleeping on a bed a foot too short and far too narrow, she'd fallen into a deep slumber.

Unfortunately, when she saw the man standing over her, some of her dreams returned to the fore and she realized that *he* had been in them. Captain Garrick

Dalton. Bare to the waist, standing sternly at the prow of a ship, his hair streaming behind him. His body gleaming with moisture.

"Captain Dalton," she croaked, wishing he had found her anywhere but here, in a nursery, lying under a tangled quilt decorated with ducks. She'd meant to awaken early and put the room to rights so no one would know where she'd spent the night. But Patience had overslept—by an hour or more if the light streaming through the window was any indication.

"You look incredibly uncomfortable, Miss Pedigrue."

Too late she realized that her feet were dangling off the end of the bed. Her nightdress was bunched up around her knees, and the covers were wrapped about her waist.

Scrambling to her feet, she hastily tugged her clothing into position and clamped a hand over the unruly mane of hair streaming down her back.

"Was there something you needed, Captain?"

He regarded her wryly, his flint-blue eyes snapping with amusement. Patience fervently wished he would turn his back to her, as a gentleman should. But he didn't. He kept staring, making her uncomfortably aware that the bright sun was probably piercing the thin fabric of her night rail.

"I came to bring you something to wear. Emaline's seamstress was able to involve three of the house-maids in some impromptu sewing." His gaze flicked up and down her body with the intensity of a burning brand. "It's a good thing I did, if that's how you planned to dress for breakfast."

Patience felt a flush steal up to the roots of her hair, but she refused to back away, just as she refused to give him the satisfaction of knowing he'd unsettled her.

"As a matter of fact, I haven't had the time to tend to my ablutions, Captain."

"Oh, really." The reply was droll.

"I was just about ready to wake Emaline."

"Emaline is in the garden."

This time there was no way to hide her embarrassment. To be caught napping while her charge ran willy-nilly through the roses was an unpardonable mistake.

"I'm sorry, sir." She could barely force the words from her throat. She'd done it now. She'd carelessly allowed a child with delicate emotions to venture outside on her own. She would be tossed onto the streets without a penny to her name, and there wasn't even a possibility of references. She'd be lucky if he didn't spread the word far and wide that she wasn't worth employing. "I'll just pack my things."

"Why is that?"

"I realize you'll be dismissing me—"

"Dismissing you? What utter poppycock is that?"

"I failed to—"

"All you failed to do was wake at four in the morning, as my sister did. She came in search of me." He rubbed at his own cheeks and she realized he was weary to the bone. "I wouldn't expect the devil himself to keep such hours. That's why I took her for a ride and reintroduced her to some of her old haunts. Then I instructed one of the grooms who mind the stables during the night to watch for her. If she leaves the house unaccompanied, they are ordered to follow her."

"I see." It was a lame reply. She didn't see. Not in the least. In fact, she was beginning to wonder what other strange practices she would be witnessing before she left this place.

"I noticed you didn't manage to give my sister a bath."

Again Patience flushed. "No, sir. She was fast asleep when I returned from dinner, and I hated to disturb her." She hesitated, then added, "But I'm afraid she must have awakened while we were dining. When I discovered her asleep in my room she was . . ."

Garrick's brow creased in concern. "She was what?"

"She was curled up on the floor. Completely unclothed."

His lips thinned. "I'll have a word with Miss Fitch. The maid she assigned to watch Emaline must be more careful."

"I'll do my best to see that Emaline bathes."

"Thank you. I'm beginning to believe that since the wreck, she's been deathly afraid of water."

Of course, Patience thought to herself. Of course! That would explain why Emaline had become nearly frantic on the ship.

Garrick straightened from where he'd been leaning lazily against the small table where Emaline would probably take most of her meals. "In the meantime, I think it's time you donned your uniform."

He gestured for her to precede him into her own room, where, on the rumpled covers of her bed, she saw a dimity gown laid out, awaiting her approval. As much as her fingers itched to touch the delicate fabric, she didn't dare. She couldn't possibly accept anything so fine.

"I don't think—"

"I don't require you to think about the uniform I've

provided, Miss Pedigrue," he said firmly. "I only require that you obey me when I order you to take it."

Obey. If he'd used any other word, she probably wouldn't have blinked an eye, but that particular concept stuck in her throat and would not be dislodged.

She turned to confront him. "I will not blindly obey anyone, Captain Dalton."

He peered at her even more intently. "Oh?"

"I will not subject myself to tyranny in any form." Her hands were balling into fists.

"Why is that, Miss Pedigrue?"

She tilted her chin to a proud angle. "I have already suffered beneath such selfishness and I will not do so again."

"Is that a fact?"

She didn't like the way he answered or the way he moved toward her, gradually crowding her against the foot of the bed.

"Tell me, Miss Pedigrue, are you always this blunt?"

"Yes."

"Are you always this open about your feelings?"

"Yes."

"And are you always this careless?"

She opened her mouth, then shut it.

"I have given you a uniform to wear," he continued in a tone that brooked no argument. "As your employer, I should be allowed to choose whatever I feel is appropriate, provided that I do not stray over the lines of taste or decorum. Is that too much to demand?"

She didn't answer, knowing that if she did, she would look even more the fool.

He sighed, clearly regretting his show of anger. "Put

on your dress, Miss Pedigrue. Then join me downstairs for breakfast. In the future I will not wait for
your company. Today I don't see how either of us can
possibly avoid it."

He left, shutting the door resolutely behind him—
not quite a slam, but nearly.

Afraid he might return as abruptly as he'd left,
Patience took the time to twist the lock. Just in case.
She wouldn't care to have a repeat of this morning's
debacle. Captain Dalton had already seen her dressed
in little more than her nightdress. He needn't see her
in her chemise as well.

The thought was enough to make her cheeks blaze,
and she pressed her palms to her face, staring into the
mirror and wondering why she became so easily
embarrassed of late. True, her father had insisted that
she and her sisters lead extremely sheltered lives. But
of them all, Patience had enjoyed the most freedom,
since she was her father's messenger and errand girl.
When instructed to visit the shops, she had always
rushed through her purchases so that she might linger
on the waterfront, stroll past the Common, and drink
deeply of sunlight and laughter.

She'd thought such activities had made her very
sophisticated and worldly-wise, but she was discovering that they did not.

Patience held the dimity gown up to the light, her
mouth forming a small *o* at the way the sun melted
through the fragile fabric. She gazed at the neckline,
seeing that it was quite low—at least it was lower than
anything she was accustomed to wearing.

But even as she considered putting on one of her
black gowns, just for spite at the captain's audacity,
she realized she couldn't do that. Not if her show of
defiance would hurt Emaline.

Since the minutes were ticking away, she tugged the

nightdress off and reached for her underthings. Just as her sister Constance had instructed from the time Patience was old enough to understand, she donned the proper number of garments in their proper order: chemise, hose, corset. Corset cover, knee-length petticoat, horsehair crinoline, and five outer petticoats. Once she felt modestly dressed from that perspective at least, she pulled on the full gray skirt with its tiny pink flowers and the matching bodice with its tucked front and pagoda sleeves.

As her fingers fumbled with the buttons, she wondered how the captain had persuaded the newly hired seamstress to fashion a garment so quickly—without measurements or fittings. Over all, the fit was quite good. The dress was slightly tighter and more tailored than she was accustomed to wearing, the skirt a trifle shorter, but she couldn't fault the picture she presented.

Rushing to the bureau, she plaited her hair in three braids, wound them in a coronet at the nape of her neck, and topped the ensemble with a fragile batiste headdress.

Glancing in the mirror, Patience could scarcely believe the transformation. Although she'd been in mourning for less than a month, she'd never really owned anything brighter than her cinnamon-colored Sunday dress. But this—this!

Her hands touched the skirt at her waist, and she turned from side to side, trying to catch every angle in the less-than-satisfactory mirror hanging on the armoire door. But when she caught herself wishing she'd followed Felicity's example and bought herself a watch-spring hoop to rid herself of the bulk of her petticoats, her thoughts came to a screeching halt.

Vanity. Sheer and utter vanity. What had this man brought her to? She was practical and intelligent—

which, in her opinion, was far more important than being pretty and vapid.

She pursed her lips and wrenched open the door. He might think she would be that tractable and easily swayed, but she would never abandon her principles.

On that thought, she swept from her garret room to the back staircase, frowning as another thought hit her. Emaline was nine years old, and although that did not mean she was an adult by any means, as far as Patience was concerned, the girl deserved something more in the way of accommodations than a nursery. A nursery that had obviously been designed with small children in mind. Children who were purposely kept far away from the rest of the house, Patience added to herself as she marched down her third flight of stairs. It was a wonder, given the way Emaline ran headlong away from any sort of discipline, that she hadn't broken her neck on the staircase during one of her flights.

By the time Patience reached the dining room, she'd worked herself into a mood that Constance was fond of referring to as a full-fledged snit.

"Captain Dalton," she began firmly as soon as she entered. But after two steps, she realized she wasn't alone. A stoop-shouldered gentleman rose to his feet, then another leaner, overly handsome man and a pretty woman near Patience's age lifted their heads and stared in her direction. Instantly Patience became aware of being studied—critically by the woman and with far more interest than necessary by the handsome man.

"So glad you could join us promptly," Garrick commented, but there was a mocking gleam his eyes that suggested he'd known she was about to rail at him again.

He motioned to a chair—the same one she'd sat in

the night before. The one to his right—the place usually reserved for important guests or close family.

The handsome man immediately sprang to his feet and pulled out her chair.

Patience took it with some reluctance, but only because the other two strangers were obviously waiting for her to do so.

"I would like to introduce a few of my colleagues to you."

Garrick began on the left side of the table, motioning to a distinguished-looking man with a splendid set of white muttonchop whiskers. "This is Asa Marcus. He manages my accounting office here on Addlemeyer."

The man nodded, then returned his attention to his food.

Garrick pointed to the man who still stood uncomfortably close to Patience's chair.

"And this is Jan Ellington, my second-in-command, and his sister, Nina."

Nina flashed her a bright smile. "It will be lovely having another young woman on the island."

"Thank you."

Jan took Patience's hand and, much to her annoyance, kissed her knuckles. "Garrick, you failed to tell us how beautiful Miss Pedigrue is. She's a vision. Truly."

A vision? Patience would have snorted if such a reaction wouldn't have labeled her common. She had never been referred to as anything but "presentable," and she had no illusions as to her appearance.

Garrick seemed no more pleased by the man's remark than Patience. While Jan took his chair, Garrick began grilling the two men about the state of the business since his departure.

As the drone of male voices washed over her,

Patience did her best to appear serene and confident, even though she wished she could have taken breakfast in the kitchen. When Bickerstaff placed a plate of fruit, eggs, and sliced ham in front of her, the fare caused her stomach to tighten even more.

"Are you from Nantucket, Miss Pedigrue?" Nina asked.

Eyeing the dark-haired, olive-eyed woman, Patience felt plain and unsophisticated in comparison. "No, I was hired in Boston."

"Ohhh," Nina drawled. "Boston." She apparently found the fact interesting, because she smiled coyly. "Then you must have been bowled over by Mr. Bickerstaff's charm when you were interviewed."

At that moment Bickerstaff returned to the dining room with an assortment of sweet rolls on a tray.

"I'm afraid Mr. Bickerstaff didn't interview me," Patience reluctantly admitted.

Nina blinked. "You mean you were interviewed by the captain himself? How fascinating! Even so, you missed a treat. Mr. Bickerstaff can be so . . . so . . . sensitive to a woman's concerns."

"Well, I—" She looked up in time to see Bickerstaff roll his eyes, and she hid an answering grin.

Turning her attention to her meal, she was able to avoid any further conversation. When finally Jan and Asa finished their business with Garrick and rose, she exhaled in relief.

"Come along, Nina. We've got work to do," Jan said.

Nina tossed Patience a rueful smile. "Men. They can be positively medieval, can't they?"

Unclear as to the woman's meaning, Patience nodded.

Delicately wiping her lips, Nina leaned toward the

Captain. "If you need my help—in any capacity—don't hesitate to let me know."

"Thank you."

Then, in a whisper of silk and the click of male boots, the trio made their way out of the room.

The captain waited until the thump of the front door signaled their complete retreat. Pushing his plate away, he leaned back in his chair and linked his fingers together.

"Suppose you tell me what caused you to be so hot and flustered when you first entered the room."

Patience didn't think that she had been in any way hot or flustered, but she didn't bother to correct the man. "I was merely wondering why the nursery is so far away from the rest of the house."

Garrick touched a fingertip to his lips, drawing attention to his slim, well-formed fingers, the nails recently buffed and tended as if he were some European gentleman and not a ship's master. "You don't approve?"

When he spoke, her attention was drawn from his finger to his lips. She cleared her throat. "I neither approve nor disapprove."

"Somehow I doubt that."

She sighed in impatience, and he chuckled. "When I was a baby, the nursery was relocated to the top floor so that my parents could make love without being heard."

The blunt statement caused her to gasp. She stared at him, then resolutely looked away, knowing that he was trying to get a rise out of her. Unfortunately he'd managed to do just that.

But she wouldn't admit that to him.

She couldn't.

"Captain Dalton—"

"Garrick, please."

"I couldn't possibly call you by your first name."

He shrugged as if it were of no importance to him either way.

"Captain Dalton," she began again, "I realize that you have been away from home for many months." She faltered, then continued, "But if I am to do my job properly, you must learn to temper your language."

"Why?"

Her mouth opened and shut fishlike for a few seconds, so stunned was she by his challenge.

"Because Emaline needs to hear how proper gentlemen speak."

He leaned forward again, bending his head near so that it took all the will she possessed not to back away.

"How *does* a proper gentleman speak, Miss Pedigrue?"

She knew he was baiting her, but she didn't see how the knowledge could possibly help her. Not unless she challenged him openly.

"I believe the instructions you gave me on the journey here included helping Emaline fit into society."

"How does my speech prevent you from accomplishing such a feat?"

"Certain things should never be mentioned in the presence of a lady."

"What things?"

"Well . . . such as . . . the intimacies that can occur . . . between a husband and wife."

"Ahhh." The drawl had returned. "So I shouldn't have mentioned that my parents didn't want to be overheard during their lovemaking."

Patience could feel the heat beginning to creep up her cheeks.

"Was that what I did wrong, Miss Pedigrue?"

She couldn't speak. Not without her words emerging as a choked strangle.

"Or was it the fact, that as one of their children, I shouldn't have known they were doing it, hmmm?"

Patience jumped to her feet, nearly sending her chair toppling backward. "This current topic is completely beyond my original point. I merely meant to indicate that Emaline is a growing child, yet she has been placed in a room—and indeed a bed—meant for a toddler. I believe she would respond to our overtures far better if we treated her in a manner befitting her age. But since I have interrupted your own work, I will leave you now while I search for Emaline."

He grinned. A devilish, dangerous grin that made her think of a cat toying with a mouse.

"Very well. We'll continue this discussion later."

No. They would not. Not if Patience had anything to do with it. But she didn't say the words out loud, no matter how much she wanted to do so.

"Good day, Captain Dalton," she said tightly as she headed to the door.

"Good day, Miss Pedigrue."

She paused, knowing he had one more thing to say to her—and praying she would have the strength to withstand whatever improprieties might be waiting on the tip of his tongue.

But all he added was "I'll see to it that you and Emaline are moved to more appropriate rooms."

She remained where she stood for several seconds until she finally realized that he didn't plan to offer anything more titillating than that.

Bit by bit, she relaxed. She even found the energy necessary to smile. "Thank you, Captain Dalton."

But as she went in search of her charge, she couldn't

escape the niggling sensation that she hadn't really won anything.

Not yet.

Indeed she had the strange sensation that she'd been maneuvered into position for the next confrontation. The battle of the moment might have been won, but not the war of wills.

Chapter

10

Nearly three hours later Patience led Emaline into the house from where the little girl had been making mud pies on the back walk, then doing her best to feed them to a resigned Oscar. Obviously, being back at Dalton Manor had distracted Emaline from her joy of learning, because she'd completely ignored Patience's attempts to coax her into the classroom.

Miss Fitch, a dour woman with pale blond hair and a nose that must have been pinched with a clothespin as a child, met her at the bottom of the staircase. "Your things, as well as the girl's, are being moved to the master wing," she said.

Patience stared at the woman, not comprehending the words, her fingers still tightly wrapped around Emaline's wrist as the girl squirmed to be free. "What exactly does that mean?"

Miss Fitch's expression became even colder, if that was possible. "It means that you've been put in the rooms opposite Captain Dalton's own chamber."

The woman turned and made her way up the wide staircase, every muscle in her body radiating a disapproval that Patience had rarely had directed her way by anyone other than her father.

The rooms opposite Captain Dalton's.

The phrase reverberated in Patience's head like a death knell.

Opposite Captain Dalton's?

The first embers of anger began to smolder in Patience's breast. Damn the man. Didn't he know that she must guard her reputation with utmost zeal? Didn't he realize that by moving her to a room in his own wing he was implying she was a woman of loose morals?

The more time she spent in his company, the more she was beginning to believe that Emaline wasn't the only Dalton she would be expected to "civilize."

Unfortunately, before she could move, Emaline took that opportunity to lean down and bite Patience on the forearm.

Swallowing a yelp of surprise, Patience unconsciously let go, and Emaline darted up the stairs.

Patience gave chase, lifting her skirts and racing behind her. She was nearly at the top when she realized that someone was coming down. Before she could slow her headlong pace, she plowed into an immovable object. One that was distinctly male. Distinctly solid.

Closing her eyes, she cursed her fate again, wondering why the ever-present witness to her impulsiveness had to be Captain Dalton.

Garrick grasped her arms, steadying her, his hands warm and broad.

"Miss Pedigrue. Fancy bumping into you here."

When she wavered on the tread, he snapped his arms around her waist, hauling her close to keep her from pitching down the stairs.

He might as well have set a spark to a bucket of kerosene. The moment his body came into contact with her own, she was reminded of the way she seemed to lose all control whenever he was near. Then she heard Miss Fitch's words, *Your things, as well as the girl's, are being moved to the master wing.*

Huffing in frustration, she yanked free, nearly stumbling in her attempt. "I'll kindly ask you not to touch me in the future, Captain Dalton."

"I suppose it isn't seemly for a gentleman to keep a woman from falling down a staircase, either?"

She opened her mouth, ready to utter a rousing retort, but all she could manage was an "ohhh" of irritation. Brushing past him, she followed her charge.

Garrick watched her go, her skirts swishing around her legs in a way that offered him quite a satisfying view of her trim, supple ankles. The kind he'd always enjoyed divesting of a layer of silk hosiery.

Enough!

He shook his head to rid it of such thoughts. Patience Pedigrue was the kind of woman who required a gradual seduction. He would only defeat himself if he continued to dwell on the woman's latent sensuality.

He made his way to the foyer, intent upon the stables and the daily gallop he took on his stallion whenever he was home. He couldn't wait to get astride Ramses and race the wind. Other than sailing, it was his only abiding passion.

"Captain?"

Swearing under his breath, he acknowledged Miss Fitch as she stepped from the breakfast room.

"Yes, Miss Fitch."

She pointed to the shaggy, mud-laden dog at her feet. "What am I supposed to do with this beast?"

He looked at Oscar and frowned at the burrs and brambles snagged in his dirty coat. "He should have been given a bath days ago, Miss Fitch."

Her lips folded into a prim line. "He was given a good grooming just yesterday. But that . . . that *child* . . ."

"Emaline?" Garrick inquired silkily, barely concealing his anger at having Emaline referred to in such a contemptuous manner.

Miss Fitch must have caught her error, because she flashed him her most gracious smile. "Yes, sir. *Dear* Emaline has taken to chasing the animal into the bushes."

"Why?"

She inhaled sharply as if to hold her temper. "I have no idea."

"Are you understaffed, Miss Fitch?"

She blinked at the sudden change of topic. "I beg your pardon?"

"Are you understaffed?"

"No, sir."

"Then assign someone to bathe the dog whenever it becomes necessary and don't bother me with the details. As for my sister, as long as the dog doesn't object, she may chase him wherever she wishes."

"Yes, sir," she said tightly, taking a stack of envelopes from her pocket. "Your mail, sir."

Garrick absently took the stack from her, tossing it onto the salver on the chest by the door. He was about to walk past when one of the letters caught his eye, the seal so familiar to him now that he couldn't have ignored its significance even if he tried.

Snatching the letter from the pile, he headed toward the study.

Damn it all to hell.

Not another threat.

Not so soon.

* * *

140

Nearly an hour later Garrick galloped his horse to the top of the rise and surveyed the town of Addlemeyer below.

He'd never had to question why his father had decided to settle here, on a small island off the coast of New England. Just looking at it, Garrick understood his father's reasons. Addlemeyer held a quaint hominess that was hard to deny. Narrow twisting streets were lined on either side with neat clapboard buildings, most of them whitewashed and trimmed in blue, green, or red. The town itself was barely two furlongs in length, but the wharf area was bustling.

Three ships had docked in the last month, all of them part of the Dalton fleet. The most notable was the new schooner *Emaline's Return*. With the ship in their possession, Jan Ellington would study the design in order to see if any of their own ships could be altered to make them faster and sleeker. In the meantime he had placed an order for five more. Enough to bring the number of Dalton vessels up to twenty.

So why couldn't Garrick take pleasure in all he saw?

Why couldn't he focus on all that was good and forget that other, darker forces were being drawn to Addlemeyer as well?

Tipping his face up to the sun, he closed his eyes, allowing the wind to play through his hair and cool the heat already gathering in his body. His mother had once stated that Garrick was born hungry. He was never satisfied with what he had. He was always searching for more.

More.

Today was no exception. He felt a restlessness inside him. One that in the past he had often confused for the need to begin another voyage, conquer another business venture. But having just returned from such a trip, he knew that wasn't what his soul needed. There was something else. Something lingering just on the fringes of his consciousness. Something that he would recognize as soon as he saw it. He was sure of it.

Growing impatient with his own thoughts, Garrick shook his head to relieve it of such nonsense. In truth, that wasn't why he'd come up here. No, he'd come to this spot because it was the only place where he could think. The only place where he could truly be alone.

Dismounting, he draped the reins over a branch and sat on a nearby log, pulling two notes from his pocket.

The mere sight of them caused his stomach to tighten and a potent fury to fill his breast. Opening them both, he noted again that the script was identical. The first had been delivered to his hotel room, the other to his home. This second note said, "I will kill you, Captain Dalton. And your sister too."

Dammit!

He threw both of the notes to the ground where the breeze teased at the edges and threatened to scatter them. Garrick would be the first to admit that he wasn't a saint. He had probably offended his fair share of people in business, and the explosion of *Dalton's Pride* was a tragedy beyond measure. But he honestly couldn't think why anyone would want to hurt Emaline.

He raked his hands through his hair in frustration. Then, scooping the offensive letters from the grass, he strode to his horse and swung into the saddle.

Now more than ever, Emaline's future would have

to be secured. He had hoped to woo Miss Pedigrue gradually. But these threats were convincing him that he could no longer afford such a luxury.

It took nearly an hour, but Patience finally found Emaline Dalton crouched in the far corner of her governess's wardrobe, her knees drawn up to her chest and her arms hugging her legs to her body.

"There you are," Patience said, relieved. After encountering Captain Dalton on the staircase, Patience had been unable to fathom where the girl could have gone. She'd been tormented by horrible images of Emaline flinging herself from the roof in a fit of pique or tumbling down the back staircase.

She opened her mouth to scold the girl for her habit of biting adults, but stopped before the first sound could be uttered. Emaline looked so forlorn, so fragile, so . . . lost.

A sigh melted from her lips, and the starch eased from her spine. Emaline was only nine, and she'd spent four years with the native tribe. Was it any wonder that she would find another change frightening? Especially after spending so much time with that awful Bodrill woman. Patience couldn't even fathom how abandoned the girl must have felt.

Emaline needed some stability in her life. She needed to know that she had come home, and home was where she would stay.

"Do you mind if I join you?"

At the question, Emaline, who had been sitting with her head buried in her knees, peeked up at her through the tangle of her hair.

She made no response, but it was obvious that she'd heard the question.

Gathering up her skirts and praying that the sturdy, oversized armoire would hold them both, Patience climbed into the space opposite Emaline.

Because of the volume of her petticoats, there was no question of drawing the door closed on her side of the wardrobe. As best she could, she drew her own legs into the same position Emaline had adopted, mimicking her posture, but not mocking it.

"This is lovely, isn't it?" she commented.

Emaline stared at her in disbelief.

"It's so quiet, so serene in here, I really don't know why I haven't tried it before."

The girl gave no indication that she agreed or disagreed with such an observation.

"You know, when I was a little girl, I used to go into the cellar beneath our house for much the same reason—but only in the summer, you understand. It was much too cold in the winter and filled with food supplies. Supplies and spiders. I can't abide the creatures, can you?"

There was no answer.

"But I digress. I was telling you of my adventures." She pretended to think, when in reality she was merely rambling in an attempt to reach the girl in some small way.

"In my family, there were three of us children, all girls. Constance was the eldest, then me, then Felicity. They weren't as fond of the cellar as I was, I can assure you. But when Papa was napping, I could persuade them to join me by telling them that the root cellar was a magic kingdom and I was the queen. I would order them to join me for a royal tea party, and we would sit on grain sacks with a crate between us and pretend we were having a luncheon. We even fashioned a set of dolls out of potatoes to be our servants."

Patience's narrative faded away. At the mention of a doll, Emaline's eyes had widened in a very real, very tangible show of interest.

"Do you have a doll, Emaline?"

Before the girl could respond, a shadow fell over the two of them.

"So this is where the two of you have been hiding."

Patience closed her eyes and silently prayed that the armoire would swallow her whole. She had meant for Captain Dalton to find her the epitome of decorum and professionalism. To have been discovered in her charge's bed dressed in a nightgown could be considered an accident. But to be found talking to Emaline while huddled in a closet, smashed against the clothing and undergarments hung from the hooks could only be interpreted as a sign of madness. Madness and complete inefficiency. Governesses were supposed to toe the line. They were supposed to hand down rules and see them blindly obeyed. They weren't to join the less than dignified practices of the children they were meant to teach.

"Captain Dalton," she acknowledged slowly, not bothering to look up.

"Miss Pedigrue."

To her surprise there was no disapproval in his tone. Glancing up, she found him eyeing her with something akin to wonder.

"Imagine finding you here," he said when the silence grew too long.

"Yes. Well, we were . . ."

"Talking," he supplied. "I can see that."

The approval in his tone caused her body to warm from the inside out.

"Thank you, Miss Pedigrue. I sense that Emaline was in need of a . . . closet conference."

"Indeed, sir," she murmured, following his lead.

He opened the door on Emaline's side. "It's time for lunch, Emmie. Are you hungry?"

Emaline nodded, and he scooped her into his arms, carrying her as if she were a toddler and not a young girl.

Emaline clung to his neck, gazing up at him with such hero worship that Patience couldn't tear her gaze away.

"Are you coming, Miss Pedigrue?"

"Coming, sir?"

"To lunch."

She stared at him uncomprehendingly. Then, realizing she was the only person still in the closet, she scrambled to her feet. "I don't understand."

"It's a meal we have, about midday, that involves—"

"I know what lunch is, Captain," she interrupted—with a little more vinegar than she had intended. "What I meant to say was that I thought I would be eating with Emaline. Here. In the nursery."

"Didn't Miss Fitch tell you? Your quarters have been moved."

"Yes, but . . ."

"But what, Miss Pedigrue?"

"I really would be more comfortable eating in the kitchen. As I've stated several times, it isn't proper for a governess and her charge to eat with the family."

"Why not?"

She didn't have an answer to that question.

"Don't bother to answer, Miss Pedigrue," Garrick said, turning to make his way into the corridor. "I don't care about tradition. This is my house, and I will decide which customs will be observed in regard to my sister. If it will make you feel better, consider yourself a temporary member of the family."

He exited the room, leaving Patience rooted to the spot, stunned.

Family? He planned to treat her as a "temporary member of the family"?

For some reason that idea brought a tightness to her chest. Except for her sisters, no one had ever asked for her company.

After a few seconds she forced herself to move, forced herself to follow them into the hall. But even as she did so, she couldn't deny—no matter how much she might want to do so—that something very elemental had changed.

In the way she regarded her position.

As well as in the way she regarded her employer.

Garrick saw to it that his sister was seated in the chair on his left, Miss Pedigrue in the seat on his right.

"Would you be so kind?" Garrick slid the silver bell toward Miss Pedigrue, watching her carefully, wondering if she would catch the significance of the gesture.

He was not disappointed. She stared at the bell as if it were a foreign object, then met his gaze.

"You wish me to serve as your hostess?"

"Please."

"But it isn't—"

"Customary? Proper?" He made a *tsk*ing sound with his tongue. "Surely by now you've caught on to the fact that I care little about such rules, Miss Pedigrue."

She was reluctant to comply, but he also sensed that she would not refuse him. Not yet, at any rate.

She waited until Emaline had stopped squirming before ringing the bell, hesitantly at first, then with more authority.

Immediately, Bickerstaff ushered a bevy of servants into the room. They carried tureens of soup, loaves of fresh bread, and platters of cold meat and cheese.

"You will also discover, Miss Pedigrue, that I dispense with the usual folderol associated with the midday meal. In most households there is a sort of system—soup, then the entrée, then whatever else is on the menu. I, on the other hand, prefer to pick and choose for myself. If I don't wish to eat something, I don't. If I do, I do."

He watched the way she stared as Emaline reached for the platters as soon as they were put on the table rather than waiting for Patience to serve her.

"I also believe that it is rude and presumptuous to let another person decide what size portions you are allotted. In the Dalton family, the midday meal has always been run using boardinghouse principles. Take what you want, but leave one foot on the floor at all times."

He waited for her to respond to the jest, but she merely blinked at him as if he'd lost his mind.

"Eat up, Miss Pedigrue."

She appeared hesitant, making one last protest. "Meals should be a time for close family . . ."

"I have already explained that you are, in essence, a part of our family, Miss Pedigrue. I have entrusted you with the care of my sister. There is no more important job in this house. Besides which, the meals we have together will be an excellent time for you to report on Emaline's progress. So eat."

Patience finally selected several small mounds of food, arranging them on her plate with a fastidiousness that bordered on being maddening.

"Captain Dalton . . ."

"Yes, Miss Pedigrue?"

She leaned toward him, offering a view of far more

interesting delights than those lining the table. He wondered if she was aware of the way the fabric of her gown stretched tightly over her bosom and of how the neckline gaped when she bent forward, so that he was teased with a tiny pair of freckles gracing the inside curve of one breast.

Tearing his gaze away from the sight, from the glimpse of the lace that edged her undergarments, he found her watching him with eyes that had grown dark, the pupils large and fathomless.

She truly was lovely. This morning he'd been a bit taken aback to find her in his sister's cot. But when he'd discovered Emaline's tattered baby blanket abandoned in the governess's bedding, he'd easily surmised what had happened. Somehow Emaline had ended up in Patience's room and vice versa. That could have happened only if Patience had willingly surrendered the comforts of her own quarters.

The thought that this woman, this grown woman with her fastidious habits, would have deigned to sleep in a child's cot had touched Garrick in a way he never would have believed possible. Finding her holed up in the armoire had impressed him even more. This woman had an enormous capacity for loving. He knew she did. And he sensed that she would understand the measures Garrick intended to take to ensure his sister's welfare.

She would understand.

But Garrick would have to see to it that she agreed as well.

"Captain Dalton," she said after several seconds. He saw the way she physically removed herself from the intimacy of their shared gaze. "I sympathize with your view of . . . dining informality. I really do."

"But you have a complaint to make."

"Well, sir . . ."

"You think it isn't healthy for Emaline."

At hearing her name, the girl looked up from the crust of bread she'd been eating.

"You think we should keep to a schedule, a regimen?"

"Yes, sir, I do."

"That way, she will know what to expect from society."

Miss Pedigrue wilted in obvious relief. "Yes," she said, exhaling at the same time. "At least we agree on that."

"No, Miss Pedigrue, we do not."

Her fork hovered in midair.

"I will concede the need for stability in Emaline's life, but I will not concede to a need for more structure than is necessary."

"More than is necessary?"

"In time, we can introduce Emaline to everything that awaits her in the world beyond us. For now, it is more important that she be reassured that she belongs here."

Patience looked down at her plate, obviously chastened. For some reason, that made Garrick feel petty, so he added in a gentler tone, "This does not mean that I wish you to indulge her every whim. As she grows accustomed to her new life, she will have more duties and responsibilities. In the meantime she has her educational schedule to adhere to and lessons that need to be learned. In fact, I have sent Bickerstaff to Nantucket this afternoon to purchase books and materials for just such a purpose. After you have drawn up a more complete list, we will arrange for supplies to be sent from Boston."

When she finally glanced his way, he offered her a cocky grin. "But I would hope that a few . . .

wardrobe sessions would also be included in her routine."

He knew by the way her lips twitched that she'd caught his double meaning.

"In the meantime," he said, directing his attention to his little sister, who was demolishing a bowl of custard—with her fingers, "I think it's time the two of us gave Emaline a bath."

The moment the words were out of his mouth, he realized his error. He should have waited for the end of the meal—or at least made his suggestion in private.

But Emaline cast him a tortured glare and jumped up, her chair toppling over backward. Then she scurried from the room as if the hounds of hell were after her.

"Damn," Garrick muttered, throwing his napkin onto the table. "Miss Pedigrue, have a tub prepared. We'll both be back in a minute."

Chapter

II

It was actually three-quarters of an hour later when Garrick reappeared, the squalling, screaming form of his sister draped under his arm like a sack of meal.

Following the captain's orders, Patience had arranged for the tub to be placed in the kitchen. Then she'd dismissed the servants, much to Miss Fitch's annoyance, she was sure. It was obvious the woman felt the encroachment into her own territory completely unacceptable.

As soon as the water had been heated, Patience put a scant six inches in the bottom of the tub, added a dash of vanilla and a few rose petals, thinking that maybe the scent and the exotic flourish might catch Emaline's fancy.

She needn't have bothered. As soon as Emaline caught sight of the bathtub, she began to bellow at the top of her lungs, her arms and feet flailing in her effort to get free.

"Stand back, Miss Pedigrue," Captain Dalton ordered as he strode into the room. But when he would have dropped Emaline in the water, she clung to him, wailing like a banshee until even Patience's ears began to hurt.

Sighing in impatience, Garrick sat on one of the trestle benches, pulled his sister onto his lap, and forced her by sheer strength of will to hold still.

"Emaline, stop it!"

She grew quiet in an instant at his authoritative tone.

"Nothing will happen to you," he said more gently. "The water isn't even as deep as the puddles in the yard after it rains."

Emaline, tears streaming down her face and streaking through the grime on her cheeks, looked far from convinced.

"Would I ever let anything hurt you?" he asked, stroking her snarled hair. "You know that I will do everything in my power to see you remain well. But you need to wash. If you don't, you'll grow sick."

Emaline didn't appear to believe him.

"Please. Do it for me, hmm?"

She trembled, her whole body racked with the convulsions.

"Come along."

He stood, taking her by the hand and pulling her to the tub. When he saw the preparations Patience had made, an approving light glinted in his eyes.

"Look at that, Emmie. Miss Pedigrue has made you a beautiful bath—one for a proper little lady."

Emaline still hung back, but it was obvious that the floating petals intrigued her.

"See? It's not so bad."

Garrick sank onto his heels, reaching into the water and swirling it into ever increasing circles. "It's nice and warm. I promise that it will feel oh, so good to wash away some of the grime."

The coaxing tone he'd adopted would have been enough for Patience to follow him through the gates of hell, had he asked, but Emaline wasn't so easily convinced.

"Suppose we take off your shift, hmm?" he said, referring to the fact that, once outside, Emaline had divested herself of the dress, shoes, and stockings, that Garrick had helped her don that morning.

When he tried to lift it over her head, she squealed in protest.

Garrick sighed, and Patience had to turn her head away to hide her own smile. Evidently she was not the only person in this room who suffered from a lack of patience. Garrick was a man who was accustomed to being obeyed, and the fact that a child—his little sister, no less—was bent on openly defying him was maddening.

"Emaline"—there was a strained quality to his voice as he spoke her name—"I really think you should take your chemise off. It won't do to bathe while you are wearing it."

Once again he touched the hem. It was a mistake. She began to squeal, sinking onto the floor until he was forced to lift her bodily and hold her over the water.

When it became apparent that he was going to drop her in, clothing and all, she became that much more ferocious in her struggles, scratching him on the cheek, the arm. The moment her toes touched the water, the volume of her shrieks increased, as did her panic, until she was splashing water over them both. When Garrick put a hand at the top of her head to force her to sit, she wriggled free, running from the room and leaving a streak of wet footprints behind her.

The sudden silence in the kitchen was deafening.

Even so, Patience could not prevent a low chuckle from bubbling from her lips.

Garrick glared at her. "I don't think it's at all funny."

"No, sir." She tried to school her features, but the corners of her mouth kept twitching with barely suppressed merriment.

"What's so blasted amusing, Miss Pedigrue?"

She shrugged. "The whole situation. Other than her feet, the only thing we've managed to bathe is ourselves." She gestured to their water-dappled clothing.

His grin was slow, but just as genuine as her own. "Maybe if we keep working on her a piece at a time, we'll have the whole child clean one day."

"By Christmas, if we're lucky."

He planted his hands on his hips, wryly shaking his head. "You could be right."

When Patience went to gather a rag to sop up the moisture on the floor, he regarded her strangely. "Any other woman would have been horrified by Emaline's antics."

"I don't think you give the gentler sex their due."

He didn't look any more convinced than Emaline had when he'd told her the water wouldn't hurt.

Patience felt compelled to add, "Compassion comes naturally to us, Captain."

"But it doesn't come naturally to men?" he prompted.

The last thing she wanted was to be drawn into an argument, so she shrugged.

He refused to let the discussion die. "Tell me, Miss Pedigrue, what do you really think about the matter?"

"In my experience, women are more likely to feel empathy, tenderness, and longing."

"What about men?"

"Their emotions are baser in comparison."

His hands fell to his sides, and he took a step toward her. "How so?"

"Men tend to dwell on ambition, displays of strength, and . . ."

"And what?" he prompted when she didn't continue.

"And conquest, Captain Dalton," she finished bluntly.

"You don't approve."

It was a statement, not a question.

"I suppose such emotions are ingrained in their nature, their upbringing. How can I disapprove of something that comes from a deep-rooted instinct?"

"So you believe that men are inherently drawn to—how did you put it?—conquest?"

He eased closer to her, and although a healthy measure of space still separated them, she had the sensation of being crowded.

"Yes, and such vices can lead to tragedy."

"They can also lead to great pleasure."

"Corporal pleasure," she said distastefully.

"Not always. Isn't there just as much joy to be gained from a job well done? From exploring unknown territories? From developing new relationships and opinions?"

The words were quite innocent on the surface, but she sensed a far more disturbing meaning underneath it all.

"I think this discussion would be better off tabled, Captain."

"You do, do you?"

He was still easing toward her, forcing her to retreat or face running into him altogether. But when her hips encountered the table behind her, all avenue of escape was removed.

"I would like to continue this conversation a little further."

"If you must."

He was only inches away from her now, his thighs pressing into her skirts and causing them to flatten between them.

"I want to know what personal experience, as you call it, has led you to such a conclusion."

"My father—"

"Who else?"

She peered up at him in confusion, seeing the way his eyes had grown darker. Flint gray and blue.

"Who else?" she echoed weakly.

"Who else has taught you about a man's ways?"

"I don't—"

He cupped her cheek, and she shrank from the contact. Except for her father, no man had ever been this close to her. Certainly no man had ever had the audacity to touch her so familiarly.

"Have you had many beaux, Miss Pedigrue?"

She wanted to say yes. She wanted to claim she'd had hundreds and hundreds, if only to salvage her pride, but she couldn't seem to speak at all.

His smile was indulgent. Mocking.

"Haven't you been taught that it isn't nice to make snap decisions about people—let alone half the population—based on little more than supposition and generalization?"

She didn't respond. She couldn't. Not when the man's hand had slid around her waist to rest in the hollow of her back, pulling her resolutely toward him.

"Miss Pedigrue," he murmured as he bent low, whispering the words next to her ear, "I do believe you're a bit of a fraud. All show and little practical knowledge."

She shivered, feeling the way his lips touched the delicate skin of her ear.

"Don't you think it's time you sampled some of the real thing?"

"Real thing?"

"Baser emotions. Corporal pleasure."

Then he was shifting, and his lips touched her own.

She was so startled by the contact that she didn't move. But as the fact sank into her brain that he was kissing *her,* his employee, she found that she couldn't shift away. The pressure of his lips was so soft, so sweet, so gentle—everything she had accused him of being incapable of displaying on the basis of his sex.

A faint moan came from her throat, and it must have pleased him, because she felt him smile.

"That's it, Miss Pedigrue," he coaxed. "Surrender to it."

When he took her hand, placing it at the side of his throat, she did not resist. Surprising even herself, she slid it around to the nape of his neck, delighting in the way his hair fell over her fingers and tickled her skin.

He drew her closer, the kiss deepening, his tongue stroking her bottom lip. Her mouth parted at the unspoken invitation, and he slipped inside, caressing her in a way that she never would have imagined possible.

When he drew back, slowly, gradually, she stared up at him as if she had never seen him before. And indeed she hadn't. Not like this. Not with an expression that held passion and a hint of disbelief.

"Miss Pedigrue," he finally murmured, the title he used sounding more like an endearment than a formality. "I don't think you've ever been kissed before."

She could have withered and died at the remark, but when she would have escaped, he held her fast.

"Do you know what it does to a man to know he is the first?"

"The thrill of conquest?" Patience was amazed at how her voice emerged so husky and wanton.

"Not conquest. Seduction."

Her cheeks grew hot. "I believe that's a rather strong term for what has occurred here."

"Is it?"

He spread his fingers wide over her shoulder blades, making her even more conscious of his strength, his power, drawing her closer and closer to the sweet torture of his hips.

"Have you never been wooed, Patience?" he whispered, caressing her back in slow moving circles. "Not even from afar?"

"Afar?" The word was but a croak.

"Yes." He bent to murmur against her ear. "Someone studying you from across the room, sweet nothings sent to you by a secret admirer."

She didn't want to admit the solitary nature of her existence. It was a matter of pride. But the warmth of his hands, the intoxication of his spirit, had weakened her will to the extent that she shook her head. "No."

"Pity." The way the word was uttered made her believe that he truly regretted such a fact. "A woman should be seduced at least once in her lifetime. She should be overwhelmed with words and unexpected kindnesses. She should be worshiped and revered."

Patience stared at him, wide-eyed, sure that he was saying such things to serve his purposes and for no other reason. But his eyes gleamed with sincerity. With utter earnestness.

He pulled the neckline of her gown down over her shoulder, bending as he did so to press kisses along her throat and collarbones as if he were stringing an imaginary necklace.

She shuddered as a wave of molten desire surged through her body, settling in the pit of her stomach with a wanton energy. She clung to his waist, his shirt clumping in her fists, her body no longer resisting him, but moving closer. Closer.

"You are a woman of passion, Patience."

"It's wrong," she moaned. But she did not move away.

"What's wrong?"

"Passion."

"Why? What could possibly be wrong about what you feel right now?"

She wanted to tell him the truth, that anything this wonderful must surely be decadent and sinful. But she couldn't speak. Not when his lips were skimming lower and lower, grazing the upper curve of her breast.

"Give in to me," he murmured against her.

"No." Her refusal was more a matter of survival than of honest intent.

Rather than dissuading him, her response made him smile. Lifting her, he straightened, bringing her face even to his so that he might kiss her passionately, completely.

The bones of her body seemed to melt beneath the firestorm of pleasure she experienced. She wrapped her arms around his neck and returned his embrace measure for measure, knowing that she had never experienced anything like this before and fearing that she would never experience it again.

When he set her on her feet and began to pull away, it was she who made a soft mew of regret. Then she whirled in embarrassment, gripping the edge of the table, disgusted at the way she had allowed her body to overrule common sense.

This man was her employer. It would not do to foster any sort of relationship other than one of strict professionalism.

She squeezed her eyes closed. Then, knowing she must salvage at least some small shred of pride, she straightened her spine and turned, raising her chin slightly so that she could look at him with as much authority as she could muster.

"Thank you for helping me prove my point."

He didn't appear the least bit dissuaded by her frosty tone, and she realized that her gown still dipped low over one shoulder. Shrugging it into place, she did her best to appear even more daunting.

"What point was that, Miss Pedigrue?"

"That men delight in physical domination."

"I believe the word you used was 'conquest.'" His eyes burned. "Perhaps I was hasty to condemn your assumptions about my sex's true nature." He grinned. Slowly. Leisurely. All-knowingly. "For I would enjoy any attempt to conquer you, Miss Pedigrue. Since such feelings are the curse of my sex, you wouldn't consider that a true vice, would you?"

"One of many."

"Then perhaps you should take the opportunity to reform me while you are here in my employ." He placed his hands on the table behind her, forcing her to bend backward to escape the clouding effects of his nearness. "My own governess always claimed that I was a bad boy. A very bad boy—a veritable rake, I believe she said once. I think you could rectify that character flaw."

He offered her one last brushing kiss across her lips. Then he was pulling away—so gently, so slowly, that she was able to get her bearings first.

But as he left the room, she couldn't prevent an old

notion from popping into her brain, echoing over and over until she wasn't sure if she remembered it properly.

Was it the reformed rake who was supposed to make the best husband?

Or was he said to be the best lover?

The night was cool and dark and deep in the shadows of Garrick's study. His father, a man who loved the sea, had instructed that the room be built on the east side of the house with wall-to-wall French doors that could be thrown open at the end of the day so that the fresh breeze could make him believe he was still aboard a ship.

Garrick had always loved this room. Even now he sometimes fancied that he could catch a whiff of his father's pipe tobacco or hear the rumble of his voice. It had become Garrick's place to think, to dream.

Bickerstaff looked up from the game of solitaire spread over the gaming table.

"What have you decided?" he asked. "Will she do?"

Garrick sighed, pushing the shipping ledger away. Trust Bickerstaff to have unraveled his thoughts.

"She certainly seems to have Emaline's best interests at heart."

Bickerstaff was obviously referring to the way that Miss Pedigrue and her charge were outside puttering around the tiny goldfish pond his mother had fashioned near the terrace. Claiming that the pond was in need of work, Patience had persuaded Emaline to help her thin out the perennials that had grown too close to the rocky perimeter. She'd even persuaded Garrick to carry buckets of the stagnant water away so that she and Emaline could move closer and closer to the bean-shaped pool. Then she'd unearthed a piece of canvas sail to line the hole.

Sensing Miss Pedigrue's intention, Garrick had waited until his sister positioned herself inside the pond's circumference. As she helped Miss Pedigrue stack rocks to hold the canvas in place, he'd begun bringing fresh water from the pump. Emaline had been calf-deep before she was aware of her situation. Even then she hadn't made a fuss. She'd merely jumped free and continued to work from the other side.

From his study fifteen feet away, Garrick wished that business hadn't called him into the house so quickly. He could hear Miss Pedigrue promising Emaline that they would see if "the captain" could find them some goldfish.

"She has a way with Emaline, doesn't she?" Bickerstaff remarked.

Garrick couldn't deny that. After the debacle with the bath, he'd thought that Emaline would go into hiding for the rest of the day, as was her habit when she was distraught. But barely an hour later he'd found her seated on the grass at Patience's feet while her governess read to her from a book of fables. The fact that the story mentioned a pool of water at least a dozen times had not escaped Garrick's attention—nor had it escaped Emaline's, he wagered. But the girl had remained where she sat, her dirty feet tucked under Patience's skirts, one arm wrapped around the leg of the bench her governess sat upon.

"I'll wager fifty pounds she has Emaline bathed by the end of the week," Bickerstaff pronounced gruffly, rising to look beyond Garrick's shoulder.

"Tomorrow," Garrick murmured. "I say she'll be clean tomorrow."

163

Leaning back in his chair, he reached for the snifter of brandy he'd left by his blotter. Holding it aloft, he watched the way the candlelight played in its depths and grew to resemble the color of Patience Pedigrue's hair. Such an interesting shade of red. Not at all repellent. No, it was warm and intriguing. Although he had not allowed himself to touch the tight braids at the back of her neck, he would have bet the tresses were silken to the touch.

". . . gone deaf as well, man?"

Garrick roused himself enough to catch the last of Bickerstaff's query. "Beg pardon?"

"I asked if you'd received any more threats?"

"Just the one I showed you."

"Maybe whoever is responsible is cooling off."

Garrick hoped so. He hoped that the obvious guards on the grounds would put an end to this nonsense before it went any further. But somehow he wasn't so sure.

A knock on the door brought his head up. No one had ever dared to interrupt him in his study. It simply wasn't done. If someone had decided to do so, it could only mean that something was wrong. Very wrong.

Bickerstaff's hand slid to the knife hidden in a sheath beneath his vest.

"Captain Dalton? May I come in?"

Garrick immediately recognized the soft tones as belonging to Miss Pedigrue and gestured for Bickerstaff to resume playing cards.

"Yes, Miss Pedigrue."

She hesitantly entered, obviously recognizing the inner sanctum for what it was—purely masculine territory.

"I'm sorry to disturb you."

"Are you and Emaline finished outside?"

"Yes. We didn't mean to work so late, but since the task was started, your sister wanted to see it finished."

"And your ability to disguise your true intent was without flaw."

She smiled faintly. "I'm glad you approve."

"Have you moved into your new quarters?"

He saw her faint frown of irritation and wondered what had caused it, but before he could speak, she said, "They are quite adequate, thank you."

Adequate? Only adequate?

"I hope the beds we secured for you were satisfactory."

The slight pink tinge to her cheeks conveyed that she'd caught his reference to finding her on the nursery cot.

"They are both quite . . . roomy."

"Which one has Emaline chosen as her own?"

Again the hesitation. Again he sensed that Emaline had somehow slipped into Patience's room and commandeered her bed.

"She has decided to try them both, Captain."

He grinned. "How very wise of her."

Thinking that she had merely come to inform him that they were both retiring for the night, he looked away. But a moment later he realized she still hadn't left.

"Was there something else that you needed, Miss Pedigrue?"

"Yes," her tone was hesitant, relaying that she was very reluctant to ask him for anything.

"Out with it," he urged.

Her posture was so rigid, so stern, so governesslike, that he wondered how she had managed to unbend long enough to respond to his kiss.

"I came to ask if Emaline had any old toys on the premises."

"Toys?"

"Yes, Captain. She is only nine, you know. Although most young ladies hover between childhood and adolescence, many of them still cling to . . . dolls."

"Dolls?"

"Yes, sir. I was wondering if there might be a doll somewhere in the house."

He shook his head. "I don't think so. When it was believed that Emaline had drowned at sea with my parents, most of her things were given away to charity."

"What a shame." She was obviously disappointed with the news. "Then please tell me where I might find a needle and thread."

The request was so simple, yet so hesitantly offered, that he sensed there was something she wasn't telling him. Something important. "Why?"

"Why what, sir?"

"Why do you need them?"

"I-I thought to do some mending."

"Of what?"

"Emaline has snagged her hose."

"Her seamstress has finished several new frocks, and we'll be taking Emaline to buy new stockings and shoes tomorrow, if I can break away from my duties at the shipping office."

"Does that mean you can't tell me where to find a needle and thread?" She was adamant about having them, even when he was sure he'd pointed out why she didn't need them.

Rather than deal with the unfathomable female mind, Garrick stood, made his way to the cabinet in the far corner, and removed his mother's sewing kit.

His thumb automatically caressed the round wicker sewing basket decorated on the top with a bouquet of ribbon roses and a finely crafted tassel.

"Here you are, Miss Pedigrue."

When he would have handed it to her, she stared down at it in confusion.

"It was my mother's," he explained lest she think he engaged in darning himself.

"But I thought you said—"

"Not everything was donated to charity, Miss Pedigrue," he explained, divining her thoughts. "I am not so hard-hearted that I didn't keep a few mementos."

She took the basket, holding it to her chest as if it were a treasure to be guarded. "Thank you. I will return it to you straightaway."

"No need. Keep it with you. If I feel the urge to do some sewing, I'll know where to find it."

He knew a saucy retort hovered on her lips, but seeing that Bickerstaff was watching them with a fascination that bordered on the obscene, she merely said, "Thank you, Captain Dalton."

She left the room, closing the door soundlessly behind her.

For several moments Garrick endured the condemning silence of his companion. Finally Bickerstaff threw his cards onto the table and pushed back his chair. "I need a drink," he said glumly. "Have you got any more of that brandy?"

Garrick glared at him. "To see your reaction, you'd think I planned to murder the woman."

Bickerstaff filled a glass with a healthy amount of the potent liquid. "It's about the same thing—forcing her to live with the likes of you for the rest of her days."

"I'm not *forcing* her to do anything."

"Aren't you?"

"She is here of her own free will. She may offer her resignation and leave at any time—of her own free will."

Bickerstaff held one finger away from his glass in an accusatory manner.

"You should tell her why you've decided to marry her. She deserves to know the truth."

Garrick waved the comment away with an exasperated gesture and prowled to the window. But there was no solace in looking out to sea. Not when he knew that everything his friend said was true.

"What exactly do you want me to confess? That I instructed my valet to find a woman who was lonely and free of family ties? A woman who was desperately in need of a home and the wages I could provide? To make sure she loved children and would understand what it meant to be a sailor's wife?" He planted his hands on his hips. "Or should I be even more blunt and convey to her that I'm not looking for a governess for my sister but for someone to be my mate, someone who can become Emaline's legal guardian should anything happen to me?"

The room echoed with absolute silence.

"Yes," Bickerstaff stated softly. "You should tell her."

Garrick pounded one fist against the window frame. "I'll be damned if I will."

"Then you'll be lying to her."

"How?"

"A lie of omission."

"How can it possibly be considered a lie of omission if everything I say and do is honest and aboveboard? I truly want to get acquainted with this woman. If I find her agreeable to my intentions, I will woo her in a grand fashion. If I discover that we are compatible, I will offer to marry her. I won't threaten her, defile her, or harm a hair on her head."

"But what about love?"

Garrick growled low in his throat. "Love is an emotion for fools."

"Your father didn't think so."

"My father was an exception. He found a jewel among women to be his bride."

"What makes you think it couldn't happen to you too?"

Garrick walked to his desk and leaned on his hands in order to make his point. "Because I'm honest enough to admit I'm a bastard through and through. The only love I've ever known has been for my family. When they were lost, I learned quickly enough what a pernicious emotion even that can be. It might be touted by poets and philosophers, but it can't bring the dead back. It can only bring more pain."

Garrick shook his head. "No. A business arrangement is the best solution." He straightened and stabbed the air with his finger. "And a business arrangement is what it will be." Then, without waiting for a response, he stormed from the room, slamming the door behind him.

"I think you're wrong," Bickerstaff murmured to the empty room, a trace of wonder in his voice. "I say this could be the beginning of a love match." He nodded his head in emphasis. "Just you wait and see."

Chapter

12

Once Patience made her way upstairs to her new suite of rooms, she closed the door and locked it carefully behind her.

The master's wing indeed.

She didn't know what the master had in mind by moving her and Emaline across the hall from his own bedroom, but she wasn't about to make a mistake and find out. She'd heard that governesses were sometimes regarded as easy prey by their employers. Hadn't Colleen Fitzwilly been sent home from New York after a scandal involving just such an occurrence? After that, Colleen hadn't been able to hold her head up during Sunday services. In fact, she'd finally moved west to live with her aunt, and there were rumors that she was in the family way at the time.

The reminder was enough to send Patience scurrying for a chair to prop under the doorknob. After the kiss she'd shared with the captain in the kitchen, she didn't think it would behoove her to offer any sort of encouragement to the man. Indeed, she couldn't think what had come over her. She was well on her way to personal independence. She wasn't about to surrender her will or her body to any man.

Uttering a soft harrumph to underscore that mental resolution, she tugged a trunk in front of the chair. Just in case.

Then, crossing to the rocker in the corner, she adjusted the wick on the lamp so that it burned brightly enough for sewing but not enough to wake the girl curled up on Patience's bed.

Just as Garrick had suspected, the little waif had stumbled through the connecting door, trailing the same bedraggled blanket she'd had the night before, her hair a mass of tangles, her feet and face filthy beyond belief. Patience's only solace was that—this time—Emaline had deigned to keep her nightgown on.

Tiptoeing to the bed, Patience tucked the covers more tightly around Emaline's shoulders. "Poor lamb," she murmured, bending to kiss a grubby cheek.

Setting the sewing case aside for the moment, she took a soft cloth from the stack beneath the dry sink. Dipping it in the water that she'd poured into the bowl some time ago, she nodded in satisfaction at the temperature. It was tepid, warm enough to do some good, yet not so cold as to jolt the girl into wakefulness.

Patience began with Emaline's face, scrubbing away the dirt and tears left from the day's travails. Then, unbuttoning the little girl's gown, she scrubbed her torso, her arms, her legs, and finally her feet, until the child was as pink and sweet-smelling as if she'd climbed into the tub as Garrick had wished. It took five different basins of water and a good deal of soap, but even though her back ached from the effort of bending over the bed, Patience was pleased with the outcome. Her only regret was that she could do nothing with Emaline's hair. Not now, anyhow. But she hoped to rectify that matter in the morning.

Replacing the covers, she put the frayed blanket within reach, sensing that it was some sort of childhood memento. Taking the sewing basket, she returned to the chair in the corner.

Easing into its depths, she rocked softly as she investigated the contents of the kit. Besides a folded piece of parchment neatly lined with needles and pins, she found an assortment of colored silk thread, gold scissors, a net bag filled with buttons, scraps of ribbon and embroidery, and a skein of red yarn.

Grinning in delight, Patience reached for a petticoat she'd ironed and set beside the chair.

"Well, now, Emaline," she whispered, not really expecting a response, "let's see what we can do about making you a doll."

It was dawn when Garrick gave up all pretense of sleeping and reached for his trousers. Sliding them over his legs, he dragged a shirt over his torso, leaving it open to his waist, the cuffs hanging loose.

If her habits held true, Emaline would soon be up, he told himself. He would see if she would like his company again this morning.

But as he let himself out onto the balcony and padded the length of the wraparound gallery, he had to admit to himself that it wasn't just Emaline who filled his thoughts. Her willowy governess was at the center of a few of them as well.

Moving to the guillotine window on the opposite side of the wing, he crept into the bedroom, noting with a glance that Miss Pedigrue had not taken his sister's bed as he'd thought she would. In fact, the covers had not even been drawn back.

Frowning, he tiptoed to the connecting door, telling himself that he was just going to ensure that his sister was safe.

When he found Emaline curled up on her side, her baby blanket tucked beneath her cheek, he smiled, then stared.

She was clean.

The girl was *clean*.

Well, almost, he amended, noticing the state of her hair. But even from this distance, he could see that her cheeks were pink and rosy. The legs and feet poking out of the covers were crisscrossed with scratches but were nevertheless free from grime.

His mouth dropped ever so slightly and he wondered how Miss Pedigrue had persuaded her to take a bath. But when his gaze alighted on the washbasin filled with murky water, a cloth carefully looped through the handle of the pitcher to dry, he grinned.

It appeared that Miss Pedigrue could be a sly one when the situation warranted it.

As soon as the thought occurred to him, he found himself wondering what had happened to the learned governess. Where could she be?

A soft sound caused him to turn, and he grew still, ever so still.

Miss Pedigrue was slumped in his mother's rocker, her head lolling uncomfortably to one side. Some time during the night, she must have fallen asleep over her work, because the sewing basket had toppled to the floor, and a ball of bright red yarn had unrolled beside her.

But that was not what captured his attention. It was the fact that he could see the cut-up remains of a

petticoat scattered on the floor, while in her lap—
very naked and as yet unfinished—lay a handcrafted
doll.

The sight of it caused a curious tightness to grip his
throat. It was not the most intricate of creations. Its
arms and legs jutted from its body like a gingerbread
cookie's. Blue glass buttons had been sewn to its head
as eyes, and a scrap of pink velvet formed its lips. In
Miss Pedigrue's lap, he could see the beginnings of a
set of underclothes taking shape, as well as what
looked like a little red wig.

She'd made his sister a doll.

Garrick hadn't even considered toys yet, let alone a
doll. He hadn't known that Emaline wanted one.

He didn't know why he moved toward Patience.
Nor could he explain why he didn't wake her. Instead,
gently removing the doll and the unfinished clothing
from her lap, he set them on the floor and scooped the
woman into his arms.

She shifted, mumbling something he couldn't decipher, but to his infinite relief, she didn't wake as he
carried her into the other room and laid her on the
bed. Not wishing to disturb her any further, he took
an extra quilt from the armoire and placed it over her
body.

How infinitely enticing she looked, lying on the
covers that way. It made him wonder what it would be
like to wake to the same woman day after day as
husbands were wont to do. He'd always thought men
who said they could be satisfied by one woman were
either fools or liars. But at this moment he wasn't so
sure.

Unable to resist the temptation, he placed a soft
kiss on her lips. To his amazement, she responded,
sweetly, innocently, before stretching and rolling to

174

her side. When she settled even more deeply into slumber, he didn't disturb her.

But this time, when he left, it was through the door.

Patience woke slowly, luxuriating in the feel of fresh, sun-dried sheets and downy pillows.

She couldn't remember coming to bed. In fact, she couldn't remember falling asleep at all. The last thing she recalled was cutting out a tiny chemise and gathering ruffles for a tiny petticoat.

The doll.

Pushing the quilt away, she hurried into the other room, but Emaline was already on the floor, cradling the toy in her arms and rocking it as she tried to attach the red yarn curls with a straight pin.

"Good morning, Emaline."

The girl looked up from her make-believe baby, her eyes wide with delight. "It's a doll," she whispered in near reverence.

"Do you like it?"

Emaline nodded.

"It isn't finished yet."

"Will she have some clothes?" The girl's comment was so hesitant, so soft, it was barely audible.

Patience sank onto the floor beside her, deciding that now was not the time to take an authoritative stance. "I've finished her chemise and a petticoat, but you'll have to help me pick out some cloth to make a dress."

"Yes. Yes, I'd like that. What about her hair, Patience?"

Patience had already made more progress with the girl than she would have believed possible, she thought when Emaline used her name for the first time, but she dared to go one more step. "She needs curls, doesn't she?" she asked.

Emaline nodded.

Patience touched the girl's hair. "Just as you need yours."

Emaline's blue eyes sparkled with a hint of suspicion.

"I would like to see your curls," Patience told her.

The suspicion grew more distinct.

"I bet you have pretty hair. Long and wavy and beautiful."

Without another word, Emaline tossed the doll to the floor, jumped to her feet, and ran from the room.

After her abrupt exit, Patience didn't have the energy to stand up. She'd pushed the child too far. She shouldn't have backed Emaline into a corner.

But after Emaline had spoken—had called Patience by name—she'd been so sure she could get her to wash her hair. She'd been so *sure*.

"Don't take it too hard."

Her chin jerked up, and she found Garrick standing in the doorway, his shoulder propped against the jamb.

Immediately she stiffened. "Good morning, Captain Dalton."

He sighed. "Aren't we past all that 'captain' nonsense yet?"

She didn't dignify that question with an answer.

"Fine. You can call me Captain Dalton until the day you die if you want to do so."

"Was there something you needed?" she asked, rising.

"As a matter of fact, yes. I came to augment your uniform."

Stepping aside, he allowed one of the servants to enter and place a box on Patience's bed.

"I really don't think—"

He silenced her with a gesture. "I believe we've discussed that particular phrase before, Miss Pedigrue. If you will remember, it is not one of my favorites."

The maid excused herself, and he resumed his casual pose. "As for the clothing, you can't possibly expect me to allow you to be seen in a single dress. If word got out, I'm sure that my reputation as an employer would be ruined."

She was quite certain he was mocking her, but she didn't know how she could call him for it. Not when he was watching her with that predatory gleam in his eye.

"Thank you, Captain."

At her unexpected capitulation, he smiled. "Does this mean that you will accept the clothing without a fight?"

"If that's what you wish."

"My, my, you must have awakened on the right side of the bed."

Her eyes narrowed. There was something about the way he said that . . .

She dismissed such a thought as nonsense. She was becoming as suspicious as Emaline.

"Emaline is looking well this morning," Garrick stated.

Patience allowed herself to be diverted. "I managed to give her a good scrubbing after she'd fallen asleep."

"So I saw. It's an immense improvement."

"Thank you. I tried to get her to wash her hair . . ."

"I heard," he said when her explanation trailed away.

Pushing away from the doorframe, he came into the room, and Patience was alarmed by the way he filled it with his presence, making it seem crowded.

177

Intimate.

"I also noted that you've made her a doll," he said, bending and retrieving the toy.

Patience cleared her throat, wondering if she'd overstepped her bounds as a governess. If there was something the child needed, shouldn't she have informed Garrick? "I had a few spare moments."

He regarded her doubtfully. "How is that possible? I'm sure it took at least an hour to bathe Emaline."

Patience wasn't sure if she was being complimented or accused of lying.

His lips twitched into a slow smile. "Admit it, Miss Pedigrue. You were up late into the night crafting this toy."

"What would possibly make you say such a thing?"

"I saw the lamplight under your door."

"Oh."

"I retired rather late myself."

"I don't understand."

"I couldn't sleep."

Patience didn't know why he felt it necessary to confide such personal details.

"You see, I kept expecting to hear a tussle from this side of the hall."

So he'd thought she couldn't manage his sister.

"I assure you, sir. I am more than capable of seeing to Emaline's needs."

"I'm certain you are, but I wasn't sure that she would *allow* you to see to them. That's why I had you moved closer to my own quarters."

Patience felt muscles she hadn't known were tense ease at the news. "Oh, really?"

"She can be quite a handful if she decides to rebel."

"So you didn't mean to—" Patience snapped her mouth closed, realizing what she'd been about to say.

"I didn't mean to what, Miss Pedigrue?"

"Nothing."

He edged closer. "No, I think there is most definitely something on your mind."

"No, I—"

"Did you think I moved you closer for . . . personal reasons?"

"Your sister is indeed a personal—"

"Let me rephrase that. Did you think I'd moved you closer for . . . carnal reasons?"

"Captain Dalton!" she protested.

"Yes, Miss Pedigrue?"

Bit by bit, he was backing her against the wall—and with each step, she was being flooded with memories of their earlier embrace. Their kiss.

"Is that what you thought, Miss Pedigrue?" When she didn't respond, he added, "Patience?"

The sound of her given name on his lips was almost more than she could bear.

"I—I don't know."

"Come now, this is no time to be shy about your feelings."

No, it wasn't. But she couldn't be bold, either. She couldn't tell him that his nearness was making her pulse race and her heart pound in her ears. She couldn't tell him that at this moment she could think of little else than kissing him again, feeling his lips caressing her own, his arms sweeping around her body to pull her to him.

Then there was no need to say the words. Either he'd read her thoughts or his own emotions were similar to hers. He hauled Patience against him and took her mouth greedily, eagerly. She wound her arms around his neck and wove her fingers through his hair, delighting in its texture, its weight, its warmth.

All thought, all coherent sense of danger, fled from her brain to be replaced by one sensation: a passion so deep and consuming that she feared she would lose her very soul to him.

Hungrily she ran her hands beneath his open shirt, caressing his firm flesh. She dug her fingers into the tensile strength of his shoulders, his chest. She rubbed his collarbone, then moved lower, delighting in the silken texture of the hair that grew there.

"You are so beautiful."

The words he spoke were directed into her hair, and at that instant she felt beautiful.

"Do you know how you affect me?"

"No."

"You must know. All you have to do is walk into a room, all prim and proper, and I have this . . . *need* to mess you up. Like this."

"No." This time she wrenched away from him, moving to the window.

She was breathing hard, but little air seemed to be reaching her lungs. She thought that must be why she continued to feel so hot, so anxious.

"Captain, this isn't—"

"Proper?"

She hadn't heard him come up behind her. He took her shoulders in his hands, forcing her to turn and look at him. His eyes burned with a blue-black intensity that made her shiver with an emotion akin to . . . fear?

"Real life is rarely pretty, let alone proper, Miss Pedigrue." His arms slid around her waist, hauling her against him, making her acutely aware of his arousal. "Real life is messy and mean."

She struggled to get loose, but he refused to let her go. Her puny will was no match for the strength of his arms.

"I've never understood why my contemporaries feel the women they associate with in public have to be prissy misses. That's not the sort of woman with whom they associate in private."

She stiffened at the mere mention of such a subject, one never spoken of in polite society.

"Do you want to know what a man really wants, Patience?"

She wriggled, knowing that she had to get away from this man before he formed images in her mind that shouldn't be there, that shouldn't be recalled late at night when there was only the narrow width of a corridor between them.

But try as she might, she could not keep him from saying, "A man wants fire, Patience, not ice. He wants a woman who doesn't undress behind a screen but tantalizes him every evening by removing her garments slowly, in a performance worthy of a French bordello. He wants a woman who delights in the feel of satin and silk against her skin. A woman who will be a temptress and a tiger. A woman who will—"

"Stop!" The word was merely a rasping moan, but he must have heard her, because he looked at her then. Intimately. Fiercely.

"You could be such a woman, Patience."

She groaned again, closing her eyes, not wanting to see herself as he must imagine her at that moment. The pictures he'd created in her own brain were far too vivid, shaming her to the core.

Because she wanted to be that kind of woman.

Deep down.

Where it mattered most.

"Please let me go," she whispered, knowing that if he didn't she would surely be consumed by the heat of their combined bodies.

He didn't move. Not for aeons. Then finally he stepped away from her, trailing his fingers down her cheek one last time.

"I'll see you downstairs for breakfast. Once I've rounded up Emaline, we'll see about dressing her in some of the things the seamstress has made for her."

Then he was gone, closing the door behind him.

Bit by bit, Patience sank to the floor, bowing her head. What had happened to her? How could she have let things go so far? She had met this man only a short time ago, but already he knew her more intimately than any man she'd ever met.

It had to be wrong.

She balled her hands into fists and closed her eyes. What was she going to do? She really shouldn't stay in this place. The air itself was rife with temptation.

But even as the thought appeared, she knew she couldn't leave. And not just because she needed the employment.

She feared she needed this place, this child . . .

This man.

Chapter

13

Knowing she would not be given much time, Patience gathered her emotions tightly together, submerging them beneath those obligations she could control—duty and decorum. She splashed cool water on her face and plaited her hair into an even more somber coronet than the one she'd worn the day before. Then, crossing to the bed, she stared at the box of clothing that had been brought to her, wondering what the captain had chosen as her uniform of the day.

She poked at the lid, dislodging it as if the box held a snake, but when she saw the sheen of blue-and-gray striped taffeta, she bit her lip and lifted the skirt from its tissue-paper nest.

Absolutely beautiful.

Drat that man, she thought. He knew the very things she would find difficult to resist.

Sighing, she pulled a second layer of tissue paper aside to reveal a tailored cotton shirtwaist and two pairs of clocked hose. Silk hose. With tasseled garters.

She had agreed to let the captain buy her a uniform—but this was the height of extravagance. In fact, she thought, experiencing a wave of dawning suspicion, with the inclusion of the hosiery, it bordered on being intimate, as if he intended to influence her, tempt her, sway her.

Well, she thought, tossing the skirt onto the bed, he was soon to see how wrong he could be. She was more than capable of accepting his offerings without a second thought.

Barely fifteen minutes had passed while she dressed in the full skirt and form-fitting blouse—but not the stockings. Nothing could force her to don anything that decadent.

Wishing to make a statement of her independence, she took a wide belt from her own stores, pinned a lace-edged handkerchief at her throat much like a frilly jabot, and smoothed her hair.

She was about to leave when she paused one last time to check Emaline's room. She saw that the child had also received a present; an identical box lay on her bed, and tissue paper lay scattered on the floor.

Automatically, Patience bent to gather the pieces, but when her toe hit something hard next to the bed, she paused, reaching for the offending item. As soon as she saw the bottle, then the label, her eyes widened in horror.

Running from the room, she raced down the staircase, intent on finding Emaline before she fell beneath serious harm.

Hearing the clink of cutlery, she changed her direction.

Miss Fitch was in the foyer, arranging cut flowers in an enormous vase on the center table, but Patience didn't even nod to the woman. Instead, she flung the dining room door wide and searched for her pupil.

When she saw Emaline at her place, her head resting on the table, her eyes glazed, she knew the worst had happened.

Seeing her, Emaline hiccuped, giggled, then waggled her fingers unsteadily in the direction of the door.

Patience opened her mouth, then noted that Asa Marcus and the Ellingtons had come for breakfast this morning as well. Seeing her, Jan jumped to his feet and hurried to pull out her chair. Avoiding the intense gaze he cast her way, Patience kept her attention riveted on the captain.

"Captain Dalton. A word, if you please," she said at the first break in conversation. "In private."

Jan's expression fell to one of supreme disappointment. When Asa half rose from his seat, Patience motioned for him to remain where he was while she completely ignored Nina's blatant curiosity.

Emaline grinned crookedly, reaching for a piece of ham and gnawing it straight from her fingers, a bright red mustache rimming her upper lip.

Patience's fingers tightened around the neck of the wine bottle she held hidden in the folds of her dress.

Only Garrick seemed unaffected. She waited for him to make some sort of comment, some mocking reply, but he didn't. After wiping his lips with his napkin, he rose with the grace of a practiced athlete.

"My office?" he inquired as he passed her.

"Fine."

Closing the door behind them, Patience took a surreptitious breath to curb her growing concern. With each step, her courage began to flag. Emaline could not have found the wine on her own, someone must have given it to her. Accusations would have to be made, but Patience was loath to be the one making them.

They moved into his study, and Garrick leaned against his desk, crossing his feet at the ankles and folding his arms over his chest. Such a broad chest.

Stop it!

"Well, Miss Pedigrue? What has inspired you to interrupt my breakfast again? If you wish to thank me—"

"Indeed not!" she inserted with more spirit than the comment required. She snapped her jaw shut at her own rudeness. Control. She must maintain control.

Turning, she closed the doors, effectively shutting out the faint murmur of conversation from the dining room as well as the sight of Miss Fitch, who had her head cocked as if to eavesdrop.

When she faced the man again, he was studying her with a wry smile. One that was much too self-satisfied, in her opinion.

"Don't tell me you desire my company so much that you would—"

"Captain Dalton," she interrupted firmly, "I wish to have a word with you about your sister."

"She looks very nice in her new dimity, doesn't she?"

"Yes . . . er, no. I mean . . ." She paused a moment to collect herself then said, "Captain, didn't you note that Emaline's behavior was changed this morning?"

He shrugged. "She seems much more agreeable than she has the past few days. When I brought her the box with her dress, she was nearly giddy—"

"She is drunk!"

His humor fled so abruptly that she was startled by the change.

"Drunk!"

It took Patience a moment to realize that Garrick

Dalton was well and truly surprised. Moreover, he was as horrified as she had been.

"Y-yes, sir," she stammered, handing him the empty wine bottle and watching the anger darken his eyes. Thank heaven she wasn't the object of his ire.

He pushed her aside as if she were of no more substance than a feather and threw open the door. Patience hurried to follow him as he stormed into the dining hall.

Garrick then turned his attention to his little sister. "Emaline," he growled, his tone gentler, but no less stern, "your governess has informed me that you have been drinking wine." He put his hands on his hips and leveled his gaze her way. "Where did you get it?"

Patience saw the way Emaline wriggled in her chair like a cornered rabbit. Her pale blue eyes widened and glimmered with sudden tears.

"Leave me be!" she suddenly shouted, jumping to her feet. "Just leave me be!"

Then, after sweeping her hand wide and sending her dishes crashing to the floor, she darted to the window, scrambled outside, and ran into the garden.

"Dammit," Garrick growled as Bickerstaff came to investigate the noise. "Help me find her and bring her back. Tell her I'm not angry," he added with honest remorse.

Asa Marcus and Jan Ellington jumped to their feet and followed the two men out, but Nina remained in her chair, idly stripping grapes from the bunch in her hand. "That girl is the devil's own seed."

Patience had heard much the same phrase from her father on countless occasions, and her gaze hardened.

"I beg your pardon?" she murmured as if she hadn't heard the woman correctly.

Nina offered a gay laugh and waved her hand

dismissively. "I meant no harm, but you have to admit she has the manners of an orphan."

A slow anger began to rise in Patience's breast. "Perhaps that is because she *is* an orphan."

Nina shrugged. "There's no need to act like a lioness with her cub, Miss Pedigrue. I haven't had your education. I'm not able to put my thoughts into words in the most poetic way."

As far as Patience was concerned, flowery speech couldn't hide a disparaging remark.

"Tell me, Patience," Nina continued as if her outspokenness was already forgiven, "do you enjoy your work?"

"Yes, ma'am, I do."

"Hmm." She chewed thoughtfully on a grape. "I once considered finding a position myself, but frankly, I couldn't picture myself toiling from dawn to dusk."

Toiling? That was one word Patience would never have associated with caring for Emaline.

"Thankfully, my brother has accrued enough of a fortune in his business with Garrick that I haven't been forced into such dire straits."

Was there a point to this woman's prattle?

"I must confess that Jan has taken quite a shine to you." She said the words slowly, as if she were sharing a secret.

Patience didn't know how to respond. Quite honestly, she hadn't given Jan a second glance since their first introduction—she wasn't even sure if she knew the color of his hair.

"May I relay to him that you would entertain his attention?"

No.

Patience barely managed to keep from blurting the word. Scrambling for a suitable reply, she finally said,

"I have been in the captain's employ for only a short time. So far, Emaline and I have begun only the most rudimentary of studies. Until she settles into a proper regimen and does not need my constant supervision, I fear that any personal activities are out of the question."

Nina scowled, but before she could press the issue, Patience quickly exited the dining room. Nina could see herself out.

Unfortunately, as soon as she'd stepped into the foyer, it was to see the captain carrying Emaline while she, in turn, was draped over his arm and holding the dog's collar, forcing Oscar to dance attendance on her.

"Enough, Emaline," Garrick said sternly, then stood stock still. "Let go of the dog."

Emaline's lip trembled, and she reluctantly let go of the dog. Free at last, Oscar scrambled for the front door and disappeared into the bushes lining the drive.

"Oscar was naughty," Emaline whispered.

"No, I think Emaline has been naughty."

She stared at him blankly.

Sighing, Garrick sat down on a bench, forcing her to look him in the eye. "I want to know if you've been drinking wine, Emaline."

When Patience would have spoken, the captain held up a hand, even though he had never once glanced her way.

"Tell me," he urged, his tone soft and persuasive.

"No, Garrick."

"What have you been drinking, then?"

Patience moved so that she could see Emaline's expression. Emaline tipped her head back and studied the ceiling with one eye closed.

"Emaline," Garrick drawled in warning.

Without warning, Emaline's lip began to quiver and

her eyes filled with tears. "Mama's raspberry cordial," she said.

At the mention of his mother, it was Garrick who grew still, a stricken expression flashing over his features. Then, with an obvious strength of will, he pushed his own emotions away and asked, "Where did you get it?"

"The back larder."

"Is that all you've had to drink?"

Emaline bit her lip and nodded. At her evident distress, Garrick pulled her close to his chest and cupped the back of her head. "There, now. Don't cry."

He began to shush and console her as if she were a much younger child in need of reassurance.

Patience stood rooted to the spot, wondering at the contrasts of this man who could be so intimidating one moment, then positively endearing the next.

When Emaline's tears had been dried, Garrick motioned to a maid who was entering the foyer with a basket of flowers.

Seeing his gesture, the young woman curtsied. "Yes, sir?"

"What's your name?"

"Martha, sir."

"Martha, would you please take my sister to her room. Tuck her into bed and read her some stories." Under his breath, he said to Patience, "Judging by Emaline's reaction to the alcohol she had on the boat, she should be due for a nap."

"Then I should be the one to—"

He halted Patience's protest with a touch of her arm. "Emaline, will you go with Martha?"

Emaline studied the maid with heavy eyes. "Will she bring the flowers?"

"If you wish."

Wriggling to the floor, Emaline took the girl's hand and tugged her toward the stairs. "Come see my new bed," she said, her distress forgotten.

Garrick waited until his sister was out of view before saying, "Come with me, Miss Pedigrue."

"But—"

He cut her off with a wave of his hand. "Emaline will be asleep in ten minutes. I think it's time you and I settled upon a formal routine for her lessons as well as a proper curriculum. Emaline is settling into her new surroundings quite well. I know I asked you to relax her schedule for a time, but I am beginning to believe you were right in proposing she have a more structured regimen to help her adapt to her new life. Besides which, I need your help."

The captain strode through the foyer, leaving her to scurry after him.

"Miss Fitch!" Garrick bellowed to the house at large.

The housekeeper had finished her flower arrangement some time between Patience's arrival and Emaline's escape, but she immediately stepped from the study, an empty vase in her hands.

"Sir?"

"Come with us, please."

He led them down a wide hall, then into a narrower corridor that led to the kitchen. As soon as he stepped into the servants' domain, all talking ceased. A pan clattered to the floor somewhere in the distance; then the area became as still as a tomb.

"Carry on with what you're doing," Garrick instructed, but it was clear that no one intended to move.

Patience wasn't sure why she had been asked to

follow, but she accompanied him down a steep set of stone steps to the cellar, which had been divided into storage areas.

Choosing the last door on the right, he opened it to reveal shelves stacked with crocks and jars of preserves. Without pause, he moved to where a dozen bottles of a burgundy liquid had been bunched together. He selected one that was half empty, removed the cork, and sniffed. Then he held up the bottle for Patience's inspection.

"Is this the same sort of bottle you found?"

"Yes, Captain."

He held it out to Patience. Immediately she recognized the fruity odor of fermented juices. "That's it."

"Miss Fitch? This is my mother's concoction, yes?"

It was clear that the housekeeper did not approve of his question, which seemed somehow to imply an accusation. "Yes, Captain. It is her famous raspberry wine."

"Where is the cordial?"

She pointed to a shelf near the top where identical bottles were filled with an identically colored liquid.

Garrick put the wine back in its place and withdrew one of the cordial containers. "Thank you, Miss Fitch. Will you please see to it that all of my mother's wine is moved to the top shelves."

"If that is what you wish, sir."

"I do. I would not like my sister to be confused by them again."

"Your sister?"

The words had barely left the woman's mouth when Garrick's expression grew thunderous. "Yes, Miss Fitch. Despite my order that the wine be kept locked up, my sister somehow found her way into this storage chamber." There was a thread of steel to his tone. "Please inspect the other compartments."

Miss Fitch rose to her full height. "I must have failed to properly inform the new servants of your orders. I will rectify the situation immediately." Two spots of color had appeared on Miss Fitch's cheeks. "Is that all you need?"

When he nodded, she excused herself, "With your permission, I'll find the stewards."

The sound of her footsteps echoed through the corridor and up the staircase. Once they had faded away, Garrick took a deep breath, exhaling slowly.

The reaction was so unexpected that Patience stared. "Captain?" she asked softly. "Is something wrong?"

He gathered his thoughts before saying, "I thought being Emaline's guardian would be the same as being her brother. Day by day, however, I am beginning to see what a difficult task it is to raise a child who has had no proper training. If she were younger . . ."

A smile tugged at her lips. "There are no manuals of instructions for babies, either."

He chuckled. "I suppose not. But with babies, at least you have a period of trial and error before they start talking back."

"From what I have seen, you've done nothing but help the girl."

"Help her? The clothes I provide are off in an hour, she's deathly afraid of bathwater, and she's taken up drinking to boot."

"An honest mistake."

"Not really. I was the first person to introduce her to wine."

"Yes, but you have also established the limits of her . . . experimentation."

"Have I?" His question held a very real doubt.

"She adores you, Captain."

Dropping his hand, Garrick took a step toward her.

"The perfect answer," he offered ruefully. "But then, you're the perfect person, aren't you?"

One of his forearms rested on the wall over her head, effectively pinning her in place.

"I am far from perfect, Captain." But it was difficult to speak when he stood so close to her. She could feel the heat of his body, smell the faint scent of soap on his skin.

"How so?"

How so what? she wondered, scrambling to remember what they had been talking about. His proximity was making it difficult for her to think at all.

"I am far too stubborn, Captain. Too impulsive."

"Those could be considered fine qualities."

"Not in excess."

"And you believe that you possess them in excess?"

"I have been guilty of such a thing on many occasions."

"When?"

He was leaning toward her, making coherent thought impossible. She could only stare at him, at his mouth. That beautiful masculine mouth.

"When what, sir?" she sighed.

"When have you been too stubborn, too impulsive?"

He was so close. She couldn't think.

But then all thought became unnecessary. So much so that she couldn't resist rising on tiptoe.

"Now, sir. Now."

She slid her arms around his neck, and he pulled her to him, their mouths melding in a furious passion that should not have been possible. Patience never would have dreamed that any man could hold her and embrace her this way, let alone anyone so vibrant and powerful as Captain Dalton.

But then all ability to reason fled. There was only

this moment and the overwhelming desire flooding her body. Her fingers plunged into his hair, and she pressed herself against him, damning the skirts that bunched up between them.

"Captain?" a distant voice called, and they sprang apart like guilty children.

"Yes, Bickerstaff?" he called, reaching for her hand. She would have smiled at his husky tone if her own body hadn't been weak and trembling with the sensations rushing through her veins.

"A messenger is here from the shipping company."

"I'll be right there."

Gently he leaned over her one last time, brushing her lips with his. After straightening, he thrust a bottle of cordial into her hands. "See to it that my sister is given a small glass each evening before she retires," he murmured, his eyes still blazing, his voice gruff with lingering passion. "Maybe that will appease her hunger for familiar things."

Patience nodded, not trusting herself to answer aloud. As soon as he left the cellar, she sagged weakly against the wall, smiling in much the same giddy manner she'd witnessed with Emaline that morning.

Chapter

14

During the next few weeks, life at Dalton Manor became more structured and calm. Emaline was told she could leave her bedroom no earlier than seven-thirty, so she began sleeping past the first hint of dawn.

Patience's nightly sponge baths had begun to register on the girl, who soon began to complete them on her own, sketchily at first, then with more precision. She had even surrendered to having her hair washed, but only if Garrick was the one to complete the task. She sat in a chair, which she allowed him to tip back as he poured warm water from a pitcher.

Indeed, she soon became as concerned with her appearance as other little girls. The seamstress, Mrs. Rogers, had seemed like some nebulous fairy godmother to Patience during those first few days. But now Emaline insisted on regular visits to the small cottage a quarter mile away, which had been converted for her use.

Several of the village women had also been hired to sew the countless garments Emaline needed, so their walks were timed to correspond with afternoon tea.

Carrying a basket of goodies supplied by the kitchen, Patience would follow Emaline as she scampered down the trail through the woods. The hour spent at Mrs. Rogers's cottage was always pleasant and full of feminine chatter as the women gladly instructed Emaline in basic needlework.

And only Patience seemed aware of Bickerstaff following them during their travels, a pistol tucked negligently in his waistband.

As for Emaline's studies, the mornings were filled with mathematics, literature, and history. After lunch, Patience schooled her pupil in the social graces—posture, table settings, etiquette, and dancing.

After tea each day, Garrick devoted his attention to Emaline—and usually to Patience as well. There were trips to the beach where he steadily weaned Emaline away from her fear and coaxed her into the shallow water. Several times, they'd gone to the wharf to pick up packages of books and supplies, and once they'd even entered the town's combined mercantile and post office.

In all, Patience was beginning to believe she had stumbled into some idyllic world. Of course, there were still minor skirmishes with her charge and disagreements with her employer, but the entire household was beginning to work together as a crew with a single goal rather than a ship with myriad masters.

And Garrick?

Patience found herself intrigued by his complexity, his patience with his sister, his confidence with his men . . .

His tenderness whenever he and Patience were alone.

Smiling secretly to herself, she returned from waking Emaline to discover a box waiting for her on her bed.

After supplying her with the wardrobe she needed for her job, Garrick had stopped showering her with clothes. But this morning he'd found some new addition he thought necessary.

Cautiously, she lifted the lid and slid aside the tissue paper.

A petticoat lay on the top. No, not a mere petticoat, but a creation such as she had never seen before, one that had pin tucks and cutwork and delicate cotton lace at the edges. Not just any lace, but machine lace. The sort that was so fabulously expensive at the mercantile.

Patience feared to touch the delicate edging, it was so fine. But her curiosity soon overcame her hesitation and she sighed in delight at the texture of the fabric. It wasn't muslin, as she'd supposed, but a soft Indian cotton, so sheer and light and delicate that it could have been used for the outer dress rather than for undergarments.

Her fingers curled around the waistband and she lifted the petticoat out of the box. It had little more weight than a cobweb—such a direct contrast to her own undergarments. Frowning, she admitted that it would be a shame to wear it over her plain woolen underthings.

But as she held the petticoat up to her waist and the flounces fell from the box to the floor, she was delighted with another surprise. In the bottom of the box lay a hoop, coiled like a magical spring.

"Oh," she breathed, barely believing what she saw. Never in her life would she have expected Captain Dalton to offer her such a thing. In fact, she probably shouldn't accept it. She should send the box right back to him with an explanation that a uniform was one thing but undergarments were quite another.

But even as she considered refusing the items, her fingers curled a little tighter around the petticoat. She'd heard that every man had his price, and she supposed every woman did too. It seemed that her price was a petticoat and a watch-spring hoop.

After donning her own chemise, corset, and corset cover, she slipped the hoop over her head and buckled it around her waist, laughing in pleasure when the wires settled into position, forming a perfect bell that twitched and bounced as she walked. Next she slid the petticoat on top of the crinoline and buttoned it securely. Regarding her reflection in the mirror, she thought it a shame that it couldn't be worn as a skirt. It was the prettiest thing she'd ever seen—and certainly the loveliest garment she'd ever worn.

After donning such wonderful scanties, it seemed a shame to cover them with anything too heavy, so she took the skirt from the day gown he'd provided and paired it with one of her finest shirtwaists. Borrowing the wide sash from her Sunday best ensemble, she tied it around her waist and pinned a brooch at her throat.

Catching her reflection in the mirror, she was amazed at how the change in undergarments had altered her posture, her whole disposition. She felt . . . free.

Free from the somber mourning clothes, from the heavy petticoats, from the suffocating heat of so many layers of clothing.

"Emaline, are you ready?" she called.

The girl bounded into the room, her face rosy from a scrubbing and her hair pulled back into braids. In an instant, Patience knew that Martha had come to help Emaline dress. The maid had doted on Garrick's sister since the unfortunate incident with the wine.

"Do you like my new ribbons?" Emaline asked.

"They're very pretty."

"Martha gave them to me."

Patience made a note to mention Martha's kindness to Garrick. The ribbons must have cost her a few days' pay.

Patience's step was decidedly light as she hurried down the staircase and entered the breakfast room. Emaline skipped ahead of her and was taking her seat when the captain rose to his feet.

Of the entire day, this was the moment Patience least liked. She'd soon realized that breakfast was a time when Asa Marcus and Jan Ellington reported to Garrick on shipping company business, and Nina invariably tagged along.

There was nothing wrong with Mr. Marcus or the Ellingtons. Granted, Nina could be opinionated at times, and Patience still hadn't forgotten her derogatory comments about Emaline, but overall, they were pleasant companions.

Nevertheless, Jan Ellington tended to stare at Patience throughout the meal, and she was growing weary of the man's attentions.

Upon taking her place, however, Patience hesitated. The other three chairs were noticeably empty.

"Where are the Ellingtons and Mr. Marcus?"

Garrick didn't immediately answer. He was watching her, studying her attire.

"I'm pleased to see that you accepted my latest gift."

This time it was Patience who adopted a teasing tone. "I was led to believe it was the latest addition to my governess's uniform."

She took her seat, having learned from watching her

sister Felicity with her new crinoline that she had to subtly reach behind her and lift the hoop so that its rings would collapse properly. Then, feeling a heat enter her cheeks, she murmured, "Thank you. It's lovely."

Knowing that she mustn't look at him or she would be undone, she turned to her pupil instead. She laid her napkin in her lap with obvious care, then looked pointedly at the girl's linen square.

Emaline, who had been reaching for a piece of sausage quickly grabbed her napkin instead and settled it over her lap.

Patience flashed her a beaming smile. Suddenly hungry—starving, in fact—she began to fill her plate with fresh berries, scrambled eggs, toast, and preserves.

"You appear to be in good spirits," Garrick commented, sipping his coffee.

"I am, thank you."

"Pressing business will keep me at the shipping office again today."

Patience's mood plummeted, and she noted that Emaline's smile had dimmed as well. "I see." But even she heard the distinct lack of enthusiasm in her voice.

"I thought the two of you could join me."

It amazed her how quickly she brightened again.

"You and Emaline could spend some time on the beach or in the dunes. Take her schoolbooks along, and I'll meet you for a picnic at midday. I'm sure Miss Fitch will ask the cook to fix us a basket, won't you, Miss Fitch?"

Miss Fitch, who had just entered the room, looked far from pleased by the assignment, but she didn't argue. "I'll see what I can do, sir."

"Good." He pushed back from his place. "I'll

201

rendezvous with the two of you at the foot of the staircase in an hour." He was at the door of the dining room when he added, "Oh, and, Emaline . . ."

His sister glanced up, obviously pleased and surprised to be addressed directly.

"You were dressed this morning before I had a chance to bring you a surprise."

Her eyes sparkled. "What sort of surprise?"

"Go look."

Grinning in farewell, Garrick left the room, his boot heels clicking on the marble floor of the foyer as he made his way outside.

"Can I go look at my surprise?" Emaline whispered.

"After you've eaten."

Emaline finished her meal in minutes, and Patience, laughing at the streak of impatience she generally saw in herself, excused the child from the table.

The clatter of Emaline's feet faded as she ran up the stairs.

Following more sedately, Patience arrived in time to see her open a box much like the one that had held her hoop earlier that morning. Inside lay a similar petticoat and crinoline, along with a complete set of underthings, a pair of shoes, and a white dimity dress trimmed in pink.

"Look, Patience, look!"

"You'll look like a princess."

Piece by piece, Patience helped Emaline put on the finery, explaining to her with each layer why there was a buckle here or special stitching there. It didn't bother her that Emaline asked questions about things she'd taken for granted for weeks. Patience delighted in Emaline's curiosity about everything that surrounded her.

When her charge discovered the pièce de résistance,

a miniature reticule, she squealed in delight, running from the room to find her brother and thank him.

Chuckling, Patience met the two of them at the foot of the staircase.

Garrick held Emaline in his arms while she chattered about her new things. Looking over the little girl's shoulder, he met Patience's gaze, and there was no denying the deep joy to be found in his expression.

Patience's steps faltered, and she paused, loath to interrupt the tender scene. There should be more children in this house.

Garrick's children?

The thought stunned her. Not with its suddenness but with the rash of gooseflesh it brought with it—as if Patience might have a hand in caring for those children. But only as their governess, of course. She would enjoy living here on Addlemeyer Island.

The fact that she was considering extending her stay beyond the required year stated in her father's will was not as stunning as it would have been mere weeks ago. Somehow, in the space of a few weeks, she had begun to feel that she was in control of her life—so much so that she didn't mind putting down roots here. Perhaps that was because she was needed.

Emaline wriggled to the floor. The moment her high-button shoes hit the marble tiles, she ran to the front entrance.

"Hurry, Patience, hurry! Garrick has promised to take us for a ride in the open carriage!"

The silence the girl left in her wake was electrified and sweet. The house echoed with her laughter and chatter.

"If I'd known that another new set of clothes would set her off like that, I would have given her something every day."

Patience shook her head. "I don't think it's the

clothes so much as . . . a sense of permanence she feels. The grown-up bed in her new room, the finery, the attention she's received from you. All of those things have reassured her that she is home."

He looked at her for several moments, his eyes growing as dark and fathomless as a summer sea—and she realized that he had not worn his eye patch in several weeks. "You left out the mention of her governess."

Patience could not bring herself to meet his gaze. "Shall we go?" she suggested brightly.

When she would have walked past him, Garrick took her arm. "You have already earned yourself a special place here, Miss Pedigrue."

It was as if he'd read her thoughts and had responded to them. "Any governess could have done the same," she murmured.

He shook his head. "I doubt that. How many women in your profession would take such a personal interest in their charges? How many would sit in an armoire to reassure her or stay up half the night to make her a doll?"

"You place too much importance on simple things."

"While you don't place enough importance on them."

When she refused to look at him, he drew her chin up. "Such a complicated woman," he said more to himself than to her. "Complicated and, oh, so beautiful."

A tightness was gathering in her throat, her chest, and lower, so much lower.

"I am not beautiful." There was a bitterness to her tone. Hadn't her father told her often enough that she was plain? Hadn't he despaired of the color of her hair, informing her that no gentlewoman should be born with tresses that shade. That it must be a reflection on the quality of her soul and she should guard against temptation all the more.

Garrick scowled. "Not beautiful? How can you think that? You must see in the mirror what I see now."

He ran his palm over the locks that fell over her ears from a center part. "Your hair is as soft and silken as a butterfly's wing. And your skin . . . so clear and fine and pure. My mother would have called it peaches-and-cream."

His head was dipping toward her. "And in the midst of it all, a delightful mouth, a winsome nose, and eyes the color of emeralds."

Garrick's lips covered hers, and the will to argue disappeared. She was aware of nothing but his arms, his strength, his passion.

Standing on tiptoe, she clutched at the front of his shirt, greedily responding to the pressure of his body, to the hands at her back, to the insistence of his tongue. There was no thought of propriety or the discrepancy in their social positions.

A crash occurred behind them and they sprang apart to find Miss Fitch standing in the parlor entrance. A silver salver, which had recently held the mail, lay at her feet. Behind her, Bickerstaff grinned widely.

Patience felt the blinding heat flood her cheeks, but Garrick merely twined his fingers between hers and drew her to the door.

"Miss Fitch," he said with a nod, bending to scoop the mail into his fist, "we'll be gone for most of the day."

"Yes, sir."

Then he was pulling Patience outside and into the sunshine.

A shiny black carriage had been drawn up to the block, and Emaline was already seated.

"Hurry, you two!"

"Can you drive a carriage, Miss Pedigrue?"

Patience regretfully shook her head. Her father had considered such conveyances an extravagance, since he rarely left the house. He'd proclaimed that his daughters didn't need one either, since they had no business going any farther than they could walk.

"I suppose I'll have to teach you."

Garrick helped Patience into the carriage. Then, instead of swinging onto the horse that was being held in check by a groom, he climbed in beside her.

"Take Ramses back to the stables, Hans."

The tall, painfully thin groom nodded, already backing out of the way.

"Hiyahh!" Garrick flicked the reins across the rump of the gelding in the traces, and they sprang into motion, flying down the pea gravel drive toward the high stone walls that marked the boundary of the Dalton estate.

Patience clung to the cushions, but Emaline had risen to her knees and was leaning forward between them, encouraging Garrick to greater speed.

They turned onto the main road, Garrick easily avoiding the ruts, and raced along the high dirt track that wound over the bluff. Below them, the sea lapped against a narrow beach, filling the air with its scent and sound.

Patience was still intrigued by the view. She'd lived near the water most of her life, but the sea seemed different here at Addlemeyer. Perhaps it was the fact that the island was not very large, but the air here seemed fresher, the beauty crisper, the scents more heavenly.

"Have you lived here all your life?" she asked Garrick, raising her voice to be heard over the clop of hooves and the crunch of the wheels on loose rock.

"Except for the sea voyages I've taken."

"You must love this place very much to return to it after visiting so many exotic lands."

He eyed her strangely, as if he were giving her statement careful consideration. "I wouldn't live anywhere else."

"I can see why."

"Can you?"

She shifted in her seat. He was paying less attention to the road than to her.

"The weather can be quite harsh here during the winter," he continued. "And we aren't completely immune to hurricanes and fierce winds."

"I doubt that any place on earth could claim perfection. Even Eden had its serpent."

Again she sensed that he was digesting her response with more care than it deserved. She was relieved when the road began its twisting descent into the village of Addlemeyer and he had to give his full attention to the carriage.

"On the way back, I'll show you how to take the reins."

She shook her head. "I don't think I could control such a large carriage on this road."

"Then we'll have to get you a governess cart."

"Pardon?"

"I've seen them quite often in England, and I'm sure we could find one here. They are very small, with enough room for a woman and two or three children. The seats face each other and the governess rides sideways so that she can see the youngsters at all times. Generally, the cart is pulled by a pony or a docile mare."

Patience thought the idea sounded intriguing and more in keeping with the sort of challenge she would be willing to undertake, but she didn't say so out loud. This man had already spent far too much money on her behalf, and to ask for more would be unthinkable.

"It isn't a crime, Patience."

She was jerked from her thoughts. "Captain?"

"It isn't a crime to accept gifts."

Once again he'd shown an uncanny ability to read her thoughts.

Transferring the reins to one hand, he clasped her chin, looking at her with such intensity she felt as if molten gold were flowing through her veins.

"Neither is it a crime to want something," he murmured.

But this time the statement was clearly directed to himself—and that fact made her shiver despite the warmth of the sunlight.

Chapter

15

The streets of Addlemeyer were busier than usual, causing Patience to look toward the docks.

"One of my ships arrived late last night. It was loaded to the gunwales, so it will take some time to distribute the goods to the companies we supply."

He gestured to barrels being hefted onto a wagon. "We brought whisky from Scotland as well as wool and malt. From England we brought paper, Indian cotton, dress goods, silver and china, machine parts, and an entire printing press for an establishment in Baltimore."

Patience was as wide-eyed as her charge, trying to see everything at once.

As they pulled to a stop at the edge of the quay, however, it became clear that Emaline was growing increasingly agitated as they drew closer to the ships. Her nervousness around water was easing, but she still had no desire to board any kind of vessel.

"Perhaps we should forgo a tour of the ship."

Patience nodded in agreement.

He negotiated the confusion of animals, sailors,

and stacks of cargo. "I'll set up a corner for you in my office to use while I'm conferring with my men."

"We couldn't possibly interrupt your work," Patience protested.

"It's no interruption. I'll be needed on the docks most of the time anyway."

He helped the two of them alight, his hands lingering at Patience's waist a little longer than necessary. Then, taking Emaline's hand and laying his palm against the hollow of Patience's back, he escorted them to a two-story clapboard building a few yards away.

It was obvious from the moment they stepped inside that the edifice had been built for business rather than aesthetics. Tall desks with scribe's chairs lined a room crowded with bookcases and tables. Men dressed in black coats and starched collars were working furiously over what looked like ship's registers and account ledgers.

"Marcus!"

The tall, bewhiskered man stood up from one of the desks.

"This is Asa Marcus's domain."

The man bowed, but did not speak. Patience was sure he hadn't directed a half-dozen words in her direction since they'd met.

"If there's anything you need while you're here, ask Asa."

Patience nodded. "Thank you, Mr. Marcus. It's very kind of you to take care of us that way."

His smile was a bare lifting of the corners of his lips. "I am always more than willing to serve Captain Dalton in any way he requires."

My, my. An entire sentence!

"This way." Garrick took them up a narrow staircase and led them into a private office.

It was quieter here. A large window overlooked the sea, and some care had been taken to impress any customers who would be entertained here. The plank floors were covered with an enormous rug, and the furniture was heavy, masculine, and built for comfort.

"You and Emaline can work here," Garrick said, clearing a space at a table near the back. "I shouldn't be gone for more than an hour or so."

"That will be lovely," Patience responded when it became apparent that Emaline had begun to explore.

Garrick hesitated at the door, obviously reluctant to leave them. "If you require materials, you can ask any of the fellows below."

"Thank you."

"And help yourself to anything you'd like here. There's ink on my desk. Paper too."

Again he hesitated, and Patience found herself wishing they could return to that moment in the foyer of his home where there had just been the two of them.

After tapping the doorframe with his hand, Garrick turned and left, the sound of his boots against the stairs accompanying him as he went.

Knowing she mustn't brood over the way his absence caused the room to lose some of its brightness, she turned to her charge.

"Well, Emaline, I think that we will avail ourselves of your brother's office, as he suggested. Shall we see what sorts of interesting books we can find?"

In the end, they chose one filled with maps for a geography lesson, another with pictures of birds, and a book to practice her reading.

The little girl seemed to understand the necessity of practicing the new skills she'd learned, but she didn't look completely enthusiastic, and Patience supposed that it must be hard for her to fathom why Latin might one day become a necessity and why it was better to study here, where it was cool and quiet, rather than running loose.

After an hour, however, Patience could see that Emaline's interest was beginning to flag. Taking the volume about birds, a stub of a pencil, and a sheaf of writing paper, she suggested they go outside and see if they could find any of the birds pictured in the book.

Not wishing to disturb the men at work, they slipped away without a word. Fully aware that the ships and the slapping waves made Emaline nervous, Patience led her toward the rolling hills on the outskirts of town and into the tall dune grass.

Emaline's exuberance soon returned, and she ran and skipped, holding her arms up to the sun and twirling in dizzying circles.

She was a study in contrasts, Patience noted. Her neatly combed hair and delicate attire made her look like just what she was, an heiress to a well-known shipping company. But in her manner when she was outside and unfettered, Patience could see that four years of living among the natives of a small island had also influenced her personality. She displayed an almost hedonistic enjoyment of freedom that would have been curbed in other girls her age.

Nevertheless, Patience let her run until her cheeks were pink and her eyes bright. Then, drawing her to a knoll overlooking a group of birds searching for food in a stagnant pond, she handed Emaline the book and the two of them searched for a match. It was only after a half hour of fruitless studying that Emaline saw the small print on the title page: *Birds of Europe.*

Laughing at their mistake, Patience tossed the book into the grass and handed Emaline the paper and pencil.

"Draw for me," she instructed the girl.

Emaline regarded her in astonishment. "What should I draw?"

"Anything you'd like."

Thinking a moment, Emaline grabbed the book, set it on her lap, and used it as a makeshift table. Then she bent over her work, the tip of her tongue poking out the corner of her mouth.

Patience leaned back on her hands, holding her face up to the sunlight. The golden glow infused her entire body, ridding it of the tension that had dwelled inside her for years, filling her with a peace and happiness she'd never experienced before.

How wonderful to have time just to sit and breathe and relax, she thought. Her father had insisted that idle hands were the devil's workshop and had required his daughters to be busy at all times.

"Patience?"

"Mmm?"

She didn't open her eyes. She could still hear the furious scratching of Emaline's pencil and knew she hadn't finished yet.

"Are you going to marry my brother?"

Patience's eyes sprang open. The tightness in her chest she'd experienced in Garrick's presence that morning returned tenfold. "Why would you ask such a thing?" she gasped.

Emaline didn't immediately respond. She was busy with her drawing. When she did speak, she startled Patience even more. "I think he likes you a great deal."

Patience found herself scrambling for something to say. Conversely, she wanted more information even as she dreaded discovering the truth.

"I remember what it was like when I lived here

before," Emaline went on. "He would bring me presents whenever he returned from a voyage."

"Oh?" The word was strangled and barely audible.

"Then he would spend all his time in town with Millie Van der Meer and her friends."

Patience didn't bother to ask who Millie was or to inquire about the woman's friends. She could well imagine.

"Mama used to sigh, but Papa would only laugh and tell her, 'Boys will be boys, madam.'" Emaline's voice had dropped to a rough approximation of her father's. "But Garrick hasn't gone to see Millie at all this time."

"Perhaps he wants to spend time with you, Emaline."

The girl's face scrunched up as she thought about that point. Then she shook her head. "No, I don't think that's it at all," she said, then returned to her sketch. "I sleep at night, so he wouldn't stay home just for me."

Her remark left Patience completely flustered.

Garrick was whistling softly as he strode up the path to the main building. By pushing himself and his assistants, he'd been able to finish the work slightly ahead of schedule, which left him with the afternoon free. He was hoping to tempt Emaline to go for a swim in the surf.

He took the stairs two at a time and rushed into his office, but a quick scan of the area revealed that he was alone in the room. A neat stack of books and some paper bearing Emaline's untrained scrawl lay on the corner of the table, as did the basket of food.

Frowning, he went downstairs.

"Asa, where have my sister and her governess gone?"

The accounting manager looked up from his ledger. "They're upstairs, sir."

The moment the words left the gentleman's mouth, Garrick felt a twinge of unease settle in his gut.

"They aren't there."

Asa's head popped up again. Bit by bit, a silence spread over the room like waves in a pool. The men in his office had been informed that they were to watch Emaline at all times, and since it was such an unusual request, they'd understood the gravity of the order without being told.

"Find them."

Garrick's command was low, but he did not need to repeat it. Immediately, the workers pushed away from their tables and scurried toward the exit. By the time Garrick had gone outside, released the gelding from the carriage, and swung astride its bare back, his employees were dotting the landscape like black ants.

Garrick quickly surveyed the area, his pulse beating frantically in his veins. Silently, he prayed that Patience and Emaline had merely wandered off, but the sharp tang of dread lingered on his tongue. He couldn't help thinking that this was the first time since Boston that the pair of them had been unsupervised.

Think, man. Think!

Spurring his horse into action, he didn't analyze what made him turn away from the waterfront and the business section of town. He began riding toward the dunes, pulled by some nameless emotion that he had never experienced before. The sound of hooves beating against the earth formed an urgent tattoo, and his gaze moved restlessly, searching the grassy expanse as he'd once searched the horizon for his first sight of home.

"Emaline! Patience!" he called, noting that somber clouds were beginning to appear on the horizon.

Why hadn't he noted the change in weather? Why hadn't he checked on them earlier?

"Emaline!"

And then, as if he'd imagined the sight, a figure rose from the grass. She stood tall, her red hair gleaming like a beacon, one hand raised to her forehead to shield her eyes from the sun.

Patience waved to him, lazily, cheerfully, not in the least bit worried or upset. Beside her, a darker head poked into view.

"Captain! How good of you to join us," Patience called.

Garrick didn't slow the pace of his mount until he was nearly upon them. Then he brought the animal to a skidding halt and swung from its back. He swept Emaline into his arms, holding her tightly against him until she protested and begged to be put down.

As she darted away to catch a half dozen pieces of paper being scattered by the wind, Garrick turned to Patience. She was eyeing him as if he'd lost his mind. Such an expression, so close on the heels of his worry, was the only encouragement he needed to grasp her around the waist and haul her close for a passionate embrace.

She was so light in his arms, so warm, that he alternated between wanting to kiss her senseless and his desire to shield her against whatever problems the world might send her way.

Too late he remembered that they weren't alone, that they had a very real witness. A very young witness. A very impressionable witness.

Drawing back, he twisted his head enough to find Emaline gaping at him open-mouthed. For some reason her stare made him more self-conscious than he'd been in decades.

"I, uh . . . I thought something terrible had happened to you both."

Patience was still trying to catch her breath, and Emaline's mouth was spreading in a wide grin.

"When I didn't find you in the office, I assumed . . ." He didn't finish his explanation. He wasn't about to tell either of them about the threatening letter he'd found in the batch of mail he'd picked up on his way out the door. The third note to be delivered since Garrick arrived home had been especially chilling:

Your continued disregard will only increase the danger, Captain Dalton. You think that by ordering your sailors to watch your house you can protect its occupants. But I know the weak links in your defenses. Just as I know that you find your sister's governess intriguing.

Go away while you are still free to do so. Take your sister back to her uncharted island and stay there with her. If you do not leave America, you will not live to see the end of the year.

Shaking away the sick dread that the memory of the letter instilled in him, Garrick returned his attention to Emaline and her governess.

When the silence went on too long, Patience said quietly, "But, Captain, we merely came out here to study the birds."

"I see."

Reluctantly, Garrick disengaged himself and reached for the pistol he'd tucked into the back of his trousers. Patience stared at the weapon, her gaze not leaving him for an instant as he pointed it skyward and pulled the trigger.

Both she and Emaline jumped at the loud report.

"Why did you do that?" Emaline whispered as if she'd done something wrong.

Garrick tousled her hair reassuringly. "I sent some men out to look for you. The shot will notify them that you've been found."

Emaline's eyes danced. "Why would you send anyone to look for us? We were right here all along."

"Because I lost you once, little one. It will not happen again."

Emaline wrapped her arms around his waist, hugging him tightly, then danced away to gather her things.

"What's wrong, Garrick?"

Patience uttered the question so softly, so carefully, that Garrick couldn't bring himself to look at her.

He was a private man, one who rarely showed his emotions, especially to someone he had known for only a few weeks. How could such a woman inspire in him emotions that no one but his sister had ever been able to arouse?

But as he looked at her, he realized that to compare what he felt for Patience with his brotherly love for Emaline was wrong, oh, so wrong. The emotions were similar only in their intensity.

"What have you done to me?" he whispered.

He knew she caught the words because she looked away, staring out at the wind-whipped grass.

"I don't understand."

But she did. He knew she did. He could see it in the careful angle of her chin and the sudden pallor of her cheeks.

"Yes," he insisted. "You do."

He saw her lashes flicker and the way her bosom shuddered as she took a quick breath.

"If my sister weren't here, I would pull you down onto that grass, and you would let me."

This time she didn't bother to protest and that fact sent a wave of lava into his groin.

"You want me to touch you, Patience."

"Yes." It was a murmured admission. One that emboldened him even more. It didn't seem to matter that Emaline stood only a few yards away or that at least three feet of space yawned between him and Patience. Since he could not love her with his body, he would make love to her with his words.

"Are you a siren?"

She shook her head.

"I think you are. You've sung your siren song to lure me off the edge of the earth."

Patience looked at him then, and he could see the pulse beating quick and hard at the base of her throat.

"You know full well what you're doing to me. How you can bend my will with a single glance."

A light flared in her expression, one that looked very much like a burst of feminine power, but it was quickly doused by her uncertainty.

"Did you offer the same speech to Millie?"

He frowned. "Millie?"

"Emaline told me today how you used to visit the woman and her . . . friends."

He grinned. "Does that upset you?"

"Of course not. Why would it upset me?"

But when he didn't speak for some time, she finally admitted, "You are a man of the world. I cannot condemn you for being true to your own set of standards."

"What if those standards have been tempered by age and experience?"

She glanced at him again, but only briefly.

"My sister was quite young when she disappeared. A great deal has happened to both of us since that time."

The breeze sifted through the dune grass, making a luffing sound much like that of the wind pushing against the sails of a ship.

"Why are you telling me all of this, Captain Dalton?"

Garrick took a deep breath, filling his lungs with the scent of brine and salt air. Unbeknownst to this woman, he hovered on the edge of a precipice. One from which there would be no turning back. He was a man of his word, and once he had given his promise, there would be no turning back.

"Just this once, won't you call me by my given name?" When she didn't respond, he added, "Patience."

She bowed her head, and he saw the way she nervously clasped her hands.

"Garrick."

The word could have been a figment of his imagination, but he didn't think so. She looked so slight, so sweet, so hesitant—and so clean. In his travels he had met many beautiful woman, some of whom were more than willing to surrender their bodies to his intimate exploration.

But this woman was different.

So different.

She was of the sort with whom a man shouldn't trifle. The sort who was meant to be a wife. A mother.

"Patience, I have never been a patient man."

Vaguely, he wondered why her lips twitched as if in secret amusement at his remark.

"I had not noticed that before, Captain."

"Garrick."

"Garrick." Her lips remained tilted in a smile.

Garrick shifted to watch his sister chasing a butterfly. "The last few years have been . . . hard." It was difficult to admit such a thing, especially to a woman, but he knew it was something that needed to be said. "Until Emaline was discovered, I feared that I would spend the rest of my life alone—and until I began doing so, I didn't realize what a dreary prospect that could be."

She was staring at him now as if she never would have believed he possessed such emotions. Taking advantage of her scrutiny, he caught her gaze.

"I do not want to be alone again."

She laughed softly. "Emaline will keep you company for years and years."

He shook his head. "You misunderstand. I do not wish to be *alone.*"

Her amusement faded, and she said questioningly, "Garrick?"

"I love my sister dearly, Patience. But she has her own life to lead. In the past few weeks, I have seen her blossom under your care. One day she will be a beautiful woman."

"That displeases you?"

"No, not at all. But it has made me very aware of my own mortality."

At long last he took a step toward her, gently caressing her cheek. "I have decided that I want more than a sister to care for. I also want children of my own."

Her eyes had grown wide and as green as the shores of Ireland the first time he'd seen them through his spyglass.

"I have much to offer any son or daughter. A thriving business, a good home, and a desire to see my offspring safely grown."

His palm cupped her face, his fingers slipping into her hair.

"All that remains is to find myself a wife."

Chapter
16

Patience stood stunned. She'd heard the words, she'd seen them come from his mouth, but that didn't make them any easier to believe.

"Captain?" she whispered, her voice choked.

He smiled at her response and leaned down to kiss her lips.

"Is that all you can say to a man when he offers you marriage?"

For some inexplicable reason, her eyes flooded with tears.

"I don't think I've ever seen you this speechless," Garrick said, drawing her into his arms and rocking her back and forth. "I would have thought you'd be bristling with objections that I would be bold enough to suggest a very civilized and sound proposition."

He made the idea of marriage sound like a business merger.

"I—I don't know what to say."

"You don't have to answer right now," he whispered next to her ear. "Just promise to think about how our marriage would provide everything that my family still lacks—a woman to fill the house with warmth, a mother for Emaline." His voice deepened. "A companion for me."

He'd analyzed the situation and decided upon a practical means of attaining his goals. The marriage would offer him enormous benefits.

But what about her?

There was one thing she had to know before she allowed herself even to consider the possibility that this outrageous proposition could actually be directed toward her, Miss Patience Pedigrue of Boston.

"Why?" she asked.

"Why should you think about it?"

"Why would you ask me?"

He tipped her chin up. "Because I've been searching for a woman like you for a very long time. Someone level-headed, beautiful, sweet. The perfect hostess for my home and business associates. More importantly, my sister adores you, and I have grown to depend on you as well. Now that I've found you, I won't let you slip away."

The foolish tears welled up in her eyes again, and she blinked them away.

This had to be a dream. Long ago she had daydreamed about marrying a wealthy, dashing man. But somehow she had always envisioned love as being part of that relationship.

Garrick released her to collect Emaline and lifted them both onto the horse, then led the animal back to the docks. Throughout the short journey, Patience kept telling herself that this man couldn't possibly have proposed marriage to her. Not so suddenly. Not so rashly.

Just as she couldn't possibly be considering accepting him.

Somewhat dazed, she allowed him to help her into the carriage and drew Emaline's sleepy body against her shoulder. As she did so, she wondered if this was what her life would be like if she stayed here. If someday she might cradle another head against her breast. One with wheat-colored hair and eyes as blue as the sea. A little boy, perhaps, who had stayed too long at his father's office.

The idea caused her stomach to do mad flip-flops, and she tried to force her mind onto something else, *anything* else. But when Garrick finished harnessing the horse and squeezed into what little space remained on the seat beside her, she was immediately inundated with his warmth, his scent, his strength.

She could do far worse than to marry this man. Her life with him would be quite content. If she left Dalton Manor, even with her inheritance, she would have to work to support herself, but if she married Garrick, she would never be forced into service. As Mrs. Garrick Dalton she would always have a roof over her head and food on the table. And she would be free to pursue her own interests and to make her own place in the community.

But at what price? There was always a price. She'd learned long ago that nothing in life came free. What sacrifice would be demanded for all that she would gain?

Once they arrived back at the estate house, Emaline was lifted from the carriage by Bickerstaff and the carriage was led away.

"Would you care to join me for a drink?" Garrick asked her as they hesitated at the bottom of the marble steps. He caught himself immediately, "Ahh, but you don't drink, do you?" He held out a hand. "Join me in the parlor and I will ask Miss Fitch to bring you some tea, then."

She followed him on wooden limbs, knowing that she couldn't possibly manage a teapot in her current condition—and she most certainly couldn't keep a cup and saucer from rattling. But she didn't protest.

Her skirts whispered across the marble floor of the foyer. Without waiting for someone to attend them, Garrick bellowed for some refreshments to be brought to the parlor, and Patience knew that the command would be obeyed.

Gratefully, she sank onto a velvet settee while Garrick adjusted the blinds to shut out the strong afternoon sunlight.

"Damn."

Her brows rose, and she wondered if he was about to rescind his offer.

Shielding his injured eye from the sun, he grimaced. "I still haven't adjusted completely, I'm afraid."

Garrick was generally so strong and filled with purpose that she often forgot he'd been wounded not once, but twice.

"The explosion must have been horrible."

He didn't immediately speak, then finally said, "Bickerstaff told you, I suppose."

"Bickerstaff, the sailors. I've heard a good many people talk about the tragedy. They have all been very concerned about your recovery."

He took a deep breath, and she thought he would change the subject, but he offered, "My leg, the burns, the eye. All of them are healed and growing stronger every day. But the fact that I lost so many men is not something I have been able to forget."

"No one blames you."

"I don't know. Of late I've wondered if an unhappy family member might be responsible for the attack in Boston."

Patience stared at him in horror. "Surely not. We

haven't received a single threat since coming . . ." Her words trailed away when she realized that Garrick had received more of the warnings but had kept her blissfully ignorant of them.

"I wondered why Bickerstaff continued to trail Emaline and me to Mrs. Rogers's cottage."

"I've also asked several of my sailors to guard the perimeter of the house, and Captain Rosemund is anchored five hundred yards out to sea to discourage anyone from attempting to land near the beach."

"You've been very thorough."

"I have to be. I could never let anything happen to Emaline. Or to you," he added softly.

Her body, which had so recently chilled, grew warm again.

"How is your knife wound?"

"Healed, for the most part, thank you. Much to Bickerstaff's relief."

"He worries about you."

"He's a good friend." Then, as if uncomfortable with the direction of the conversation, he said, "We forgot about our picnic. You must be starving."

She was about to reassure him that food was the last thing on her mind when he stepped into the hall and bellowed to the cook to fix them some lunch as well.

Returning to a spot in front of her, he said, "I promised you time to think, and I will give you that much at least. So this afternoon we will speak of other things. That way we can get to know each other better."

The thought was enough to make her panic. If he knew more about her, he might change his mind.

Miss Fitch chose that moment to enter the parlor. It was clear from her frosty-eyed stare that she didn't think a governess should take tea with her employer.

But then again, Patience thought with a sigh, Miss Fitch probably hadn't approved of their kiss in the foyer either.

"Thank you, Miss Fitch."

"Will there be anything else, Captain?"

She asked the question as if she expected him to request bedding and some pillows, Patience thought, her hands beginning to tremble.

"No. That will be all."

The woman turned on her heel and left in a crackle of starched skirts. Once in the foyer, she was careful to close the doors with much more caution than was actually necessary.

"You don't like her very much do you?"

Patience started. She hadn't realized that her feelings were so transparent. "I don't know her."

"You don't have to know a person to discern whether or not you are compatible."

With one simple phrase, he brought her thoughts back to the decision looming ahead of her.

"Why don't you go ahead and pour yourself a cup?"

"You don't want any tea?"

"I prefer something a little stronger."

Standing, he moved to a cabinet in the corner, removing a bottle and a crystal glass. Splashing something into its depths, he returned.

"Would you care for a sandwich?" Patience asked quickly, trying to remember how to play the proper hostess. For some reason, habits that had once been second nature seemed to have deserted her in her hour of need.

He leaned close, selecting one. In doing so, she was sure that she could detect the scent of salt and sun and summer clinging to his skin. She closed her eyes briefly and tried to control the way her pulse leaped in response, but her body seemed to have developed a will of its own.

Rather than returning to the chair he'd been in before, Garrick sat beside her on the settee, turning sideways so that his shin pressed into the folds of her skirts. He rested an arm along the back of the couch.

"Your tea," he reminded her.

She managed to pour a cup of the brew. Her fingers were stiff as she lifted it to her lips, and the tea was scalding hot, but she didn't care. It revived her somewhat, helping her organize her thoughts.

Garrick took a bite of his sandwich, the tiny, crustless fare looking far too dainty for his hands. He had strong, slender fingers dusted ever so slightly with golden hair.

Would those fingers touch her intimately? Would they stroke her skin and arouse her to a fever pitch?

The thought shot through her like a lightning bolt, and she nearly dropped her cup. The images her mind had created crowded fast and strong into her head, becoming impossible to banish.

"Tell me about your family," Garrick said.

"My family," she repeated, grasping on to the subject as if it were a lifeline. "I have two sisters."

"Older?"

"One older and one younger."

"What are their names?"

It was amazing, but she actually had to stop and think, even though she was sure she'd told him about her sisters long ago.

"Constance. Constance is the eldest."

"And the other one?"

"Felicity."

"What did they say of your coming to work here?"

She shrugged. "I don't suppose they really thought

about it one way or another. Our father wanted us to earn our inheritance, so—"

"He didn't think the way you cared for him was enough?"

"Apparently not. Felicity was sent to serve as a teacher in Saint Joseph. She was quite excited about the prospect. She'd always wanted to go west."

"What about Constance?"

"She was ordered to serve as a seamstress for a theater in New York."

"An odd request from a pious man."

"I suppose. But Constance has always had a fascination for the theater."

"So your father was, in essence, granting each of your sisters a wish."

She'd never thought of it that way, but she supposed it was true.

"What about you, Patience? What did you wish for?"

She couldn't say it aloud. He would recognize the similarity to her present situation.

"Tell me," Garrick urged, his fingers toying with a lock of hair that had fallen from her tidy coiffure.

"I had some silly notion about supporting myself, traveling, seeing the world."

Garrick took the cup and saucer from her hands and set them on the table. Then he caught her face in his palms.

"You could do those things if you married me," he whispered, speaking of the very thing he had promised he wouldn't mention. "The only thing that would ever tie you to me would be my name. Beyond that, you would have the power and money and influence to devote yourself to whatever causes please you."

"As long as one of those causes is you?"

"Of course. But I wouldn't force your loyalty. I would earn it."

"How?" The question was but a whisper against his lips.

"Like this."

The kiss was slow and sweet and tender. The sort that had the power to break a woman's heart with its poignancy. His lips worshiped hers, displaying such adoration that she could scarcely believe it was directed to her. Patience Pedigrue. Spinster. Governess. Woman.

Her hands splayed over his chest, and he smiled against her, tipping his head to kiss her cheek, her jaw, then nipping the side of her neck.

She gasped as a bolt of sensation shot through her body to pool deep in her loins.

"I can show you the world if you want it, Patience," he whispered into her ear. "London, Paris, Venice. Or I can bring it to you if you'd rather."

His fingers were plucking the pins from her hair, and she uttered a soft sound of distress, one that was quickly absorbed by his mouth. By the time he lifted his head, she could feel the plaits falling loose and his fingers combing through the strands. Within minutes her hair lay crimped and shimmering over her shoulders.

Patience saw the slow smile that crept over his face. "I knew it would look like this." He scooped up a handful of her hair as if it were something precious and allowed it to flow between his fingers.

Bit by bit, he laid her back against the arm of the settee, then settled beside her, his body pressing against hers. Warm. Heavy. Hard.

"I shouldn't be doing this, Patience."

She didn't know how to reply to such a statement.

"I swore I wouldn't pressure you. But you get into my blood." His voice grew rough and guttural as if he resented that fact. Resented it and reveled in it. "I've tried so hard to go slow and not to startle your delicate sensibilities." He looked at her then, directly, so that she couldn't escape the heat she saw in his gaze.

"You should know from the start, however, that I'm not one of those pomaded gentlemen who have been taught how to take things by degrees."

He was leaning toward her again, his mouth hovering over hers. "The fact of the matter is, I've been months without female companionship of any kind."

Her eyes grew wide, her breath coming in spurts. It was not necessary for him to explain his euphemistic statement. She could feel the urgency in his body as much as she could feel it in her own.

"Ordinarily I would avail myself of the services available in town."

"Millie," she whispered.

"Yes." His grip on her arm grew fierce. "But I find that there is only one person who can slake my hunger. You, Patience. You."

Then he was kissing her with a fierceness that he had not displayed up to this point, a passion that Patience would not have thought possible. It should have frightened her.

Should have.

But it didn't.

Her own arms swept around his shoulders and she pulled him tightly to her, absorbing his weight, his urgency. When one of his thighs slipped between her legs, she gasped, pressing against him, expressing the very carnality she had once condemned in the male sex. But with every minute that passed, she was discovering that she knew nothing of passion.

When he reached for the buttons of her shirtwaist, she didn't protest. Nor did she argue when he tugged at the buttons of her corset cover, popping them free. She needed him, ached for him. So when his hand slid under the barrier of her stays, she gasped, arching against him.

Her fingernails dug into the skin of his neck, then moved lower, raking over the hard muscles of his chest.

"Our life together could be like this, Patience, full of passion and promise."

Passion. No mention of love, of affection, or even of a potent fondness.

Pushing against him, she managed to free herself and jumped to her feet. With trembling hands she tried to repair the damage done to her clothing and her hair. Then she stood at the window, her back to him, her body trembling.

In her mind's eye, she was seeing a rainy afternoon long ago when she'd crept into the attic of her father's house to amuse herself. She remembered pulling a dusty trunk from the corner and lifting the lid to expose a beautiful wedding dress.

Enchanted, she'd slipped it over her head. Although she couldn't have been more than thirteen or fourteen at the time, she'd felt like a queen in that dress. Seeing a tarnished mirror poking out from beneath a quilt and a stack of baby clothes, she'd pulled it free, and a letter had fluttered to the floor.

Patience pressed a finger to the ache gathering between her brows. She shouldn't have read it. If she had left it where it had fallen, she wouldn't have discovered that her mother had never loved Alexander Pedigrue, that she had been locked in a loveless marriage to a cold, unfeeling man.

"Patience?"

Garrick was standing just behind her, yet she hadn't heard him move. It was merely one more sign of how deeply he could affect her senses.

Gazing at him, Patience knew that the moment had come. There would be no waiting. Either she would refuse this man and resign her position as Emaline's governess . . .

Or she would agree to be his wife.

"You've made your decision, haven't you?"

"Yes."

He waited, his body tense. Even then she saw no hint of desperation. No indication that if she refused him, he would be devastated.

But that was absurd. Garrick Dalton could never be devastated by a mere woman.

Taking a deep breath, she said, "Before I give you my response, will you tell me one thing?"

His gaze was so direct that she knew he had anticipated her request.

"Do I love you?" he said aloud.

She nodded.

"No."

The bluntness of his reply hurt more than she would have thought possible, so much so, that she actually took a step backward.

So that was to be the price of such a match, a little voice whispered.

"But I am extremely fond of you, I enjoy your company, and I look upon you as a friend," Garrick continued. "Can many marriages claim such things?" He took a step toward her. "Moreover, we have known each other only a short while. Who knows what depths of emotion have yet to develop?"

Despite common sense, Patience found herself clinging to his final sentence.

Garrick could love her.

In time.

Garrick shifted, standing straight, tall. Proud. The evidence of their ardor was there in his tousled hair and the faint scratches on his neck. And even at that moment, after he had assured her quite plainly that his desire to marry her was based on sexual attraction rather than love, she was drawn to him in a very elemental way.

"Will you marry me, Patience Pedigrue?" he asked slowly, holding out his hand palm up. "Will you become my bride?"

Chapter

17

"**Y**es."

As soon as the word was spoken, the die was cast and her future was set. Patience knew there would be no going back.

Why she had agreed to such a lifelong proposition, she wasn't sure. There were those who would consider this the height of irrational behavior. But she could argue that Garrick Dalton offered her everything she'd ever longed to have—security, adventure, passion, and a chance to love.

"You won't regret it." He smiled, cupping her cheek with his hand and pulling her close for his kiss.

But even as he did so, she felt a tiny twinge of sadness. Because the emotion she'd seen in his eyes hadn't been relief or adoration.

It had been triumph.

New York

"Louise?"

Louise Chevalier woke by degrees, lulled by the

warm air that flowed through the billowing curtains and swirled around her bed.

Her lashes fluttered, and she smiled sleepily when she discovered Étienne Renoir leaning over the side of her bed.

How many times had Louise awakened to find him watching her that way? As always, his formidable features lost their severity and filled with a gentleness and love that his fellow bodyguards would have found odd in such an intimidating man.

"Come, *chérie,*" he said, his voice a mere whisper.

Étienne drew back the covers, then waited as she swung her feet to the floor and shrugged into a silken wrapper.

"You'd better eat the food Babette laid out for you on the terrace. It's nearly noon, and you have a costume fitting in an hour."

Louise grimaced. Not because the mention of her duties at the theater had interrupted her private life, but because she longed to sleep more.

After discovering that her youngest daughter Felicity had encountered problems in Saint Joseph, Louise had delayed her journey to New York and the opening of her latest production. The situation had involved several days of worry and tension before Felicity was safe. Louise smiled, recalling that her efforts had been well rewarded when Louise had finally met and been reconciled with the daughter she'd last seen as a baby.

Remembering that Étienne had promised to bring her updated reports on her other children, she said, "Tell me, *mon cher,* what have you learned about Patience?"

A smile flicked across his lips, and Louise marveled as his craggy features were warmed from within. The first time she'd interviewed the man for a position as her bodyguard, she'd doubted Étienne had the ability to look anything but forbidding. In the dozen years since, she'd discovered that first impressions could be misleading.

At first she'd tolerated Étienne's presence since his job was a necessary one. He shielded her from her adoring fans, provided a feeling of security and safety. With each month spent in his company, she'd grown to accept him, to adore him, then to crave him. At long last she'd known that he was a man to be trusted, and in their time together she'd confessed more secrets to Étienne than to any priest.

Any other man, she knew, would have judged her. But not Étienne. No, he'd treated her like a friend, then a brother, and then . . .

This past year he had been openly adoring, and she knew that it was only a matter of time before he declared his love for her and insisted on a commitment, physical and emotional. Especially now that Louise was free to marry again.

"Louise? You're woolgathering. Pray tell, are you thinking of me?"

Étienne gazed at her with eyes that were inky black, and she smiled even though her heart pounded with a mixture of anticipation and dread.

Not yet, Étienne, she prayed silently. *Don't say it yet. Don't ask me to tell you I love you. Not until the demons of my past have been exorcised.*

It took all the will she possessed to react as if she hadn't seen the passion in his eyes. Summoning a nonchalance she didn't feel, she rose and sauntered onto the terrace. There she sank into a white iron chair and laid a snowy linen napkin on her lap.

Étienne touched her shoulder as he crossed to take the seat at her left. That casual gesture told Louise eloquently enough that Étienne had read her panic and was willing to wait.

For a short while.

Then he would demand she surrender her heart and her body.

"Étienne, please. We've wandered from our original discussion." She helped herself to the fruit from the crystal bowl in the center of the table. "What news do you have of my little girls?"

Étienne took a slip of paper from his vest pocket, and when she saw the telegraph receipt, she immediately brightened. "You've heard from one of the children already?"

Louise supposed that any other actress her age might have craftily hidden the evidence of offspring and her advanced years. She had even heard of cases where performers sent their children away to be raised and introduced them to society again as nieces or cousins.

In Louise's opinion, such behavior was shocking. Had Alexander not kidnapped her daughters, Louise would have found the courage to escape her marriage—and take her children with her. Now that her girls had been found, she was more than willing to accept the role of mother to three grown women. Perhaps one day soon she would even be a grandmother.

"This was sent by the man I asked to inquire about Patience and to learn whether she was happy and safe." He paused before saying, "It seems that your daughter has agreed to be married. The news was announced in the *Addlemeyer Gazette* only this morning."

Louise froze. "What?"

Étienne grinned. "You heard me. Patience plans to marry her employer."

"Does she love him? Does he love her?"

Étienne offered a Gallic shrug.

239

"But—"

Étienne's lips twitched in amusement. "You needn't look so stunned. She *is* a grown woman, you know."

"But she's known him only a matter of weeks!"

"Not everyone waits years." His response was a subtle rebuke, but she didn't have the time to respond to it. Jumping to her feet, she announced, "Book us on the next ship to Nantucket. From there we can catch a ferry to Addlemeyer."

"You have a play opening in a week!"

"My understudy can take over. She'll be thrilled."

"The director won't be."

"I don't care." She took Étienne's hand and pulled him into the house. "We're going, Étienne. And we'll stay in Addlemeyer until I know my daughter is well and happy."

The next few days passed in a flurry of preparations. Garrick insisted that Mrs. Rogers be brought to the house so that Patience and Emaline could be fitted with new wardrobes. Then there were meals to plan, appointments to keep, and the legalities to be seen to.

Garrick took charge of the whole affair. He decided who would attend the service, what foods would be served afterward, and which day the ceremony would take place.

Ordinarily, Patience would have been irritated by such high-handed behavior, but with so many things demanding her attention, she was actually relieved to have someone else shoulder all of the responsibility.

Through it all, Emaline was sometimes ecstatic that her prediction had come true and sometimes bewildered by the fuss such a simple event could inspire. She took to trailing her governess around the house like a shadow as if she feared that in all the commotion, Patience would forget about her. Therefore, it was with some surprise that Patience emerged from her final fitting to discover that the little girl wasn't in the room.

"Where is Emaline?" she asked the seamstress, who was already bent over the pale blue bengaline suit that was to be Patience's wedding gown.

The woman mumbled something around the pins she held between her lips.

Patience didn't bother to try and decipher the comment. It was obvious that Mrs. Rogers didn't know where the girl had gone.

"Are you finished with me for an hour or two?"

The seamstress nodded, and that was all the encouragement Patience needed to escape. She would be the first to admit that she loved beautiful clothing. It was one vanity that she supposed she would never be able to conquer. But she was not the sort who could stand for hours on end being poked and prodded as if she were a human pincushion.

Rubbing at a spot on her arm where Mrs. Rogers had accidentally pricked her, she began her search for Emaline in the garden. When that proved unsuccessful, she moved into the kitchen, but seeing Oscar lying peacefully by the fireplace, she knew that Emaline hadn't been in here. If she had, she would have coaxed—or bullied—the dog into joining her.

Annoyed, Patience went upstairs to look in her room and Emaline's, but the girl was nowhere to be found.

Sighing, she stood in the hall, her hands on her hips. Where in the blazes could she be?

A slight noise alerted her to a partly open door across the hall.

Garrick's room? Emaline couldn't have gone in there, could she?

Another creak of the floorboard was her answer,

and Patience harrumphed in irritation. She'd purposely avoided looking in that room since being moved into this wing. Even after her engagement to Garrick had been announced, she hadn't so much as peered across the threshold to see where she would be sleeping by the week's end.

A rash of gooseflesh peppered her skin. Trust Emaline to force the issue. To make her enter the place she least wanted to go.

Castigating herself for putting too much emphasis on a room that was no different from any other in this house, she strode to the door and threw it open.

"Emaline, I don't think that your brother would approve of your—"

Miss Fitch whirled from where she had been bent over one of Garrick's drawers.

"Miss Fitch!"

The woman started, dropped something back into the drawer, and whirled.

When she saw Patience, her eyes widened briefly and her mouth thinned. Then she bumped the drawer closed with her hip. "Was there something you needed, Miss Pedigrue?" the woman asked stiffly.

Patience was ready to ask the same thing of the housekeeper. She opened her mouth to chide the woman for invading Garrick's privacy, but realized in time that she didn't have the authority to do so. Not yet. Not until she'd laid claim to the title Mrs. Garrick Dalton.

"I am looking for Emaline."

"I believe she was headed for the nursery."

Patience's brows rose. "The nursery?"

"Yes, ma'am."

Patience hesitated, then asked, "You don't like me, do you, Miss Fitch?"

"No, ma'am."

The woman's honesty was completely unexpected. "May I ask why?"

"Because I think you intend to marry the master for his money."

At least the woman hadn't bothered to disguise her feelings.

"I assure you, Miss Fitch, my reasons do not include money."

The woman snorted. "That remains to be seen, doesn't it?" Then she flounced past Patience, her head held high.

Patience finally found her charge in the nursery, curled up in a corner, huddled over the crude doll, which had been left behind during the move. Books and toys were strewn around the room, and since Patience had put them away before she and Emaline moved, it was apparent that the child had recently tossed them to the floor in a fit of pique.

Hesitating in the doorway, Patience tried to decide the best way to handle the situation. Her first instinct was to comfort the girl, but she sensed that it wasn't quite the right approach in this instance.

"My, we must have had quite a wind in here," Patience commented.

The child didn't look up, strengthening Patience's impression that Emaline had known she was there.

"I believe it's time for our Latin lesson, Emaline."

The girl didn't move.

"Yesterday we began to learn the irregular verbs, I believe. I think we will continue on that course for a time."

Emaline looked at her then, her eyes wide and accusatory. "Why?"

"Why learn Latin?"

Emaline shook her head. "Why bother? You won't

be giving me my lessons for long. Why start something you won't finish?"

"I am not in the habit of quitting, Emaline."

"But you'll be marrying my brother."

Patience shrugged. "How could that possibly interfere with your Latin lessons?"

"He'll hire another governess."

With that statement, Patience finally understood. Emaline had endured so many changes in the last year. The thought of beginning again with another teacher was looming over her head like an ax.

"I don't think that will be necessary, do you?" Patience asked. "There's no sense hiring someone else to do the job if I'm already here."

It was clear that Emaline didn't believe her.

"I don't remember any rule in society claiming that it would be improper for a *sister* to instruct you."

The girl's eyes narrowed. It was clear that she hadn't thought about that.

"Sisters help one another, don't they?"

Again, a suspicious look.

"So I think we'd best get started."

Patience held out her hand.

Sighing as if severely put upon, Emaline stood up and stalked out of the nursery and into the hall. Watching her, Patience supposed that an afternoon of studying would probably be in vain, judging by Emaline's current mood. But at least she could take comfort in one fact.

Emaline had taken the doll.

The evening shadows were gathering when the man finally managed to make his way back to Addlemeyer. Checking carefully behind him, he wandered through the streets in an apparently aimless manner before making his way to the abandoned warehouse behind the shipping office.

After climbing the outer steps, he used a brass key to unlock the door, then let himself into the room that he had commandeered for his exclusive use.

The faint glow of firelight from the next room drew him through the desks and bookcases piled with maritime logs and ledgers. Once in the archway leading to his sleeping quarters, he paused.

"So," he drawled. "You've heard the news."

The woman standing in front of the faint fire bristled, whirling to face him.

"Why didn't you tell me things were proceeding so quickly?" she demanded.

He shrugged. "As far as I knew, the captain had developed a healthy lust for the woman, nothing more."

"That lust has brought with it an offer of marriage," she snapped.

"You've spent more time at the house than I. You were supposed to uncover Miss Pedigrue's secrets. Don't blame me for this turn of events."

She balled her hands into fists. "Dammit, what are we going to do?"

The man shrugged. "The answer is simple. We stop the wedding."

"How?"

He crossed to the cabinet where he kept his liquor, then frowned when he noted that the brandy bottle was half empty. Scowling, he splashed a healthy measure into his glass, then stalked toward the man slouched in the wing chair and staring into the flames.

Jan Ellington nervously licked his lips, attempting to shield his own glass in the shadows.

Disgusted, the other man leaned over him, bracing himself on the chair and effectively trapping Jan.

"This is your fault, you know. We put *you* in charge of wooing the woman."

Jan couldn't hold his gaze. "I tried, but—"

"You *tried?*" A sneer weighted his tone. "Casting sheep's eyes across a table has had little effect. While you've been planning a seduction, the captain has been completing one."

Standing, he backhanded Jan across the cheek. "Damn you, I expect you to try harder. I want you to convince the woman of your undying love. Sweep her off her feet. Failing that, I want you to get rid of her, *do you understand?*"

Jan drained the glass, then rose unsteadily to his feet. "Yes, sir."

"Get out."

The two remaining conspirators waited until they heard the slam of the door. Then the woman sidled up to her lover and caressed his chest. "Do you really think he'll be any help at all?"

"If he isn't, I'll kill him."

He looked down, expecting to see a shocked expression. Instead, the woman's eyes burned with desire.

"You're so masterful, so . . ."

Ignoring her, he sank into the chair Jan had vacated.

Kneeling between his legs, she reached for the buttons on his shirt. "What are you plotting, my darling?"

"We've been too easy on Garrick Dalton. With all the sailors he's posted around the house as guards, I've allowed our mission to be delayed. I've sent ineffectual notes and bided my time—but no longer!"

She made a soft purr of delight. "What do you need me to do?"

*   *   *

Garrick stood on the terrace outside his study, staring out at the midnight sea, watching the moonlight glitter off the waves as the spray dashed against the rocks of the inlet like a flurry of diamonds.

He loved the ocean, loved its mystery, its vastness, its inscrutability. He'd been drawn to it as a boy, and that fascination hadn't changed through the years. But as of next week, he would abandon it, turn away from its allure like a lover breaking off a relationship with a lifelong mistress.

He took a sip of whiskey, drinking straight from the bottle, more than aware that he was brooding—and that he would probably get drunk before the night was through. But knowing such a fact didn't stop him. He already had his sister to care for, and soon he would have a wife. He could no longer sail willy-nilly all over the world, following whatever impulse spurred him on.

His father had found a means of compromise by taking his family with him on his voyages, a practice that Garrick had relished as a boy. But he was not his father. The wreck of his father's ship had taught Garrick that lesson well. Garrick knew the rigors of maritime travel, and he wouldn't subject a woman and child to such danger.

Not Emaline.

Not Patience.

He snorted, taking another swig from the bottle. Married. He'd never thought that such a word would apply to his name. Had it not been for the conflicts he'd faced, he wouldn't have considered such an option. But lately he'd become increasingly aware of his own mortality.

The wreck, the explosion, and the threats were not the only impetus for his change of heart. In fact, he'd shrugged off the notes that appeared in the mail as little more than the drivel of a lunatic until he was attacked in Boston.

A soft tap came from the door behind him, and Garrick's lips twitched in a wry smile. He knew without looking just who it would be. No one else dared to disturb him here when the door was closed.

"Come in, Miss Pedigrue."

He didn't bother to face her, but continued to look out at the ocean, absorbing the prickling sensation that entered his veins as soon as he heard the whisper of Patience's skirts and the snap of the latch behind her.

"How did you know it was me?" she asked, and he was sure it galled her that he'd spoiled her entrance. No doubt she'd come to confront him about something, and he'd taken away the element of surprise.

Turning to rest his spine against the doorjamb, he studied her intently, noting the gown she was wearing, a simple white cotton printed with sprigs of tiny blue flowers. The seamstress must have finished some of the dresses Garrick had told Patience to order.

He liked her in blue. It brought out the flashing glints in her eyes that told him she wasn't quite as poised or unaffected by his presence as she would have liked him to believe.

"Captain Dalton—" she began.

He didn't allow her to continue. Stepping inside and setting the bottle on his desk, he prowled deliberately toward her, liking the way her eyes widened and her breath quickened. He loved to see her this way, flushed and anticipating the worst.

The worst?

No, the best.

She was staring at him as if he were a wild beast and she the innocent prey. But there was more to it than that. So much more. Her cheeks flushed, her mouth parted.

His hand slid around her neck, drawing her to him. "Do you want me to kiss you, Patience?"

She didn't speak, didn't nod, but her lashes flickered ever so slightly in submission.

"Why did you come here?" he asked, bending, his lips brushing her own.

"I . . . needed to talk to you."

"About what?" The question was little more than a whisper. His mouth grazed her cheek, her jaw.

"To see"—she took a shuddering gulp of air—" if you had changed your mind."

"About what?" He began to explore the tender skin on her neck. Beautiful. So beautiful.

"Marrying . . . me."

He suckled the spot where her shoulder and throat met, and he felt her shudder. She gripped his waist.

"Have *you* changed your mind, Patience?"

After only the slightest hesitation, she shook her head.

"Then what makes you think I have?"

"N-nothing. I just wanted to be sure."

"I'm sure. I'm very sure." Then he swept his arms around her back and hauled her against him, flattening her skirts, plundering her mouth for the sweetness to be found there.

Her response was instantaneous. She stood on tiptoe, wrapping her hands around his neck and clinging to him as if he were the last stronghold in a furious storm. The reaction was enough to send his blood racing through his veins. Never had he imagined that a woman who appeared so pure and unaffected on the outside could be hiding such a wantonness on the inside.

But just when his own desire threatened to consume him, Garrick forced himself to draw away. No. Not yet. In a few days they would be wed. He could wait until then.

She appeared dazed and tousled, and the effect caused him to smile indulgently. What a treasure he had found in this female.

"You are so beautiful," he whispered, brushing her lips with his.

She blushed again, and he chuckled.

Patience stepped back, stumbled slightly, then bumped her way to the door.

"Good night, Captain."

So he was still to be referred to as "Captain."

He waited until she was nearly out the door before saying, "Patience."

"Yes, sir."

She didn't quite meet his gaze.

"You realize that I do not intend this to be a marriage of convenience."

"Captain?"

"Our marriage will be consummated. On our wedding night."

The words had the power to make her cheeks flame.

"You are aware of that, aren't you?"

She nodded. Slowly but not reluctantly.

"I would also like to have a son one day."

"Only a son, Captain?" she asked primly.

He could have applauded. Even in the height of her obvious embarrassment at his frank speech, she still had the will to be impertinent.

"For a start."

"And if your first child is a girl?"

She'd said "your," not "my." He hadn't missed that fact.

"Then *we* will have to keep trying." He put a slight emphasis on the pronoun.

This time her smile was slightly flirtatious. *"We* shall have to see about that."

She closed the door then, leaving him slightly out of sorts. After all, he was the one who would make such decisions.

Wasn't he?

Chapter

18

Patience tiptoed into her room, then realized that silence was not necessary. For the first time since returning home, Emaline was not sleeping in Patience's bed.

Moving to the adjoining chamber, she discovered the child curled up beneath her own blankets, the bald doll held close to her chest, the red wig a patch of color on the patterned rug.

"Well," Patience whispered to herself, "will wonders never cease."

She adjusted the covers and tenderly pushed a lock of hair from Emaline's eyes, then returned to her own quarters.

For some time she stood still, slowly turning in a full circle to examine all she saw. By this time next week, everything would be different. She would become Mrs. Garrick Dalton. She would move to the master suite. She would become his lover.

A shiver coursed through her body as she absorbed all the nuances that particular situation would entail. Before Garrick had issued his warning, she had not been so naive as to think that her status as a virgin would persuade him to carry on a platonic relationship. The embraces they'd shared in the past would have convinced her to the contrary even if she had been foolish enough to delude herself.

She moved to the guillotine window and stepped out onto the gallery, hoping that the cool sea breeze would ease the heat in her cheeks and the sudden storm of sensation raging through her body. But the whisper of sea air merely reminded her of the way a man would soon touch her as the wind did. Intimately. Completely.

When Patience began her journey away from home, her only consideration had been the fact that she would be away from her father. Now she was engaged to a man she barely knew.

Was she merely exchanging one sort of domination for another?

Even as the doubt appeared, it fizzled away to nothingness. She couldn't defend her actions, and she was glad her sisters weren't here to demand an explanation. But somehow, in her soul of souls, she knew she was doing the right thing. Her destiny was intertwined with that of the Dalton family, no matter how odd such an idea might seem to others.

An imperceptible creak alerted her, and she glanced to the side, seeing the shape that stood there, recognizing the form even though it was too dark to see the features.

Garrick Dalton.

She wondered if he knew how much he had changed her. He had transformed her from a spinster bent on strict independence to a woman preoccupied by the joys of the flesh.

"Pleasant dreams, Patience."

The wind brushed against her skin and toyed with the strands of her hair. She pushed the tresses back, staring at the man mere yards away, feeling the way she was drawn to him even then, her body thrumming with a hunger she never would have thought possible.

"Pleasant dreams to you, Captain," she murmured, turning and moving inside while she still could.

A scream shattered Garrick's restless slumber, and he swung from the bed, his feet hitting the floor and his hand clasping the pistol at his bedside before he was even aware of being awake.

Another cry, high and piercing and bloodcurdling, had him bolting across the hall and bursting through the opposite door. But Emaline was not in Patience's bed, as he'd supposed. Instead, the governess herself was reaching for her wrapper, her eyes wide and terrified as they met Garrick's.

"Emaline."

The whisper had barely crossed her lips when a third scream split the silence.

Lifting his revolver, Garrick slammed through the door to his sister's room. The little girl was sitting bolt upright in bed, clutching the covers to her body while around her on the pillows lay the remains of her hair.

"Take care of her," Garrick shouted, already leaping out the window, but as he ran across the gallery and peered into the darkness below, he could see little more than the scurrying shape of an escaping figure.

A half dozen sailors and grooms were running toward the house and Garrick motioned to the fleeing shadow. "After him!"

The men changed direction immediately, and Garrick strode back into his sister's room, intent on assisting the sailors. He'd taken little more than a dozen steps before Patience called out,

"Let your men give chase. Emaline needs *you*, Garrick."

The child was hysterical, her cries coming in choked gasps as she struggled to draw air into her lungs.

Garrick paused at the door, slamming his fist against the wall. As much as he wanted to follow the bastard who had done this and have him drawn and quartered, he knew that he belonged here.

Hauling his sister close, Garrick carried her to a rocker in the corner of the room, purposely positioning it with his foot so that the bed would be out of Emaline's line of sight.

Wrapping his arms around his sister, he began to rock, shushing her and stroking what remained of her hair. Her lovely hair. It had taken so long to persuade her to wash it, but after that, she'd kept it clean and shiny, the brilliant wheat-colored strands tumbling to her waist and held back with the pink satin ribbons Martha had given her. Now little remained, except for the jagged wisps poking out from her head at all angles.

Behind him he vaguely noted that Patience was gathering the severed strands from the pillow, brushing them into the center of the bed. She stripped the sheets from the mattress and pulled the corners to the center. At one point he thought she'd hidden something bulkier there as well, but before he could get a good look, she was lifting it all away and carrying the bundle into her own room. She returned with fresh sheets, putting the bed to rights in an amazingly short time.

Bit by bit, Emaline grew calm. Her fists grabbed hold of his shirt, and it was then that Garrick realized he'd fallen into bed fully clothed—a lucky fact, judging by the events of the early morning hours. Usually he retired nude, and he would have hated to have taken the time to pull on a pair of breeches.

"Emaline?" He spoke as softly and as gently as he could. "What happened?"

"Matumba," she whispered. "Matumba."

His brow creased. He had no idea what that word meant. "Matumba?"

She nodded, her grip tightening. "I've been bad. I've been bad. He's come to take me away."

Vaguely, Garrick realized that Emaline must be speaking of some pagan deity that she had come to fear during her stay on the island.

"No, sweetheart. No one's come to take you. You're going to stay here. With me. Forever."

She shook her head. "Matumba. Matumba."

Then she squeezed her eyes closed and began to sob again, so heavily and pitifully that Garrick had to lower his own lashes to block out the sight of her pain.

A soft hand touched his shoulder, and he didn't need to look up to see who had come to his side.

"I've spoken to Bickerstaff," Patience said, making him wonder how long she'd been gone. "The sailors lost the intruder at the cliff."

He nodded, more concerned now with the havoc that the unknown assailant had brought to his home.

"Bickerstaff has assigned an extra team of sailors to guard the house and the stables. He's given them weapons from your supply. I have asked some of the house servants to watch the upper and lower halls, especially the entrance to this wing."

Garrick squeezed her hand, wondering how this woman had so easily perceived his need to strengthen the security of the manor. "Thank you."

She nodded, reluctantly disengaging herself from his grip. Crossing to the cupboard, she withdrew a quilt from the stack and settled it over Emaline's shoulders.

"D-doll," the girl croaked, between hiccuping sobs.

Patience's tender ministrations stilled, then her hand stroked Emaline's head. "It's being cleaned, sweetie. I'll bring it to you as soon as I can."

It was clear that Emaline was less than pleased with the news, but since there was nothing more to be done, she wrapped her arms around her brother's neck and clung to him, muttering an unintelligible litany of words that Garrick began to fear might be some sort of prayer to the fearsome Matumba.

Dipping his head closer to her own, he clasped Emaline tightly, feeling the same helplessness he'd experienced when he was informed that she was dead. Silently he cursed himself for dropping his guard, for thinking that the danger of the threats had passed.

It was hours later before Emaline fell into a deep, exhausted sleep. Garrick's body ached from holding her so tightly, from rocking her, but he was loath to let her go.

A shadow fell over his face, and he glanced up, realizing that dawn was pinkening the horizon and seeping into the room.

"Emaline would be more comfortable in bed," Patience murmured.

She'd dressed sometime during the crisis. How odd that he hadn't even known she was gone. He'd been too deep in his own thoughts, his own fears.

"No, she's—"

"She's not fine," Patience interrupted. "And neither are you. Put her to bed where she can rest properly." When he didn't move, she added, "There's something you need to see. Then I'll dispose of it before Emaline awakens."

The addendum to her statement persuaded him to stand. Emaline grunted but did not awaken, even when he tucked her into the feather bed and pulled the quilt up to her chin. Emaline whimpered, then nestled into the comfort of her pillows.

Backing out of the room, Garrick raked his hair away from his face as Patience closed the door behind them both.

"What is it that I need to see?"

She gestured to the bundle of linens, which she had left on her bed. Sighing, he wearily approached them, tossed back the corners, then grew still. Cold.

In the center lay the doll Patience had made for his sister. The head had been all but torn off and a stiletto blade had been plunged through its chest.

"We are lucky that the madman who did this didn't harm more than Emaline's hair."

Garrick's stomach began to roil.

"What's happening?" Patience asked. "Who would do such a thing? This is the second time someone in your family has been attacked—you in Boston, and Emaline here."

He shook his head. "I don't know who is to blame, but I've received a few troubling notes."

"Threats? Like the one delivered to your hotel?"

He nodded.

"What are we going to do?" Patience asked.

We. She'd said "we."

"Tomorrow I'll hire extra guards as well as someone to personally protect Emaline until we can get to the bottom of all this."

Patience clasped her hands together. "Then . . . you'll be postponing the wedding."

"No." Was it relief he saw? "No, we will be married as planned."

"You're sure?" she asked.

He took her chin in his palm, holding her face up to the light, wondering what he saw there. Fear? A little.

Awareness, certainly. But there was more, so much more. Emotions that he couldn't begin to fathom.

"Do you want me to postpone the marriage ceremony?" he asked, wondering if the threats to Emaline had made Patience reconsider her rash decision to tie herself to him.

"No," she whispered.

"Good." He still held her face, still stared intently at the pallor of her skin, the deep green of her eyes. They would have beautiful children, he thought. And if they inherited half of their mother's spirit and courage, he would be a happy man.

Happy?

Yes, he could be happy with this woman.

"I'm going to lie down with Emaline," he said.

She nodded and he released her, striding from the room while he still could.

For if he stayed, he would have to hold her. And such embraces could no longer be satisfied with a simple kiss.

"You rang?"

Bickerstaff let himself into Garrick's study the next afternoon. He wore his usual livery and somber mien. But the moment the door closed, he set the lunch tray on the desk, then retrieved the plate of sandwiches and slouched in a chair, balancing the food on his stomach.

"Any leads?" Garrick asked.

Bickerstaff shook his head. "We lost the man at the cliffs. He must have scrambled down to the beach, but with high tide, there were no tracks to follow."

"Damn."

"I've implemented the extra security measures you requested. Jan Ellington helped me round up some villagers willing to conduct a search as well."

"Good."

Garrick absently selected a sandwich for himself, then leaned against the desk.

"What are you thinking?" Bickerstaff asked.

"That whoever is responsible has to be on the island."

"Unless he had a ship to help him in his escape."

Garrick shook his head. "Captain Rosemund and his men were anchored near the reef. If there was a ship out there, his watchmen would have clearly seen it in the moonlight."

"So our attacker is hiding somewhere on Addlemeyer."

"Yes," Garrick replied slowly. "And I think it's time to flush the miscreant out into the open."

"What do you suggest?"

"A party. This time we'll lure him into our midst," Garrick answered grimly.

Emaline was noticeably quiet during her lessons, and Patience couldn't fault her. She and the girl had spent nearly an hour trying to trim her hair into some semblance of normality. But several patches had been cut close to her scalp, revealing a glimpse of her pale skin.

"Enough Latin," Patience announced. She had hoped that their lessons might help Emaline to think of other things, but the girl was clearly distraught. In the past, only one thing had helped to lift Emaline from such a mood.

"Why don't you go find your brother? I saw Bickerstaff carrying a tray into his study."

"What about my lessons?"

"We're declaring a recess for today. Go on."

"I'd rather play with Oscar," Emaline announced, ambling toward the kitchen.

"Don't chase him into the bushes, Emaline. Not in your new dress."

But whether or not the girl heard her, Patience wasn't sure.

"Miss Pedigrue?"

She sighed silently to herself, turning to face the housekeeper with a smile that she didn't feel. "Yes, Miss Fitch."

"Some mail has come for you."

"For me?"

The announcement was more surprising than it should have been, and Patience's spirits immediately improved. After all, in her eyes, getting a letter was as exciting as receiving a gift at Christmas.

The woman held out a silver salver, and Patience took the three envelopes.

"Will you bring me some tea in the parlor, Miss Fitch?"

The housekeeper's lips thinned, but she nodded. "Yes, madam."

Madam. That form of address would have made Patience smile under any other circumstance, but at the moment, her attention was diverted by the correspondence she clutched in her hand.

Altering her direction, she made her way to the parlor.

Settling onto a brocade settee, she read the return addresses on each of the envelopes. One was from Felicity, another from Constance, and the third unmarked.

As she read Felicity's letter, she was deeply involved in the minute-by-minute account her sister had provided of her adventures in the West. Patience was informed of Felicity's journey and the fascinating man she'd met on the train. She was given a complete description of the house provided for Felicity's use, and humorous descriptions of the hoodlum children who lived next door.

Then the letter became curiously vague. There was a sentence describing the fact that because a slight "difficulty" had arisen, Felicity had been unable to begin her job at a local school. Patience felt a moment's misgivings, then forgot them again when Felicity began a narrative of the delights to be found in Saint Joseph and the differences between life in the West and life in Boston.

Constance's letter was far less informative. She had been delayed in her journey to New York, but she spoke longingly of her sisters and of her hope that they would soon be reunited.

Patience squeezed her eyes closed. Little did Constance know that there would be no permanent reunion once Patience had married.

Sighing, she reached for the third letter. The script on the envelope was unfamiliar, and she would have assumed it was a note of congratulations on her nuptials if it hadn't been addressed to her alone.

Sliding a single sheet of paper free, she gasped when a lock of red hair tumbled into her lap. A single handwritten sentence leaped out at her: "Next time it will be you, not the doll."

The note fell from her fingers as if it had caught fire, and she stared down at the lock of hair, automatically lifting her hands to her head.

Had someone come into her room while she was sleeping?

A bolt of fear shuddered through her body at the realization that someone could have stood over her as she slept. Someone had meant to frighten her—and had succeeded. But who? *Who?*

She scrambled to cover the page as the door opened and Miss Fitch entered with the tea tray.

"Where would you like it, madam?"

For several seconds Patience couldn't answer her. Then she pointed vaguely to the table near the settee.

She waited until the woman left, then pushed the letter deep into her pocket.

"Hello, Miss Pedigrue."

She jumped, a hand flying to her chest. Discovering Jan Ellington in the door, she fought her annoyance.

Garrick rubbed at the tension gathering between his eyes and tried to focus more intently on the ledger in front of him. He'd been working over these same books since he returned home and the figures didn't add up. Damn it all to hell, the columns wouldn't balance.

Growling in irritation, he pushed away from the desk, leaned back in his chair, and pressed the palms of his hands to his eyes. He had to be overlooking something. Something obvious, but try as he might, he couldn't understand why the goods being brought from Europe were not fetching the profits they should have garnered here in the States.

What was he missing? What item from the registry had he overlooked in the accounts? Even Asa Marcus seemed bewildered by the shortfalls.

Damn it. He wished Jan Ellington were still here. Jan had a talent for numbers and would see in an instant what was wrong. Garrick would have to send a note to town and ask him to come to the house. Even with that decision made, Garrick found himself bending over the ledger again, returning to it like a dog worrying a bone.

A soft tap sounded at the door, and thinking that

Patience had come to distract him, he smiled, barking, "Enter!"

But it wasn't his fiancée who peered inside, it was Miss Fitch.

"Miss Pedigrue asked for tea in the parlor, sir."

He stared at her blankly, wondering why she would feel it necessary to announce such a thing to him.

"Fine, Miss Fitch."

"Mr. Ellington has joined her."

"Really?" Jan must have read his mind.

Patience did her best to appear calm, but she was actually very irritated with Mr. Ellington. At breakfast that morning, he'd been trying to arrange a moment for them to speak. The hangdog expression he wore, however, had persuaded her to ignore him. If he was disappointed about her engagement, she could not help him. He might have expressed—through his sister—an interest in courting her, but Patience had never been interested.

His eyes were mournful. "If someone had told me that Garrick Dalton would marry, I never would have believed such a thing. Still, you must know that I rue his choice in brides. I'd hoped to have you for myself."

"I see." It was a lame reply, but she couldn't think of anything else to say. Certainly nothing to diffuse the situation.

"But then, I have always been an old-fashioned sort. I was taught to believe that a courtship should last for years, not weeks."

She could not escape the silent recrimination in his tone.

Jan pushed away from the wall, approaching her with a noiseless grace that she had never associated with anyone but Garrick before.

She clasped her hands in front of her, wondering why she felt uneasy. There was nothing improper in the two of them meeting in the parlor this way.

"I have a little gift for you," he said.

"For me?"

He shrugged. "It was actually intended as a token of my esteem. I suppose now it's a wedding present." He held out a tiny box. "Consider it a token of my appreciation for your hospitality each morning."

Patience reluctantly accepted the package, still feeling a niggling unease.

"Open it."

She lifted the lid and gasped when she saw the delicate gold bracelet.

"It's lovely, but . . ."

When she held it out to him, he pushed it back.

"Don't tell me you can't accept it. Don't tell me it's too personal or too frivolous or too much. It would hurt me terribly if you didn't take it."

Since he'd worded his request in such a manner, she didn't know how she could graciously refuse. "Thank you."

"Shall I help you put it on?"

Again she didn't know how to say no.

She stood quite still as he took the bracelet from its bed and slipped the box back into his pocket. She held out her arm, wondering why she shivered as his fingers grazed the inside of her wrist.

Once he'd fastened the clasp, she nearly snatched her hand back, then hid the movement by pretending to examine the intricate chain and filigree charm.

"It really is beautiful. Thank you, Mr. Ellington."

"Jan."

Patience hesitated, uncomfortable with the familiarity. "Jan."

"Since I will be off on a business trip during the

nuptials, I wonder if you would grant me one more request."

"What?"

"A kiss from the bride?"

Again she felt the niggling unease, but she didn't know how she could refuse. If Jan had been here the day of the wedding, he could have asked Garrick to give him permission for such a thing.

She nodded, lifting a cheek. But before she knew what he meant to do, he brushed his lips over hers.

"Congratulations," he said woefully. "May you have many happy years ahead of you." Bowing, he made his way to the foyer and out the front door.

Patience wilted, trying in vain to remove the bracelet from her wrist.

"Jan seems very taken with you."

She started, seeing Garrick in the doorway, his eyes dark and hooded.

"You scared me," she breathed.

"Did I, love?"

He didn't move, didn't speak for some time, then held out his hand. "Let me see it."

"What?"

"The bracelet."

Reluctantly she approached him, holding out her arm.

He grasped her wrist, twisting it this way and that. "I'd watch out if I were you. It will probably turn your skin green."

Then he released her.

"Jan said it was his wedding gift," she explained hastily, although she was beginning to believe that Garrick had overheard the whole exchange.

"How thoughtful of him."

He moved to the settee and poured himself a cup of

tea. "Tell me, Patience. What do you think of our dear Jan?"

Why did she sense that the question was loaded?

"I don't really know him."

"But you've been with him every morning. What do you think?"

Patience shrugged. "He has very nice manners."

"Manners?" Garrick chuckled. "You should see him in a brothel."

She shot a glare his way. "Meaning that you've been there as well."

He grinned, rising from the cushions and prowling toward her, sliding an arm around her waist and pulling her against his chest.

"Did you think I was an innocent, Patience?"

Innocent. That was one word she never would have associated with Garrick Dalton.

"You haven't answered me, Patience." His hand pressed her waist, the heat of his skin burning through the layers of her clothing and underthings. "Why is that?"

"I think you know," she whispered, barely able to catch her breath as his fingertips grazed her breast.

"So you think I've had a wild past, hmm?"

"In . . . a manner of speaking."

He leaned low, his lips brushing her neck, her bare shoulders. "I love the texture of your skin, did you know that?"

She could only shudder in pleasure as he suckled the spot above her collarbone. There would probably be a faint mark there in the morning, but she didn't care. Not when it offered her so much pleasure now.

"You smell so good. What is that scent?"

"Lilac water."

"Lilacs. That's it. We shall have to plant some in the garden."

"What?"

"Lilacs. We shall have to plant some in the garden."

"Yes."

But she didn't care. She didn't really care.

Twisting in his arms, she pulled him down for a kiss, and this time she was the aggressor, the one who wished to have her needs met and fulfilled.

When he drew back, breathing hard, she saw the invitation in his eyes. Nodding, she allowed him to pull her from the parlor, up the stairs, and into his room.

As soon as the door was closed and locked, she was back in his embrace. Vaguely, she felt his fingers at the back of her bodice, heard the faint popping sounds of the hooks as they came free. Then he was divesting her of her skirts, her underclothing and her foundations until she stood in front of him wearing little more than a wrinkled chemise.

When she would have drawn it over her head, he stopped her.

"No. I want to see you this way. Clothed in a wisp of fabric. Silk." Even as he spoke, he was unfastening the button between her breasts so that the chemise gaped nearly to her waist.

Then it was her turn to strip him of his jacket, his shirt, but she was not nearly so adept, and he was forced to help her.

A breeze wafted through the open window, and Patience prayed that it would cool her heated flesh, but she doubted such a thing was possible. Not when her heart pounded so hard, sending the blood coursing through her veins.

Only once did Garrick pause. Resting his forehead on hers, he looked down at her body. His gaze raked her form from head to toe, causing her skin to burn in the wake of his scrutiny. Then he scooped her up in his arms and carried her to the bed.

"You are so incredibly lovely," he said next to her ear, the words barely audible.

He set her on the plump feather mattress and stood back, divesting himself of what few scraps of his clothing still remained.

She watched, barely daring to breathe as, bit by bit, he exposed the tan, hardened expanse of his chest. He was muscle and brawn and strength. It was enough to cause her belly to tighten in pleasure at the mere sight of it.

"You work very hard, don't you, Captain?"

One of his brows lifted in silent query.

"It shows."

He shrugged the comment aside, saying instead, "I thought we'd determined that you would stop calling me Captain."

She smiled coyly. "I suppose."

"A more intimate form of address won't prove painful, I assure you."

Her own lips twitched in a smile. "Very well . . . Garrick."

He sat on the bed beside her, framing her face with his palms. "I like the sound of my name on your lips. I have waited so long for you to say it regularly."

Then he was leaning forward to brush her mouth with his. A sigh burst from her throat. This was what she had been waiting for. His loving.

But there was no need to worry about such things any longer. His kiss was long and slow and drugging, causing the embers of desire to flutter, then flame to life.

Her fingers curved around his shoulders, then swept over his back. At his slight hiss, she drew away, sure that she'd upset him somehow, but he merely said, "Careful of my scars. They can still be sensitive."

She wanted to investigate further, but he didn't allow her such leeway. Instead, he pushed her into the bed, framing her head with his elbows.

"I am glad that you came into my life, Patience."

It was an unexpected statement and was therefore that much more precious.

"I know we'll be happy together."

She nodded, unable to speak for the tightness that suddenly gripped her throat. Then she could not talk at all because he bent to kiss her shoulder, then moved down, down, down, seeking the tight bud of her nipple through the silk of her shift. When he took it into his mouth, she gasped, clutching at him.

But he had not finished with her. Just when she feared she could bear no more, he moved lower, skimming her body with his lips until he hovered over her navel.

"I should take more time, build you to a fever pitch."

"I am at a fever pitch already," she said, her hands gently sweeping down the line of his spine, reveling in the warmth of his skin and the freedom she had to touch him.

"I hope so," he whispered against her ear. "Because I can't wait much longer to enjoy your sweetness."

Then he was moving against her in a way that caused her to moan. His body was strong and hard against hers, rubbing and pressing into her softness in a way that made her lose all reason. She could only absorb the sensations coursing through her body, the fire.

"Please," she gasped next to his ear.

She wasn't sure what she begged of him, she only

knew that if this sweet torment didn't stop soon, she would surely die.

Her eyes closed, and she reached above her head to grasp handfuls of the bedding as she felt his arousal pressed intimately against her, pushing, entering, filling her, slowly at first. After encountering the resistance of her maidenhead, he paused, allowing her to grow accustomed to the strange sensations. Then, just as she feared he would not continue, he withdrew and thrust into her again, filling her completely with his heat.

She cried out in pleasure and pain, sure that the act was completed, but he began to move against her, slowly at first, then harder and faster until her mind whirled and her body seemed to have taken on a life of its own. Coherent thought fled, and instinct took over. She was grasping his shoulders, pulling him tightly to her body, answering his rhythm with one of her own.

Somewhere deep in the center of her being, she felt the onset of an incredible joy. Her body tightened indescribably. Without warning, a pleasure such as she had never experienced before burst within her body, and she cried out, clutching at Garrick as he plunged deep inside her.

It was some moments later when she became aware of the afternoon sunshine, the cool breeze, the quiet room, and the man who was still poised above her.

She blinked at him, the last few moments returning again and again to her mind's eye and bringing with them a joy she would not have believed possible. But as she stared up at him, looking at those crystal-blue eyes, tousled hair, and sweat-dappled skin, she realized that she cared for this man in a way that she had never felt before. She might even call it . . .

Love.

Something of what she thought must have conveyed itself to him because he asked, "Are you all right?"

She nodded, offering him a slow smile. "Yes."

He settled onto the bed beside her and drew her into his embrace. Patience went willingly, snuggling against him. As he stroked her hair, she reveled in the pleasant throbbing that occupied the most intimate recesses of her body.

"That was incredible," she sighed.

He chuckled. "Why, thank you."

She pinched his side. "That comment was not meant to increase your conceit."

"What a pity."

He wound his arms about her shoulders, and the silence settled comfortably between them. It inspired them to share confidences and secrets, but at the moment, Patience couldn't seem to concentrate enough to talk. After the bustle of the past few days, she found herself growing weary. Oh, so weary.

"Patience?"

"Mmm?" She heard his voice from far away and was sure she responded quickly enough.

"Patience, there is something I need to tell you . . . about my reasons for hiring you."

"Mmm. Mmmm."

She tried to concentrate. She really did. But the deep timber of his voice seemed to waver and fade.

Then there was nothing.

Nothing but the deep contentment infusing her body and the pleasant dreams that came to keep her company.

Garrick watched her nod off to sleep and didn't have the heart to wake her again. Not when she looked like a disheveled angel in his arms.

He kissed the top of her head, amazed by the depth of passion he'd felt in her arms, a joy that he'd never experienced with any woman except this prim and proper governess.

He yawned, knowing there were things he should be doing. He really couldn't afford to sleep. The problem with the company's books demanded his attention, and there were orders to fill, letters to be answered.

But as Patience snuggled closer to his side, he realized that his work could wait until later.

Chapter

19

Patience was stunned at how quickly the house was prepared for Garrick's impromptu celebration. Soon there were flowers in every nook and cranny and every surface gleamed from a recent polishing.

Before she knew it, the night of the ball had approached and the house was filling up with guests. An orchestra had begun to play downstairs, and the air was filled with music.

"You look lovely, my dear."

She smiled as Garrick bent to kiss the hollow of her shoulder.

Sliding the last jewel-tipped hairpin into place, she smoothed a hand over the emerald-green silk of her gown.

"You don't think the neckline is too daring, do you?" she asked, indicating the lace-edged bertha that swept low over her bosom.

"You will merely make every man envious of my position as your husband-to-be."

A knock sounded at the door to Patience's bedroom. "The guests are beginning to assemble in the ballroom, sir," Bickerstaff informed them from the other side of the door.

"Thank you. We'll be right down."

Even as they heard Bickerstaff padding down the hall, Garrick hesitated.

"Patience, I want you to know that I have grown to care for you. Quite deeply, as a matter of fact."

She was stunned at the spontaneous admission.

"But I also want you to know that I will not detain you if you aren't happy."

"Not happy?" she echoed in confusion, but before she could say more, he was taking her hand.

"We'll talk about it later. Now isn't the time."

Patience wanted to beg him to stay and explain, but she had no opportunity. He was ushering her into the corridor and down the stairs to where a group of people waited for them.

From that point, there was barely enough time to ponder his statement. Every second was filled with rich food and drink, dancing, and conversation. Patience was flooded with introductions and spent a good deal of time on the dance floor.

When she finally withdrew to the shadows of the terrace to catch her breath, it was with a certain amount of relief. She would stand here in the shadows near the steps leading down to the garden. No one would think to look for her here for at least a minute or two.

"Have I told you how beautiful you look, Patience?"

She squeezed her eyes shut in annoyance. No one, that was, but Jan Ellington.

Balling her hands into fists, she buried them in her skirt so that he wouldn't see them. Turning, she offered him her frostiest stare. "I'm glad you are enjoying yourself, Mr. Ellington."

He offered her a courtly bow. "I've come to give you some sad tidings, I'm afraid," he said.

"Oh?"

"I'll be leaving in a few days."

Patience's heart leaped with gladness, but she tried to school her features into a calm mask. "What a pity," she murmured.

What a pity you didn't leave earlier.

Ellington suddenly grasped her shoulders, pulling her into his arms. "We can go to England together, you and I!"

"Mr. Ellington, please," she protested, trying to push him away, but he was too strong for her.

"I'll treat you like a queen, shower you with diamonds."

Finally she wrenched free. "How dare you?" she hissed. "My fiancé has offered you nothing but hospitality and friendship, and this is how you repay him?"

"But you love *me*," he insisted.

"No, Mr. Ellington, I do not. As a matter of fact, I am very much in love with Garrick."

The night echoed with her pronouncement, and Patience mourned the fact that she had spoken those words aloud for the first time to this man.

He straightened by degrees, his features revealing an icy determination. "Then that is your last word on the subject?"

"Yes, sir, it is."

He'd grown stiff and grave. "I believe, then, that I will take my leave of you. It's time that I moved my things to the sloop in preparation for my departure."

With that, he spun on his heel and disappeared into the ballroom.

Patience put a hand to her chest, struggling to breathe. Out of vanity, she'd laced her corset extremely tight. A faintness was gathering at the fringes of her consciousness, but she couldn't give in to it now. Not when someone could step out onto the terrace for a gulp of fresh air.

"I thought you handled that very well."

She jumped as Bickerstaff stepped from the shadows, a silken shawl held loosely in one hand.

She blanched, realizing that he must have heard everything, but he didn't chide her. In fact, he seemed to be quite pleased with what he had overheard.

"I saw you step out onto the terrace, and I thought you might need a wrap."

He gestured for her to turn, and when she stood looking out over the moonlit rose garden and the gleaming steps, he settled the silk over her shoulders.

"I think you will discover that the captain's moodiness will lighten considerably once Ellington is gone."

"Do you think so?" Patience immediately regretted her query. It revealed far too many of her own insecurities. But she supposed to deny them would be pointless with this man. He understood her somehow. He'd been as much of a friend to her as he'd always been to Garrick.

"You've changed the man so much already," Bickerstaff said. "He's more—"

"Possessive and ornery?"

He chuckled. "That too. But you must understand that love does not come easily to him. Since the death of his parents and his brothers, he has never allowed himself to trust or to love anyone. He will offer his money to whoever is in need, his home, his hospitality, his ships. But his heart . . . that is one thing he keeps hidden from the world. Only Emaline has been allowed into that secret circle."

He offered a pat to her arm. "Stay here. I'll bring you some punch and a few tidbits from the buffet table. You look in need of some refreshment."

"Thank you, Bickerstaff."

As his footsteps faded, she wondered why she felt so heartened by all that he'd told her. Most people wouldn't put much stock in anything of a personal nature being revealed by a servant. But Patience instinctively sensed that he had voiced the one thing she had been unable to fathom for herself. She had always wondered why Garrick held a part of himself back and why he felt she would be tempted by Jan's attentions. It wasn't so much that he didn't trust her; it was that he didn't trust himself to care.

And he did care for her. He loved her. She knew that now.

Footsteps were moving toward her again, and she said, "Bickerstaff, would you be so kind as to ask Captain Dalton to join me? I'd like to talk to him."

There was no answer. Only an eerie silence.

"Bickerstaff?"

She was about to turn when something hard slammed into her head. Stunned, Patience scrambled to regain her footing as the stone staircase swam before her. Then, when the pain came again, she could do little more than scream.

It had been easy to gain entrance to her daughter's party. Simpler than Louise would have thought possible. After appearing in a stunning carriage, wearing an equally stunning dress, she had been admitted into the ballroom without a second thought.

Once there, however, the night had not been nearly as smooth. Several upstart sailors had begun conversations, which she later realized were a subtle attempt to inquire whether she had any sons, nephews, or godsons, who had been sailors.

Sons? If only they'd altered their line of questioning. Louise might have allowed herself to admit a portion of the truth. As it was, Louise had spent the evening alternating between watching her daughter with hungry eyes and resisting the urge to burst into tears.

Patience was so beautiful. So serene.

So much in love.

At least in that respect, Louise had been reassured. But that didn't dampen the niggling concern that danced over her nerve endings time and time again. Although Patience and her fiancé appeared to be the picture of happiness, Louise guessed that there was something wrong. Especially whenever that Ellington fellow was near.

"So what have you gathered from the other guests?" Louise inquired under her breath as Étienne approached her, a cup of punch held in his gloved hand.

"Not much. From what I've been able to discern, the captain and his fiancée are very private about the details of their courtship, and their servants are very close-lipped."

"Hmm."

"I don't like Ellington, however."

It shouldn't have surprised her that Étienne's impression echoed her own, but it did.

"What do you think is wrong with him?"

Etienne grinned. "I do believe the man is stupid enough to try to poach on another's preserve."

Louise's mood immediately lightened. The undercurrents she'd felt all evening were due to jealousy, plain and simple.

She smiled, taking a sip of the elderberry punch, quite pleased with the whole idea. It wouldn't hurt if Captain Dalton had to fight for Patience's attention, provided the conflict didn't go too far.

"Keep an eye on him, Étienne," she instructed.

"Which one?"

She offered him a playful grimace. "On Ellington. Let me know if he becomes too much of a bother."

"And if he does?" Étienne inquired. "How far are you willing to go to ensure his cooperation?"

Her spine grew steely, as did her voice. "As far as necessary."

Étienne opened his mouth to respond, but a scream tore through the room. Louise shuddered, gripping Étienne's arm. With a mother's instinct, she knew who had uttered the sound.

"Patience," she whispered in horror. "Dear God, it's Patience."

Emaline knew that she shouldn't have come down to the garden. She'd been allowed to spend one hour at the party; then Martha had come to fetch her and take her to bed. But after persuading Martha that she was tired and wanted to sleep in her room alone, she'd crept out onto the balcony and made her way down the back steps. Even so, she knew that Martha would come to check on her in a half hour at most.

Only Oscar had seen her creep into her mother's rose garden. He'd barked and set off in the opposite direction.

Knowing he would alert the sailors Garrick had posted around the house, Emaline gave chase. "Oscar!" she whispered fiercely. "Come here, you nasty dog. Oscar!"

Emaline scowled as the animal displayed an uncharacteristic burst of speed and scampered down the narrow path leading to the beach.

Huffing in impatience, Emaline scrambled to follow, wondering why the guards who were usually there were absent. Hearing a faint scream, she wondered if one of the guests had twisted an ankle dancing and the men had rushed to investigate the fracas.

"Oscar!"

Reaching the sandy beach, she searched the expanse, wondering how such a large dog could disappear in such a short time.

Cupping her hands around her mouth, she shouted, "Oscar!" The tide was encroaching on the narrow strip of sand still remaining. The rushing noise of the waves made it difficult for Emaline to hear, but she thought she detected a faint bark.

She moved in the direction of the noise, grateful for the full moon that lit her way with a wash of silver. After several minutes she noted the narrow fissure in the cliff's face and she realized where the dog had gone. There was a shallow cave through there. One she remembered from her earlier childhood.

"Come here, Oscar," she ordered. Because of the width of the hoops she still wore, she found it difficult to navigate the slender opening, but she finally made her way inside the cave. When she did, her eyes widened.

Why, there were trunks in here! Trunks and crates and all sorts of things. She could see only a few feet into the cavern, but judging by the dark shapes in front of her, the entire space was filled.

Entranced, she forgot about the dog, forgot about the guards and Martha and the party. Taking a rock, she managed to smash open one crate and pull out the stuffing.

There was nothing inside but bottles of liquor. Garrick must have put them in the cavern to keep them cool.

Her interest died as quickly as it had been aroused.

It was a shame really. This hole in the earth would have made a lovely playhouse.

When Oscar bounded toward her, she snagged him by the collar and dragged him toward the opening. "Come on, Oscar," she said sharply. "It's time for you to go home."

She was about to head to the path leading back to the house when she saw a pair of figures making their way down toward the beach. One of them was struggling to carry the other.

The moonlight illuminated a reddish glint from the person being carried.

Patience? Had Garrick brought her here for a late night swim?

Emaline frowned, ducking into the shadows.

But as the figures approached, Emaline noticed that Patience was still wearing her green ball gown. And she didn't move, even when the man lowered her onto the sand, then stretched his back and tried to catch his breath.

Emaline's eyes skipped from the dress to the shadowy shape of the man to the pallor of Patience's skin in the moonlight.

Matumba.

Matumba had come to take Patience away.

"No!" Emaline whispered. Matumba had wanted to take Emaline, but he'd settled for Patience instead. He was bent on punishing Emaline for not taking her lessons seriously.

Dropping to the ground, Emaline hugged Oscar's neck. "He can't have her," she half sobbed. "I have to stop him."

She pursed her lips. What was she going to do?

The figure was already reaching for Patience, throwing her over his shoulder and obscuring his features when Emaline would have looked at him in order to see death's face.

Matumba, the soul-robber.

Panicked, Emaline watched him head for the docks. He had come in his huge black boat, just as the islanders had said he would.

Emaline trembled at the mere idea, but there was no time to go back to the house. She had to stop Matumba. She had to be brave like the island warriors who danced and chanted and practiced their war skills to keep Matumba at bay. Barring that, Emaline had to make sure that her brother came to find them both.

Emaline closed her eyes and scraped her finger over a sharp rock. When it bled, she pressed it to one of the ribbons Martha had given her, which she'd worn in honor of the party. Then she tore the ribbon free from it's halolike arrangement and tied it to the sheepdog's collar.

"Go home, Oscar," she ordered, pushing the dog into the night. "Go find Garrick."

Then, keeping close to the rocks, Emaline trailed Patience's every move.

Garrick rushed into his study and inserted the key to his gun cabinet into the lock. But at the flare of a match, he froze.

"It won't do any good, Garrick. She's gone for good."

He tried to turn the key, but the click of a revolver's hammer being cocked made him lift his hands and slowly turn.

Jan kept his gun aimed and slowly backed behind the desk, eyeing the account book opened on Garrick's desk.

"Have you found what you're looking for yet?" he inquired, his usual quiet manner gone. In its place was a glittering hardness.

"You've been skimming liquor from the supplies sent from Europe."

Jan smiled, but it was a tight, sad smile. "Bravo."

"Where do you plan to sell it?"

"You'll have to ask my sister. She's the mastermind behind this whole plot. It was she who taught me how to juggle the numbers. For now, our cache is hidden in the cave by the beach, but she'll sell it for a handsome profit by and by."

He sighted more carefully down the barrel of his revolver, but Garrick noted that his hand trembled, making the gun shake.

"Please understand, Garrick, that none of this is personal. It's business—and I want out. Nina has assured me that if I complete one last task for her, I can leave this place with my money and find a quiet corner of the world to putter with my boat designs."

Garrick allowed his hands to drop to his sides. With a little luck, he could divert Jan's attention and lunge at him. "You and Nina are responsible for the threats and the attacks?"

Jan's brows rose. "They were my sister's idea."

"I should have guessed your intent as soon as I heard Patience scream. You followed her onto the terrace. You carried her away."

Jan offered a sheepish grin. "Actually, that wasn't my doing."

"I should have confronted you about your dishonesty before the party, as I'd originally planned."

"You mean you finally found proof of my juggling the numbers in the books?"

"Yes. Mere hours ago. I got to thinking, to reexamining my papers. It was then I realized who would inherit Dalton Shipping if Emaline and I were gone."

Jan sighed. "Yes, I suppose I was the most logical choice there. First me, then my sister. But Nina knew I wasn't up to the messiness involved. I would have been content to force you and your sister to relinquish your hold. That's why she hired her lover, Asa Marcus, to arrange for your accident on the way to England. Asa removed some of the floor planks from your ship and filled the space beneath with rotting alcohol kegs. It was only a matter of time before someone opened the hatch, held a lantern up to peer inside, and caused the cargo to explode."

Garrick's body grew numb with horror.

"You really should have died in that explosion, but I suppose no plan is perfect."

Garrick's blood began to boil with a white-hot anger. He'd been such a fool. Jan had been stealing him blind, and Nina and Asa had been plotting his death. Emaline's reappearance had inspired them to concoct new plans on her behalf.

"Why?" Garrick growled.

Jan's features grew pinched with his own brand of suffering. "Because half of Dalton Shipping should have belonged to me. My father and yours were going to be partners."

"That kind of talk was abandoned long before I was born, Jan! You know my father would never have passed on the business to anyone but family."

"It wasn't just talk! My father worked himself to death for Dalton Shipping. He died of a stroke right in the middle of the countinghouse floor. And what did he receive for his labor?"

"You were always well—"

"Dammit, I'm not talking about money. I'm talk-

285

ing about power, a true stake in the game. The shipping business should have been ours, and now it will be, do you hear?"

He lifted the revolver.

Garrick dived behind the settee, but even as he did, a shot echoed through the study.

Then there was silence. An awful, echoing silence.

Garrick squinted into the hazy cloud of gun smoke and waited to feel the pain.

But it didn't come.

"Good thing I've taken to carrying a bit of protection inside my waistcoat," Bickerstaff murmured from the door at the other side of the room, a smoking gun in his hand.

Glancing Jan's way, Garrick saw his longtime partner lying dead in a pool of his own blood. He dropped his head to the floor in relief. "Hell, man, I thought they'd be digging my grave."

Bickerstaff grinned. "They would have been if I hadn't heard your voices."

Garrick frowned and pushed himself to his feet. "Find Emaline and reassure her that everything is all right. Then assemble the men into a search party. We have to find Patience."

When Bickerstaff didn't move, Garrick felt a coldness ease into his chest. "What's wrong?"

Bickerstaff held up a pink ribbon. "Miss Fitch just brought this to me. Martha checked on Emaline and found her room empty. When she saw Oscar running from the direction of the beach with the ribbon tied to his collar, she notified the housekeeper."

He paused before adding, "Miss Fitch was the first to see that the ribbon was stained with blood. Worse yet, Rosemund sent a runner to inform you that one of his watchmen saw Patience being carried aboard

Ellington's sloop by none other than Asa Marcus. Minutes later, Emaline sneaked aboard."

Garrick strode to the gun cabinet. The key had been lost in the fracas, but he didn't bother to look for it. Breaking the glass with his elbow, he snatched a brace of pistols.

"Tell the runner to—"

Bickerstaff stopped him in mid-sentence. "Rosemund will meet us on the beach with one of his skiffs. If we hurry, we can head Marcus off before he realizes Jan isn't coming back and sets sail."

Patience's awareness of life swirled around her in waves of black and gray until, bit by bit, her eyes were able to focus and she saw the moon hanging over her head.

The moon?

Groaning in pain, she touched the spot at the back of her head that ached, and her hand came away sticky. In an instant she remembered the man who had rushed toward her. His features had been hazy, but judging by how quickly he'd attacked her after Bickerstaff's departure, there could only be one person responsible.

"Jan? Jan, are you here?"

Biting her lip against the pain, she struggled to her feet, slowly becoming aware of her surroundings. She'd been brought to Ellington's boat.

"Jan!"

Patience frowned when she received no answer. She wound her arms around her stomach in an effort to stave off the trembling that racked her body.

She had to get out of here.

Lifting her skirts, she stumbled toward the dock, but a shape stepped out of the hatchway, and an arm snapped around her waist.

"Don't move, don't make a sound."

A pistol appeared in front of her eyes even as she squirmed to see her attacker. But when she recognized the grim Asa Marcus, the accounting manager from the shipping office, she was stunned into silence.

"That's right," he said. "Stay nice and quiet, and I won't have to shoot you."

Chapter

20

"**M**r. Marcus?" Patience murmured, recognizing her captor.

"Quiet!"

Behind him, another figure stepped into view. Nina Ellington.

"I'd take him seriously, my dear," she advised. "He has a nasty temper." The idea seemed to delight Nina. "We're merely waiting for Jan. When he arrives, we'll be gone."

She swallowed. "Why?"

"Because he's gone to dispose of that bastard fiancé of yours and his little sister, that's why. Garrick's family all but stole the shipping business from our father, and we mean to get it back. I've promised Jan a reward if he will help us get rid of the bodies in such a way that no one on Addlemeyer will doubt you're dead."

"But—"

"Hush!" Asa hissed. "Don't you understand? There's nothing more to be said. Jan has gone to kill the last remaining Daltons, and I am about to kill you."

"No!"

Before Patience knew what was happening, Emaline burst from behind a pile of barrels, but before she could dash forward, Asa twisted Patience in his arms and put the pistol to her temple.

"Not another step, you little brat."

Emaline froze, her eyes widening even more as an object fell from Asa Marcus's pocket. An ivory pipe carved like the head of a woman.

"Get down those steps. Since you've been foolish enough to put your nose where it doesn't belong, you'll have to pay for your folly."

Emaline's eyes widened in terror and she turned to Nina in supplication, but when the woman ignored her, she did as she was told, reluctantly moving down the hatch and into the hold.

Marcus forced Patience to follow. Her head was thudding unmercifully, and she was sure she was going to be sick, but she fought the blackness invading her consciousness.

"That door at the stern," Nina instructed. "Go inside."

With one last regretful glance, Emaline did as she was told. Then Asa pushed Patience forward into the storage cabin with such force that she fell to the deck.

"Good riddance to both of you!"

He slammed the door. The lock clicked, and footsteps thundered away.

"Patience?" Emaline knelt beside her. "What do we do now?"

Fighting to remain conscious, Patience could only say, "I don't know, Emaline."

The boat began to rock, and Patience realized that Asa was setting sail. She could only pray that their destination wasn't far, and that she could find a means of escape once they'd arrived.

Crawling toward the wall, Patience braced her back against the boards and held out her arms. "Come here, Emaline."

The girl willingly complied.

"Are you mad at me for following you?" Emaline murmured. "I thought that Matumba had come to carry you to the valley of the dead."

So Matumba was similar to Western society's Grim Reaper.

"No, sweetheart, I'm not mad at you," Patience replied stroking Emaline's hair. "I just wish you were someplace safe, that's all."

Much later they heard the rattle of a chain. Then the motion of the ship altered, and it seemed to sway from side to side in a gentle rocking motion.

"We've stopped," Emaline murmured. "He's dropped anchor."

From some distant point, they heard the scuffle of feet, then nothing. Just an unsettling silence.

A sudden explosion knocked Patience to the deck, and she automatically reached for Emaline, shielding her slighter body as shards of wood rained down on their shoulders.

For several minutes there was an ominous quiet, broken by the tumble of wood and the grate of shattered beams toppling to the deck above. Then, just when Patience felt she could breathe without choking on the dust, she heard a distant roar.

"What's that?" Emaline yelped.

Patience shushed her into silence, but there was no need to do so. She knew what it was. Water was rushing into the hold.

"Come along, Emaline."

She didn't wait for an argument—not that she would have received one. Emaline scrambled after her to the door of the cabin.

But when she yanked on the door, it wouldn't budge.

"He locked us in," Emaline wailed. "He locked us in!"

Patience gazed frantically around them, wondering what she was going to do. They had to get out of there—now—or be drowned like rats.

If only there were a porthole. But the cubicle was as tight as a drum, airless, windowless, with only a guttering candle for illumination.

"Look, Patience."

Following Emaline's pointing finger, she saw the water beginning to seep beneath the door. Around them the ship creaked and moaned in obvious distress.

"Hurry, Emaline! Help me find something to bang a hole in the wood."

The two of them scrambled through the supplies that lined the narrow cabin, but with each moment wasted on the search, the water became deeper, thicker, colder. Even if they managed to break open the door, Patience feared that a wall of water might await them on the other side of the planks.

"Patience!" Emaline held up a hammer that had probably been used to secure the lids of the crates.

Patience grasped the tool, knowing that it would be ineffective in breaching the thick slats, but realizing that it was their only real chance.

Their only chance.

Rosemund's men grunted in unison to the dipping oars, causing the small boat to cut through the waves with more speed than anyone would have thought possible.

By the time Garrick had reached the beach, Asa Marcus had set sail. Then, curiously, he'd anchored only a hundred yards from shore and escaped in a skiff of his own. Nina was also aboard the skiff. When she caught sight of Garrick and his men, she'd pointed and begun shouting for Asa to hurry.

Within minutes Garrick and his men were within hailing distance of the sloop, and it was then they became aware of a muted thumping.

"He's locked them inside," Bickerstaff said, his brow furrowed with worry.

Garrick's instincts had also begun to scream in warning. The whole area was too quiet.

The explosion knocked Garrick from his standing position so that he lay prone in the bottom of the skiff. Automatically, he lifted his arms, trying to shield himself from the flying debris. Then he stared in horror as a hole opened up in the bow of the sloop and water began to rush inside.

"Dear God, no," he whispered aloud, panic clutching his breast. His sister was on that ship. And . . .

His wife-to-be.

Spurred on by terror and by the fear of losing all he loved yet again, he didn't bother to help his men scramble to retrieve the oars that had been thrown free. Diving into the waves, he swam toward the ship, panic adding speed and strength to his arms. Even so, it seemed like hours before he closed the distance, before he was pulling himself onto the listing deck.

"Patience! Emaline!"

But there was no answer. He scrambled to the hatch, praying that they hadn't been knocked unconscious by the blast and that he could get to them in time.

But halfway down the ladder, he realized that the water was swirling in fast. In most areas it was already waist deep, and toward the stern of the boat . . .

Without warning, he was reminded of another explosion, another ship.

No. He couldn't think about any of that.

"Patience! Emaline!"

He waded through the waves, straining for some sort of answer. It was then he heard the pounding again, as well as a muffled shout.

Sweet heaven above, it was coming from the portion of the sloop already filling with water.

Altering his direction, he swam toward the sound. The current rushed against him, making it difficult to gain any progress at all, but he soon realized that the noises were coming from the storage cabin. The tiny space was sometimes used as a temporary holding cell when disciplinary measures were needed. Because of that, the doorjamb had been outfitted with a heavy crossbar.

Diving beneath the water, Garrick prayed that he had arrived quickly enough, that he would be able to get both of his loved ones out before the ship went down.

The water had caused the crossbar to stick in its slot, but he yanked savagely, freeing it and twisting the doorknob. The door was stuck, and he had to lift his feet and kick it open.

The sea immediately whirled around him, greedily spilling through the opening he'd created and making it difficult for him to see.

"Swim out! Now!"

He saw Emaline first, paddling like a dog, her hair plastered to her face, her eyes wide with terror. He couldn't help thinking that this must be horrible for her. Completely horrible. A repetition of the first wreck she'd endured.

Knowing Emmie wouldn't have the strength or the wits to get out, Garrick grabbed her arms and drew her close. "Wrap your arms around my neck and don't let go, you hear?"

She nodded, gripping him with such force that she nearly knocked the air from his body.

The water was less than a yard from the ceiling at this point. At this rate, the storage cabin would be completely filled in less than a minute.

He was growing tired, his arms trembling with the effort it took to fight the current and support his sister. But he couldn't stop now. He mustn't.

He reached out and grasped Patience's wrist to help her fight the sucking force of the current.

"Follow me," he ordered, swimming toward the hatch.

"I can't swim."

The words chilled him to the bone, but he didn't have time to question her. Horrified, he realized that even if Patience had known how to help herself, she probably had not recovered sufficiently from being attacked to fight the undertow dragging her back into the cabin.

"Hold on to one of my legs, understand? Don't let go. No matter what happens, don't let go."

Patience nodded to show she'd heard, and he grappled his way to the hatch.

"Captain!"

Eager hands reached down, grasping his sister and tearing her away from his neck.

Ignoring Emaline's cries for them to get Patience as well, Garrick wrapped an arm around the ladder and reached for Patience's wrist. "Up you go."

More hands reached out to help him, drawing Patience free. Shuddering in relief, Garrick rested his head against the rough wood, then found the energy to drag himself onto the deck.

The boat was listing heavily to starboard, the glubbing of water signaling that it wouldn't be long afloat. Half sitting, half skidding down the sloping deck, Garrick took Patience's hand, urging her behind him.

"I'll climb aboard the skiff and help you jump across the gap, all right?"

She nodded, wedging her feet against what had once been the side rail. He winced at the pallor of her cheeks and the blood that seeped down her neck. Just as he'd suspected, she was on the verge of collapse.

Garrick jumped into the shallow skiff and turned to reach for her.

"Come on, love. Hurry."

Garrick held his arms out. He saw her respond. Then there was a horrible wrenching sound, and the deck beneath her feet collapsed.

She was thrown into the sea even as a rushing wave consumed the ship whole.

"No!" His voice was a hoarse whisper, then a scream. *"No!"*

Hands reached out to hold him back, but Garrick shook them off and dived into the water. He could not stand there and watch Patience drown. He should have seen to her safety first. She'd told him she couldn't swim. He should never have left her on deck alone.

His eyes stung from the salt and his heart pounded. His lungs felt as if they would explode as he dived deeper and deeper, trying to see through the wreckage. She had to be nearby. She had to be.

Then he saw her. A rag doll of a form being pulled deeper and deeper by the weight of her skirts.

Filled with an energy he would not have thought possible, he moved toward her, dots of color swimming in front of his eyes.

Somehow he managed to grasp her hair, that beautiful red braid that he had once seen spread over his pillow. Wrapping the plait around his wrist, he pulled her to him, then slid his arm around her chest and kicked for the surface.

Hold on, Patience. Hold on, he prayed.

But her body was so still, so slight, that he feared he was too late.

He burst through to the surface near the skiff. "Take her," he gasped.

One of the sailors gazed pityingly at him.

"Take her!"

They did as they were told, scooping her lifeless body from the ocean and pulling it aboard. Then they were reaching for him—and he was glad, because he didn't think he could have found the strength to board the skiff by himself.

Vaguely he noted that Emaline sat pale and shivering in the bow, held close to Bickerstaff's body for warmth and comfort. He saw the sailors bending over Patience while two more rowed toward shore as if their souls depended upon it.

Growling, he pushed them all aside—mere babyish swats, he was sure, but they parted nonetheless, allowing him to scoop Patience's body into his arms.

"Live, damn you," he growled. "Live."

A blue tinge had begun to darken her lips, but when the skiff scraped against sand, he carried Patience ashore and set her on the beach. Rolling her onto her stomach, he pressed at the small of her back, forcing the water from her lungs.

"Breathe, dammit," he ordered, his voice growing choked and garbled.

Dear Lord, please don't take her from me, he prayed. *I can't live without her. Please don't ask me to try.*

Sobbing, he thought he heard something.

A cough.

Sinking onto the sand, he pulled Patience into his arms. Her body was racked with spasms, and supporting her head, he helped her to relieve her stomach of the salt water she'd swallowed. Then he was cradling her against him, rocking her.

"Gar-rick." It was a mere croak of sound, but it was one of the sweetest he had ever heard.

"Shh, my love. Don't talk. Everything will be all right." He sobbed again, wondering, now that it was all over, why he felt ready to weep. "Everything will be all right."

"Ema . . ."

He pressed his lips to hers in a quick kiss. "She's fine." He held out a hand, encouraging his sister to approach. "See? She's just fine."

Emaline sank into the sand, her small hand touching Patience's cheek.

Patience smiled—the sweetest sight Garrick had ever seen.

"I prayed you would find us."

He kissed her again, her cheek, her forehead, her mouth. "I know, sweetheart."

He shot a grateful glance at his sister. "Thank goodness little Emaline decided to even the odds a bit. You stowed away, didn't you?"

Emaline nodded, and he reached out to ruffle her cropped hair to show he wasn't angry.

"It's a good thing you did. Oscar alerted us to where you two would be. Martha saw him running from the direction of the beach with that bloodied ribbon. That was ingenious of you, Emaline."

She grinned sheepishly.

Garrick continued his explanation for Patience's benefit. "Nina proved to be the author of these tragedies. She persuaded Asa Marcus to help her arrange for my ship to explode. Had we not run into bad weather, we would have opened the hatches sooner and foundered midway across the Atlantic. Then, when the explosion didn't kill me, she engineered the mysterious attacks—on me in Boston, on Emaline and her doll, on you at the ball." He cleared his throat of the gruffness that lingered there. "I'm sure she promised Asa Marcus a percentage of the shipping business if the two of them managed to rid the world of Dalton heirs. With my family dead, the business would become Jan's—and ultimately Nina's."

"But . . . why?" Patience croaked.

"Their father worked for mine long ago. Jan and Nina believed that the man should have received a better settlement at his death." He could not prevent a note of anger from feathering his tone. "All this grief was the result of greed, Patience."

She squeezed her eyes closed, making him realize, belatedly, that now was not the time for explanations. Later, when they were alone and she was well again.

"I came as quickly as I could," he whispered, noting the color slowly returning to Patience's cheeks. His fingers trembled. "But I never should have allowed any of this to hurt you or Emaline. At the first hint of trouble, I should have arranged for you and my sister to—"

"Shh." She pressed a finger to his lips. "Never apologize for bringing us home."

Her smile was one of the most beautiful things he had ever seen.

He bent close, whispering next to her ear, "I love you, Patience."

This time her eyes brimmed with tears of a different sort.

"Oh, Garrick."

Seeing her joy, her infinite, unfathomable joy, he held her close, proclaiming loud enough for one and all to hear, "I will love you forever and beyond."

As Emaline whooped and jumped to her feet to proclaim the news to all of the inhabitants of Addlemeyer, he smiled. He didn't know why the Fates had seen fit to bring this woman into his life, but he thanked Providence that she had come. With her stubborn pride and winsome ways, she had healed Emaline of her fear, and Garrick of his sorrow.

But more than that, she had taught an old sailor how to love.

And that was the greatest gift of all.

High on the bluff overhead, Louise Chevalier wiped away the tears that streamed down her cheeks. She'd been drawn to this place by the commotion, and the moment she and Étienne had arrived on the scene, she'd known that her daughter was about to die. The horror she'd experienced had been so numbing that she hadn't been able to breathe until now. Had it not been for Étienne, she would have sunk to the ground.

"She is all right, *ma petite,*" Étienne whispered reassuringly.

Louise blinked away the tears, willing her body to cease its trembling.

Étienne held her close. "You cannot rush down there. Much as you might wish to do so, your appearance would prove to be an even bigger shock."

"I know," she whispered, inundated by another sort of loss.

"We will wait until she has recovered," Étienne said, leading her away.

"Yes," Louise echoed, looking one last time at the

couple on the beach. Then, turning and stiffening her spine with renewed determination, she offered, "They are very much in love, don't you think, Étienne?"

"Yes, my dear. I quite agree." His arm snaked around her waist, pulling her close. "They are very much in love."

Chapter

21

The foyer at the manor house was all but deserted. Save for Patience, Emaline, and a few scattered servants, everyone had gone to the quaint stone chapel in Addlemeyer, where the master and his bride were to be married. Afterward there would be a huge feast in the garden, with dancing and revelry to compete with anything the tiny island had ever known before.

"Are you ready, Emaline?"

Emaline was hopping from one foot to the other. Dressed in a gown of pale blue to match Patience's suit and a matching bonnet, she looked so grown up that Patience couldn't help comparing her to the disheveled waif Patience had retrieved from Miss Bodrill's School for Young Ladies.

"Where are my petals?" she said in sudden worry. "And my dolly?" she added, referring to the porcelain creation Garrick had ordered from Boston. Since being given the doll, with its red hair and green eyes, Emaline had refused to leave it behind for more than a few minutes.

"Here, Emaline."

Patience stiffened when Miss Fitch entered the

foyer and handed Emaline the basket of rose petals that she would scatter on the aisle.

"Go get in the carriage, dear," Patience urged, sensing that the housekeeper had something to say.

As soon as the little girl was outside, Patience directed her attention to Miss Fitch. For the first time since meeting the woman, she noted that the housekeeper was not dressed in gray, as was her habit. Indeed, the pale rose suit gave her cheeks a certain color that had never been there before.

"Before you leave, ma'am," Miss Fitch began, "there is something I need to say to you."

Patience braced herself for more accusations of gold-digging.

"I'm sorry," Miss Fitch said.

The words were so unlike what Patience had expected, that her mouth gaped.

"I treated you abominably because I thought you would be like all of the other women who were introduced to Master Garrick. They saw him as a prize to be won, not a man with a heart—of late a broken heart."

After several beats of silence, Patience managed to say, "Thank you, Miss Fitch."

"I also want to explain why you found me searching the captain's drawers. Since I am in charge of handing the mail to him, I was aware of a certain seal on some of the notes. Each time he received something with that seal, he became incredibly worried. The script used in the address seemed vaguely familiar to me, and I had hoped to find one of the notes to discover the author. My behavior was completely out of line, but I pray you will understand that my intentions were good." Her chin shook. "If I had pursued my suspicions, none of this . . ."

Patience squeezed her hand. "You've done everything in your power to help this family, Miss Fitch. Even if you'd discovered that Asa Marcus was sending the notes, he and the Ellingtons would have found another way to complete their plots."

Miss Fitch smiled—actually smiled. "You're very kind."

Reaching into her pocket, she withdrew an envelope. "This came for you while you were recuperating. I wanted to give it to you earlier, but the captain said to wait until today. Since I thought it might be important, I hope you'll forgive me for delivering it now rather than after the ceremony."

Patience took the envelope, and after nodding in her direction, Miss Fitch went outside to climb onto the bench of the carriage with the driver.

Impatient for her wedding to begin, Patience nearly put the letter in her own pocket. Then, seeing a very familiar name included with a Canadian return address, she tore open the seal. Seeing that the date it was written was a mere week earlier, she wondered how the mail could have arrived so quickly.

Canada
1859

My dearest Patience,

I pray that this letter arrives quickly, and knowing its messenger, I'm sure it will. I sent a note only yesterday to explain the changes that have occurred in my life, but since I posted it through the regular mail, I doubt you have received it yet.

I have recently been notified of your engagement, and I wish to offer my hearty congratulations. As you will discover when my letter arrives, I have also found love amid my adventures. I am now Mrs.

Logan Campbell and can think of nothing else I would rather be.

I regret that you and Constance could not attend my wedding, but I am thankful that Mother was able to stay long enough to be there with me.

I can sense your reaction to the news. Yes, dear Patience, our mother has found us. Finally I understand why she has been absent from our lives all these years, and you must know the details as well.

We always suspected the veracity of the tale our father told us of mother's abandoning us. The truth is that he spirited us away from her, and she has spent years trying to find us. Had it not been for our father's death, she might never have located us at all. . . .

Feeling weak, Patience sank into a nearby bench.

Our mother is now a well-known actress, and it was she who discovered our father's will before it could be read. She bribed a clerk to bring the document to her, and she replaced it with the testament arranging for each of us to have an adventure. I was originally slated to be a missionary in India, and you were to work in some dreadful asylum or foundling home.

So that was why Alexander Pedigrue seemed to have had a sudden change of heart.

Meanwhile, by marrying Logan, I have forfeited my inheritance. But even on that point, Mother plans to thwart our father's plans. She has already begun proceedings to contest the will, stating that our father was not of sound mind when it was dictated.

Patience could almost hear her sister giggle.

Dear Patience, Mother means to visit you next. Please listen to what she has to say and decide for yourself whether or not she is telling the truth. As for me, I have no doubts.

I pray that Providence will allow us to see each other soon, and for once, I believe that my wish will be granted. After all, I know we both have a guardian angel with power enough to grant our wishes.

Love,
Felicity

Carefully folding the letter, Patience mulled over what she'd read.

Their mother had returned?

It was *she* who had arranged for their employment?

"Are you ready, Patience?"

She started, glancing up at Bickerstaff. Setting aside her confusion until she had time to reread the letter from her sister, she gathered her bouquet from the table in the foyer and hurried outside.

The carriage sped over the dirt track on its way to Addlemeyer, and amid Emaline's chatter, Bickerstaff's teasing, and the beautiful day, Patience nearly forgot the astounding news she'd just received.

As they turned into town, Patience was amazed at the number of people who had come to wish them well. Mrs. Rogers, Martha, the household staff, Edda Gray from the postal counter, and the village women who had helped Mrs. Rogers with the sewing.

Last of all, waiting on the steps of the church, was her bridegroom.

In an instant her body filled with an effervescent awareness—one compounded by the fact that he had not made love to her since the afternoon after the attack on Emaline. But he had already promised that, as soon as possible, they would take their leave of their guests.

As the carriage approached, there were cheers of congratulations, especially when the master of the island helped his sister, and then his bride, alight.

"You see, my dear," Garrick said, kissing Patience's hand. "They love you as much as I do."

Since Patience had opted to defy tradition by having her bridegroom escort her down the aisle, the guests began milling into the chapel. One or two stopped to offer their best wishes, but for the most part, Patience and Garrick were given a moment alone.

"I have a surprise for you, love," Garrick said, leaning close to murmur the words in her ear to prevent anyone else from hearing.

"Not another gift." She had already been offered a governess cart and a beautiful gray dappled pony with a promise from Garrick to teach her to drive. Then he'd given her the stunning sapphire bracelet and brooch that adorned her gown as well as a matching engagement ring.

"This time, the surprise isn't my doing—although I suppose I should have thought of such a thing."

Patience was stymied. What possible detail could he have overlooked?

"Over there," he said, pointing to a pair of women waiting beneath a large tree.

Instantly Patience recognized her sister Felicity—and was stunned by the change in her. She looked so very grown up and alive with happiness.

Patience's gaze bounced to the next figure—and locked there.

"Mama?" she whispered. In her mind's eye, she had a flashing memory of a woman who had filled her childhood home with laughter. Louise's eyes were older, sadder, but there was no denying the blatant love shining through her tears.

In an instant Felicity's words ran through Patience's brain: "We always suspected the veracity of the tale our father told us of mother's abandoning us. The truth is that he spirited us away from her, and she has spent years trying to find us."

Without conscious thought, Patience knew the words to be true. This woman would never willingly have left her children. And if it had been in her power to find her daughters, she would never have allowed Alexander Pedigrue to treat them so abominably.

Garrick nudged her gently. "Go to her," he urged. "From what I've been told, she's been watching over you for some time."

Without further encouragement, Patience ran into her mother's arms.

And as the familiar scent of jasmine and spice from her mother's sachet enfolded her as tightly as Louise Chevalier's arms, Patience knew that at long last, her circle of happiness was complete.

Epilogue

1859
Addlemeyer Island

My dear Constance,

It is with great pleasure that I announce to you my marriage to Captain Garrick Dalton, my former employer. Please rest assured that I am healthy, well cared for, and deliriously happy.

As you will recall, I took a position as governess to Garrick's sister, Emaline. Having been raised by natives on an uncharted island, Emaline had difficulty adjusting to the mores of society. However, soon after returning to her home and the care of her brother, she began making enormous strides toward her education and her training as a young lady. She is now strong, enthusiastic, and ever concerned about her impression as a proper gentlewoman.

From the beginning, Garrick has shown nothing but adoration and empathy for Emaline, which is one of the things that caused him to win my affections. That and his overwhelmingly good heart—something he tries too hard to hide from the world.

He has since confessed to me that I was hired because I was "the first presentable female to be interviewed." He had planned on marrying whoever became his sister's governess, in order to secure an alternate guardian for Emaline. According to Bickerstaff, Garrick's closest friend, however, I was the only candidate ever interviewed by the captain, and he was besotted with me from our first meeting.

Imagine, Constance . . . someone being besotted with me at first glance.

My only regret is that Felicity and Mother were unable to find you and bring you to the wedding as well. Evidently, you were en route to New York at the time, having been delayed in your journey a number of times. I pray that you have finally arrived safely.

I am sure that you caught my reference to Mama. Please, please, Constance, you must keep an open mind. Mother has explained to Felicity and me how she quarreled with Father and he stole us away. She has spent years searching for us, and I can only thank Providence that we have been reunited.

She is already on her way to New York, and I am sure she will contact you. Please meet with her and decide for yourself whether she is being sincere.

In the meantime, I can hardly wait to hear of the adventures you've encountered in New York. I know that you have long dreamed of seeing the workings of a theater, and your job as a costume seamstress should offer you some thrilling insights.

To that end, my dearest older sister, I pray that your—dare I say it?—Bostonian prudishness and adherence to the rules of society won't prevent you from enjoying yourself. After all, you may discover that the owner of your theater is someone dashing and mysterious. . . . Considering the twists of fate

Felicity and I have encountered, I would not discount a possibility. You may very well find yourself being swept off your feet by a man who will not say no to passion.

If this has already happened, do tell all.

Warmest love always,
Patience